1

# A WOLF NAMED BOWZKURT

BY

Marshall B. Thompson Jr.

Order this book online at www.trafford.com
or email orders@trafford.com

Most Trafford titles are also available at major online book retailers.

Printed in the United States of America.

ISBN: 978-1-4907-1510-0 (sc)
ISBN: 978-1-4907-1509-4 (e)

Trafford rev. 09/20/2013

Trafford PUBLISHING®  www.trafford.com

North America & international
toll-free: 1 888 232 4444 (USA & Canada)
fax: 812 355 4082

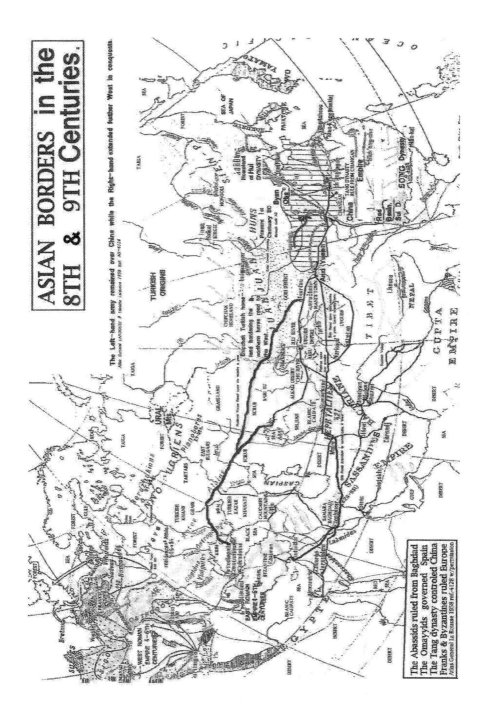

# ASIAN BORDERS in the 8TH & 9TH Centuries.

The Left-hand army remained over China while the Right-hand extended further West in conquests.

The Abassids ruled from Baghdad
The Omayyids governed Spain
The Tang dynasty controled China
Franks & Byzantines ruled Europe
Atlas General La Rousse 1938 ref 4128 w/permission

# TABLE OF CONTENTS

## # CHAPTER  * MUSIC  *  ILLUSTRATIONS  *  PAGE #

## AUTHOR'S OPENING

At the end of a braided piece the individual strands separate and taper off or are cut off. All stage plays require a denouement (de noo' mah) as part of the end. A definition of this French word is "the final revelation or occurrence which clarifies the nature and outcome of the plot." In life, we also have a personal denouement in which we clearly demonstrate the choices and purposes of our lives. The author has done this with the characters of this book. In our society, we call this denouement by various names: old age, end of the trail, last stand or perhaps the last breath of life. It is the final result of group or individual striving, planning, hoping and praying. Popular legend says you see your life flash before your eyes in the last moments. In this Gray Wolf Series, we have three basic stories, each with its own print font and denouement. In this last book A YOUTH NAMED YEET, the physical presence between the stories is not as close as before, yet none can exist without those closer, earlier relationships. Each has deeply affected all the others.

Contrary to many of the American Western Cowboy movies' traditional endings, people do not simply ride off into the sunset. Life, then and today, is not that simple. In our stories, each strand of the braid ends up where they would never have thought they would go. Life typically shows itself filled with unexpected twists and turns. I have tried to portray these moves faithfully for your instruction and enjoyment. Fiction can be so true to life! Read and enjoy.

Marshall B. Thompson Jr.

PS: The glossary and foreign words are *italicized* and spelled to help readers of English. They are not always spelled so in their dictionaries.

# MID-ASIA TIME LINE

At the beginning of the ninth century of the present era, the empires east and west were in a state of recuperation from the previous internal struggles. Upheavals in the East with the expulsion and successful restoration of the Tang dynasty brought China into a retreat toward earlier traditions. In the far West, Barbarians: Teutonic and Slavic peoples convert as they settle into parts of the old Roman Empire. Byzantium was recovering from religious controversy and Islamic aggression. Islam had its own upheavals in civil wars. The first division was the Kirbala split between Shia and Sunni. War brought separation of the Umayyad dynasty still ruling Spain from the Abbassids, who had long since departed to Baghdad. Both dynastic and territorial wars continued in the Indian peninsula. Korasan had become the seat of power in this expansion against the Rajput's frontier marches beyond the Indus River. Northward the Caliphs had found their progress blocked by the formidable Turkish tribes in the grasslands of Central Asia. The Caliphate could hardly hold the agricultural areas and the Turkic Uigurs resisted strongly on the east of the dividing Tien Shan or Tanra Dah range of Mountains. Everywhere, wars were perennial, but success in conquests was small. Warriors were in constant demand. Therefore, life expectancy was low; consumption exceeded production in every sector of the world.

In all these circumstances religious affiliation was a part of the conquest structure. Yet, as always, the personal element was present to speed or retard the process. Each empire had an official language, religion, law, and ruling capital. It was dangerous to oppose the ruling dynasties and their opinions. Yet, then, as now, minorities continued to exist and practice those things dear to their hearts and traditions. They practiced such in secrecy or publicly at a high risk and material cost to their group. The pliant majority at the behest of the ruling classes often penalized their success and occasional prosperity. Force, in all its human guises, was prevalent then, as now. Even in the face of logic, need or compassion it usually continued. Virtue was as rare a human commodity then, personally and collectively, as it is today.

It is our purpose to explore such a world and understand its ancestry to our own situations, both in Central Asia and around the world. We live with the results of these encounters and their ideological positions. The outcome of historic clashes resulting in victories or defeats have proven to be durable in nature. The game continues however, God has yet to lead the *finale* that brings down the curtain on uncertainty and striving: to take His children home for a tasty snack and warm bed before the awakening to a new day.     MBT

## PEOPLE, PLOTS & PLACES IN CHAPTER 1

Aziz: chooses to fight for his land and send Baja home.
Baja: scatters her enemies with only one major loss.
Erly: is now involved in peace negotiations with an army.
Gerchin: the warrior chief seeks the freedom he has lost.
Kadir: a vigilant guide of caravans seeks a lost friend.
Korkmaz: is an orphan who grew-up with smugglers.
Mandash: is leader of the irregular volunteer Uigur force.
Mangore: leads troopers to unsettle disputed borderlands.
Manson: is part of a border gang supplying drugs and girls.
Mookades: is the Toozlu preacher and priest of the tribe.
Nooryouz: taken from her baby and offered for ransom.
Sesli: understands the nature of threats made by a fool.
Tayze: must learn to keep pace with the camel caravan.
Twozan: the leader must pay his tribes passage money.
Yavuz: looses a friend but gains a valuable hostage.
Yeet: faces travel hardship with friends from his past.

GLOSSARY:
*Bock, ordu gelior*: Look, an army comes.
*booy roon*: here we are; here it is; behold.
*hanum*: title for a woman, (used after the name).
*hitch*: never; not at all.
*yav room*: my baby; my little one.

## HOSTAGE THREATS

"Why do you watch the road from this hiding place, Kadir bey?" asked fiesty, little Korkmaz, "It's time for food."

Kadir, the vigilant, replied, "This quiet road has become much traveled these last weeks. I have heard news of much activity at the army base. I expect some word from your grandfather, Aziz bey. He'll go to fight Uigurs. He owns land near Almati. The trouble caused by Yavuz goes on, fights, jail, murder and escapes: that means police and vigilantes are rushing around. We're exposed and at a central point between these troubles. Precaution is required. Riots and refugees are everywhere in the Syr Valley west of here. The Tuzlu Turks are retreating to the Chu River. They are going to their homeland north of here. Our Issyk Kool Lake is near enough to be endangered by all these troubles. It's a time to be careful. Vigilance is life: carelessness brings death."

The boy nodded, "Baja calls, food is ready." They moved down the hill through the bush and toward the hidden house. Beyond a clump of trees, there was a crashing of brush as three men appeared with knives.

"*Koo mool dah ma*, don't move, keep your hands open and in sight." Yavuz's voice was harsh and penetrating, "Now my fine, little men, we'll take your weapons and you can go on to the house. I knew you would be watching the road, so I came by the lakeside. Hold their weapons boys, but don't keep them where Baja *hanum* can see them." They moved slowly, normally to the impatient Baja.

The arrivals surprised her. "Yavuz bey, what are you doing here? Did Aziz come with you? No? How nice to have you drop by, what's the news at the base?" News was the main interest of all the villagers.

"Fine Baja, let me in, I want to meet your friends."

She smiled, "Come and meet the daughter of my cousin across the line. It's her first visit here. We did not want her sent back with the refugees leaving two weeks ago. She has a dear friend here with her." She went to the kitchen. "Nooryouz and Sesli, here is a friend of the family: Yavuz bey and his workers." The girls greeted them cordially.

"I didn't know your cousin had a daughter with a baby. These girls are really too pretty to be related to you Baja. I see no family resemblance."

Baja drew herself up in anger, then, changed her mind.

"I wouldn't want any of them to look like you -- or me." Baja joked walking to the stove.

"I don't believe these girls are related to any of us. I think this is the work of Aziz to cut in on my business." He hissed, venomously, "I intend to take them over and hold them until we know the truth."

"You shouldn't joke about such things, Yavuz, it's rude. I know you've been importing girls for the pleasure palaces for army coins, but Aziz would never permit such in our family; as you well know."

"He's no saint. I always suspected his pretenses and I know these girls are part of his gains. He brought them over the night of our last caravan. They smuggled them over under my nose, no less. I'm taking them now!"

"You will never, I repeat, never, be welcome in my house again. Get out of my kitchen this instant, Yavuz bey. I'm Manichean enough to shun you forever." She grabbed a yard-long, thin one-inch-thick stick used for rolling the flat bread. She whipped it around her head flexing her wrist, holding it in her fist so the stick, like a wooden sword, passed over her head and descended to eye level. She moved toward Yavuz and friends slowly as the stick moved faster. It started to whistle dangerously. They all moved back step by step. Kadir and Korkmaz broke and ran for the door to escape and the workers followed, leaving Yavuz alone. Baja did not stop,

"If you are willing to lose an eye, Yavuz, the fault rests with you alone." He turned with a curse, and dodged under the whirling end. He dived to catch Nooryouz round the waist and stood behind her. He took out his knife, and roared out his anger.

Nooryouz moaned crying, "Please, remember my baby. Don't hurt me for his sake."

"Stop Baja, you don't want her hurt. Stand back."

She slowed. "You let her go and I'll let you leave now."

He grinned, "Now listen to that, she can talk nice, when she faces a determined man." He motioned to Sesli, "You come here now."

"*Hitch*, never, you'd kill me too,"

He waved the knife, "I'll kill your friend here." Yavuz put the knife to Nooryouz throat. Nooryouz flinched.

12

Sesli backed up behind Baja. Sesli screamed, "If you got me, you'd kill me too. There's no use both of us dying. One or two makes no difference to you. You'll never get your hands on me."

He glared at her trying to scare her into obeying him. "You little whore; I know why they brought you here. Come here and I'll get you a good set up with an officer. How about that? No customer line ups."

Baja moved over and picked up a butcher's knife from the table, She waved it back at Yavuz, and advanced shouting, "You kill that girl, and you've lost your shield. She's the Umayyad ambassador's daughter. I'll never let you out of here alive."

He knew she meant it, and backed away. He turned and fled out of the house pushing Nooryouz before him. His boys had brought the horses to the door and he was out and up on one. Manson grabbed Nooryouz and pulled her up before him as they rode away.

"*Yav'room*, my baby, my little one's in there," she cried.

"Forget it," Manson laughed, "we'll give you another one."

"He's not weaned yet, he's not ready to eat food."

They rode fast and were soon out of sight. There was a moment of silence.

Then there came the sound of many hoof-beats on the road. A troop trotted up. "*Booy' roon*, here we are," Aziz's voice filled the lakeside. "Kadir, Korkmaz, Baja where are you?" He dismounted to enter the house. Sesli was holding the baby. Baja was rummaging in a trunk, she pulled out a bow, arrows, quiver, sheaths with swords.

She was surprised, "Praise all Saints and heavenly emanations, Tanra has sent you, Aziz."

He looked curiously at the strange woman holding the child. "Who's your guest, Baja?"

"Where are the boys?" she cried out. "Yavuz has kidnapped my guest, she had to leave her baby. He threatened to kill me. He's crazy and they just rode off."

"Easy now, where are the boys?" his voice was calming.

"I heard two horses leave right after the others rode away," Sesli reported, "I think they must be following the ugly little man and his gang." She paused, "They couldn't have found weapons."

"Those two wouldn't let a little thing like that hold them back."

"How did you come here?" Baja inquired, "Are you alone?"

"The army is reinforcing the Chu River fort and the fort near Almati. They abandoned the Illi River fort and the withdrawing forces reported you here. So I came with the new troops."

Baja pleaded, "You will follow those evil men? Get Nooryouz back?"

"You must promise to return to the base. The country is too wild with so many troops loose."

She shook her head, "Only when she's safe, then you can come back and we'll go."

"Not good enough. Go now!"

She bowed submissively, "You go now, hurry. We will go, too."

He eyed her suspiciously, then nodded his assent and left.

As they left, the women sighed. "Take the bow, dear, or the sword if you like it better," Baja instructed her companion. "We must be able to defend ourselves from other intruders, while the baby learns to eat. It's too great a trial to attempt on the road." She shook her head, "And it's too difficult to explain to any man."

### > - - - - - >BY THE CHU RIVER> - - - - - >

The column of refugees and Toozlu trekkers had spread themselves along the watercourses of the Chu River, banks and lagoons made of temporary snowmelt from the high country. Local residents were few for the flow ceased at the end of winter until late summer when the high mountains thawed and spread their liquid life over the arid plains again.

The first hours after arrival were spent unloading goods and recovering from the anguished days spent crossing the dry barren country above the Syr River Valley. The relief was real, but the river was only a relief stop on their move to the homeland.

Twozan the khan gathered the leaders together. Mookades, the priest, Erly, the acting yuzbasha, and their families, rode across. They had a moment of thankful prayer and a hymn for the occasion. They had survived the crossing and arrived at the recognized borders of the competing Uigur and Abbassid empires. They sang with joy.

> Father, thank you for your mercies,
> Sparkling water, daily bread.
> By your bounty and provision
> All are comforted and fed.
> Yesu we have shared your suffering,
> Faced temptation, too.
> By Your love and perseverance,
> Help us keep on serving You.

## SPARKLING WATER

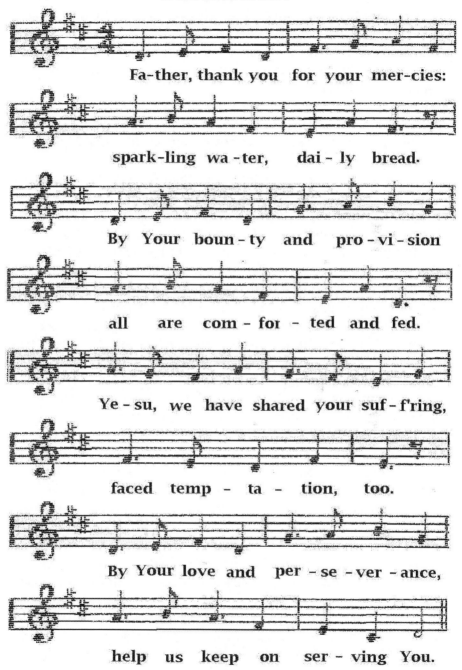

Fa-ther, thank you for your mer-cies:

spark-ling wa-ter, dai-ly bread.

By Your boun-ty and pro-vi-sion

all are com-for-ted and fed.

Ye-su, we have shared your suf-f'ring,

faced temp-ta-tion, too.

By Your love and per-se-ver-ance,

help us keep on ser-ving You.

Far on the horizon to the northeast a dark blob resolved itself into a large body of horsemen, riding four abreast, in a long line stretching back behind where a cloud of dust obscured the end of it all. Unnoticed by all, excepting a few, the armed column of troop swept down toward the joyful, noisy, celebrating mob, bent on drinking, washing and replenishing water supplies on their carts.

The small fast-moving blob grew into the battalion of horses in column, ridden by men in hardened leather armour.

"*Bock, ordu geleyor*, look, an army's coming. It's not a tribal levy, they're troopers; hundreds are coming!"

Erly's warning came none too soon. Khan Twozan reacted quickly. "Mookades go with Erly and ask for a truce. Learn their purpose and terms. I'll try to get some kind of defense organized with our men here. Setchkin, you women pray. Only Tanra can get us through this."

Twozan ran his horse over to the nearest Toozlu families and shouted, "Unpack the animals, we need time to recover. Keep the women and children busy. It's the best thing they can do with their time; work and pray. Arm yourselves men and watch if I signal." It was evident that the men were too scattered and busy watering and setting up camp to affect anything. Each would have to defend his own. The assembly had spread in order for each family to have its own pool for uncontaminated water. Twozan's horse had drunk heavily and over-watered. They were hardly able to run even a minute. Riding back, he felt his best move at this point was to join the parley. As bugles were sounding alarms, he rode out to his small group now surrounded by three times their number, talking.

Mookades introduced them. "This is the leader of the Uigur battalion, Mangore Efende. Here is our Khan Twozan, who leads the column." They exchanged greetings and then settled down to negotiate passage.

"I and my men are regular troops sent to back the irregulars." Mangore explained. "We profit only slightly from our assignments. The Father of Lights gives us our reward for a job well done, just as Mani tells us. He is the spirit of holiness sent to lead us into all truth. However, our brothers, who serve both Mani and our Emperor without reimbursement, need something for food, and families."

The leader of the irregulars, Mandash, spoke, "We serve winter and summer alike to keep the Abbasids in their place below the rivers, and we protect all our farmers and grazers from the clutches of those religious exploiters and raiders. We are forced to live on what we can forage. There will be Muslims and Abbassid coins among this mob. We'll know how to deal with both."

"The leader of the column alone has the right to search men's properties and collect coins," the priest, Mookades, said. "Any such matters must be agreed on here among leaders. Individual collections would result in many deaths and wounds. Have pity on these poor transients and let them return to their lands. They have suffered much under the neglect of the Abbasids. Remember the suffering of the children of Israel under the Pharaohs and have compassion for those in like circumstances."

The Uigurs exchanged glances and one whispered a number, while a Yuzbasha put in an urgent word of correction. "Moses served under the Jehovah of Wrath, not the Father of Lights under whom Yesu served. They are not parallel examples."

"Mangore wonders if a gold coin per man would be a just fee?" demanded the chief of irregulars.

"There are many families of men and grown boys that fought their way out of their village or farm. Others were robbed before leaving."

"A gold coin for each family might be a reasonable sum." Mandash suggested.

"What can we do for the penniless and families that lost adults or children? Most left everything behind," Erly protested.

"The Toozlu are a prosperous sept of the famous Chipchak nation. Tanra has prospered you with goods and animals, you can, in Christian charity, help to meet the needs of the destitute," suggested Mangore.

Mookades, bobbed his head angrily, "We gave our coins to that part of the tribe that separated to go a different way. We have no funds left."

A chief spit, "I'll bet we could find five thousand coins if we do our own searching. There'd be girls and goods worth that much."

Erly said hurriedly, "Let's not get hasty about this. I'll wager we might get three thousand, but it's going to cost time. We have no moneylenders among us. Leave a squad and we'll work on it."

Tension subsided and several heads nodded. In the distance, a troop of horses drew up into a column of a hundred and started walking toward the Uigur column. Behind them, another group of men ran with weapons and animals to form up.

"I think we have a deal here," the Khan affirmed. "We'll get three thousand together and you come back in a week and we'll pay it over.

However, you must protect our rear as we withdraw north. Keep the Abbasids off of us."

Neither side was happy with the sum, but it seemed to sweeten the encounter. Twozan noticed that the regulars were only about two hundred and the rest were untrained irregulars. He wondered aloud, "How did you hear about us way out here?"

"One fort has resisted all our attempts to attack it directly with irregulars, so we were going to make a circuit and invade the mountain country beyond the Chu River, go to its sources and cut them off from their base," Mangore reported. "We are not to attack directly, but try by maneuvers to encourage them to leave. It worked well on the Illi River. We want it to work here," the captain concluded.

"So your presence at our arrival on the river was just by chance and not by your design?" Twozan asked, preparing to depart.

The Uigurs laughed together, "Destiny and the wheel of life have brought you to water and us to wealth. We'll come back in a week for the gold." Mangore shouted.

Twozan moved his horse back toward the camp. "Erly, get several teams of men and send them back with water-bags to pick up stragglers and bury any corpses. We don't want more scavengers following us."

"Mookades, we have to have three thousand in gold. Register what every family gives, but appraise what they should be able to give. We may have to pay passage money to others later. Contact outriders to form an inspection team to keep sanitation and quarantine procedures in place. Let's pray that any future chance encounters will be less dangerous and more profitable for us."

> - - - - - >CAMEL CARAVAN TO BAGHDAD > - - - - - >

"Was it only yesterday that we were together with Leyla and her new husband Kerim?" Yeet wondered out loud to Tayze, as they struggled to keep pace with the caravan behind the loaded camels. Only the night before they had partied in a family reunion with loved, long lost friends.

"Yes," agreed Tayze, "I was shocked by all the scars on Leyla's sweet little face. She jumped into a thorn thicket. She had them all over her. Kerim rescued her. He reminds me of one of Kaplan's boys, Kynan. Looks like him, but acts different.

18

Yeet could see the new friends Jon and Maril ahead. They walked with Kardesh, who carried the crippled Sevman on his broad shoulders. Tash, now an Onbasha, army corporal, through the help of friends was supposed to guide all. Yeet, however, had known him as a member of a market gang bossed by Kardesh. He had reason to distrust Tash in any matter involving gain or goodwill. He did trust Derk bey the Sultan's agent who taught him to throw knives. He directed the express caravan bound for Baghdad. Derk, at least, had always shown himself a friend. To-day Derk bey seemed preoccupied and worried; Yeet had concluded that Tayze might need his help as they learned to keep pace and hoped to avoid the need of using the camels as personal transport. Just the thought made him dizzy. He had always wanted to get as far away as possible from his mother's work at the rug factory, but did that mean going to the heart of the Sultan's empire? His mother's death had cut off any desire to return home. Yet the sacrifices of travel experienced personally since they had left the quarry tired him. He would go where his hero and idol, Kardesh, went. He began to count the cost now.

"Leyla said they would follow the Amu River north to home." Tayze commented.

"Kerim said they would go to the East Bulgars first." Yeet corrected.

"They may have to live as outsiders in a strange land." Tayze sadly observed.

"We, too, may have the same experience," Yeet added.

> - - - - - >NEAR SAMARA THE CAPITAL > - - - - - >

Gerchin, warrior, leader of the right-hand sept of the Toozlu clan, hero of battles, sat on his great lion-colored horse staring into the distance. The palaces of Samara were in sight on the one hand. On the other, the distant haze of Baghdad signaled its presence. A sea of people lived on the plains of Mesopotamia. A man would drown if he sunk among them.

The high meadow and cool breeze refreshed him. It reminded him of his homeland, which was lost to him forever. Now he was captain of the palace guards. He was a slave with control of who would or would not be admitted to the Caliph's august presence. He held the power to ignore or

19

delay most applicants. He found a rich source of revenue by skillfully using his position.

He viewed the mountain. It met his need for retreat and recovery from that which he was forced to be. His herding heritage still shaped his desires, so he decided this mountain must be his. One part of his life could find freedom to follow customs and practices dear to his heart. The whirling heavenly procession of home and the New Year celebrations would continue. He knew Tanra would still rule their lives, even within the confines of Sharia law, Islam, Allah and palace slavery.

>- - - - - - -> ISSYK KOOL LAKE > - - - - - >

"Now, you've chewed it long enough, take a sip of mare's milk, mix it, and touch his mouth with your lips pursed. Let a little bit seep into his mouth. If he sucks let some more go. If he spits it up clean his lips with you finger and touch his lips, he'll suck and perhaps get some of it down." Baja stood over the two protesters protectively. One cried and the other made faces, but the lesson went on and on. He would cry-- suck a bit of strange mix – spit --suck a finger coated with the same mix. Exasperated, Sesli swallowed to clear her mouth and said, "Are you sure *bulgur,* boiled wheat, isn't too much for him to digest? Maybe just the mare's milk alone would be enough."

"He'll be eating wheat in some form the rest of his life. It's a good staple. Mare's milk does not taste the same as mama's, so he will taste a difference anyway. Better he understands that this is a new, if difficult, progress in life." Sesli cried out in protest.

"Just look at me, I'm wet and messy everywhere, and he's all wet too. He swallowed some of it and I've had enough."

"You'll be married by Summer time. You need to learn these things." Baja shook her head in despair and took the crying child on her lap. She took a corner of cloth and put it first in an open bowl of honey and then in a wooden spoon with milk and pureed bulgur and inserted it in the babies crying mouth. He paid no attention until the liquid caused him to swallow and cough. He clamped his mouth on the sugared cloth and sucked. Baja's laugh was loud and victorious. "Girls aren't what they used to be, maybe, but always experience wins. His world is expanding, there's good outside what his mama provides." When he finished the flavor and good of the cloth, he cried again and they repeated the process. Baja sighed, "Teeth and a new diet mean we won't get much sleep, but we'll be glad in a few more days that we put him through it all." Sesli was at the door. "I hear more horses on the road, Baja. Should we hide?"

"Not with a crying baby. Which way are they riding?"

"North, we could go down by the lake."

Baja laughed, "We'd have to put the baby under water to silence him. North means base soldiers reinforcing the forts. They are not looking for us. We won't likely hear horses if someone comes looking for us. Did you practice today?" Sesli shrugged and picked up the bow and quiver and sheathed hanjer. She protested again.

"It seems such a futile exertion; I get the target half the time."

"It might just save your life or someone else's for that matter. Would you argue with someone who could get you once in two shots? Would you rather them know that they can do anything they please to you because you're too weak for any defense?" Slamming the door Sesli went out into the cold to shoot arrows at the target or any tree that aroused her hostility. She fussed at the world.

"I have to look after a baby not my own. I have to hide and wait to get a decent husband someday, whenever that may be. The ones I like all leave me. First Manly, then, Bolben; he never looked at me. Now, Kadir runs after the troublemakers, and I'm alone when I want to be wanted. I think now, after all this; I would marry the first man to ask me; if he can shot straight." Her arrow, shot in anger, went straight to the bull's eye.

**MANGORE'S VISIT**

21

# PEOPLE, PLOTS & PLACES IN CHAPTER 2

Adem: guides a Bulgar named Kerim to the Mooktar.
Aziz: returns to take his family back to the base.
Baja: strives to take care of her guest's baby.
Derk: The Sultan's agent finds that he missed news.
Erly: recommends a move toward the fort.
Kardesh: carries a friend in the camel caravan.
Kerim: engages his guard in sensitive conversation.
Mookades: favors an impressive display at the fort.
Nooryouz: is the object of greedy speculation.
Sanjak: the supply officer visits Abbasid forts.
Sergeant: has information that Sanjak needs.
Sergeant Major: runs a fort while his Captain searches.
Sesli: learns how to teach a baby to eat food.
Setchkin: the Khan's wife finds safety is a memory.
Twozan: the Khan readies his forces for display.


GLOSSARY:
*barish*: peace; truce; no violence.
*Bera ket ol'son*: let there be blessings; bless you.
*esen lik ol'son lar*: may there be tranquility; peace.
*Salaam Allahy kum*: Peace to you; Arabic greeting.

**BUSY KHIVA ROADS**

"Have all the riders contact their group's leaders," Twozan explained. "Get the last arriving people out of the valley so the stream will not be muddied and contaminated. Otherwise, we will have sick people and animals within a week. None can camp beside it. Everyone must set up tents and yurts on the dry, north slope. The valley meadows are reserved for grazing. Every family must finish digging the trenches so that they have a place of defense against riders. Put in stakes to keep them at a distance. Make sure every family has weapons for every person strong enough to use them. Get the men or women of experience to teach the others. They must take time for practice every day. Any questions?"

"We're getting people claiming the convenient watering holes and quarreling over its use with neighbors. How do we handle it?"

"Leaders of ten and twenty families should have authority here. They can work together to enclose or build a well or trough for water control together. Even a stepping-stone path will keep the water cleaner. All watering places are communal in use and ownership. Apply fines if fighting or resistance breaks out. Bring back reports from the leaders of thousands as to the amounts of gold and other coins collected. Keep records of everything. We will have labor instead of coins from those who are without valuables. We need stone workers and builders. We need reports of this information before two more days pass."

23

The riders exchanged glances. It was a full day's ride to the end of the marchers' yurts now stretched along the slowly diminishing river. Ten thousand throats and three times that number of animals had lowered the level of the lakes and ponds by a hand's depth. Over the last few days the last of the stragglers had been brought in, many in pitiful condition. They reported areas of fighting behind them. Families who left unprepared were frequent victims.

As they talked, a fast riding group of men was approaching from across the river. They rode across a shallow lake disregarding the herders' protests, and the clean water tradition of all nomads. All eyes rose to watch.

"A column approaches from the south," a scout rode up to report.

"The Uigurs must be returning, it's too early," shouted Twozan, "the trenches aren't finished." The scout held up a restraining hand,

"Abbasids, the banner is black." Shock registered on all faces.

"Send one messenger along the line. Everyone arm and get in the trench, ready or not. We'll ride forward and see if there are terms or conditions that we can meet." He signaled the riders to accompany him. They were careful to ride across the marked paths between the lakes and streams to meet the army on the south side of the river.

"Barish, *esen lik ol'son lar*, Peace, tranquility be yours" Twozan shouted as they approached.

The Abbasids were alert, but not hostile as the handsome young Arab lieutenant returned the greetings. "*Salaam Allahi kum*. We have reports that the Uigurs are in this region. You are the Toozlu Turks we expected. You seem more than we were told, but we were instructed to give you passage and helps if needed." The riders exchanged quick looks.

"We saw Uigurs almost three days back," explained Twozan, "they shook us down for gold, but allowed us to camp on the promise of more to be collected. We're at the bottom of our resources."

"We keep reserves of money to bribe the irregulars from destroying Muslim villages. They tax and exploit their own villages. They would loot ours, if it weren't for the pay. The policy is not one I like, but the Mooktar and army agreed; chasing irregulars is like swatting gnats in summer. How much do you need?"

"They thought three thousand would be right, but we can't pile up enough to stay them. They threaten us with looting if we fail."

"I'll consult our commander; we haven't paid this quarter because of their working with troops. This area has been an almost neutral zone and

24

they want the villages under their direct supervision. We are obliged to see you out of the district, so who knows what the captain will think. We expect reinforcements and you'll not likely see the Uigurs again."

"Greetings to your commander." Twozan smiled cordially. "I'll send a couple of scouts with you to show you their trail. Your men can take it from there." As they rode away, he noticed that most of the troopers looked Turkish.

Mookades chuckled and asked Twozan, "What did you see?"

"Troops are out of practice and out of condition for a fight. Even the irregulars might take them. They'll need reinforcements. If they truly have that money there they might get hit at the fort while out here."

Erly came over for the end words and suggested, "We could get our money from the same source."

"Don't play the devil's advocate with me Erly. It's not the kind of repay for kindness I'd expect from you or anyone."

"Satan has need of lawyers. Potential losers always do. Let's get it."

"Has it occurred to you that the Uigurs may be using this shake down as a test to see how rich we are? They don't want our poverty. We need to be too poor for vandalism, but mean and feisty enough to cost them dearly in wounds. Appeasement money has come easy for them up to now."

"We're qualified on the poverty side. Only three hundred gold coins have come in. We'll need that to buy enough stock to get back to grazing for a living."

All those who listened agreed unanimously. "We can't give that up to the Uigurs, they'll only squeeze us for more. Better to fight them."

Twozan looked at them severely. "If you choose to fight, you must prepare your people. You have your instructions, Tanra give you wisdom."

> - - - - - > AT A MOUNTAIN CABIN > - - - - - >

"We got us a gold mine here boys. This little girl is worth a fortune from either side. The Uigurs want her to prove that the Emperor cannot be defied and lose face with escapees from the harem. The Abbasids want her because she's Umayyad and can fit into deals with Spain. We'll sell to the highest bidder." They were riding in high mountain country with Nooryouz now seated pillion behind Yavuz bey. Yavuz's little rat face was lit up with excitement. The two men were slow to see any advantages from a ransom from distant governments.

"Houses of pleasure pay right up, boss, but all governments take; they don't give money to people. Besides, how do we know Baja's not lying, she made up that cousin visiting stuff. I think she put out this

25

Umayyad stuff to keep us off her." His sidekick nodded agreement, "We can try her out and pass her on."

Yavuz chuckled, "Would you feel different about a thousand in gold each?" That's the lowest figure. Baja only tells little lies to hide big important things, she wouldn't endanger her immortal soul with a whopper." He snickered derisively, "We'll do it my way boys, and if it fails we can always go back to the other plan." The boys agreed.

"Now, each of you has to make contact with the customers. We'll meet at the peak mountain grazing pasture. No one's there in winter and I'll watch. If you come with one man alone, I'll meet you. If a group comes I'll know they made you tell and aren't willing to pay. They'll never see us. You get to the place to meet them with the money and we'll make a fair exchange of valuables. Believe me we've made the best decision."

> - - - - - >THE BUSY KHIVA ROAD> - - - - - >

"How long will it take us to reach the Mooktar, Adem bey?" Kerim asked their guard and guide.

"*Efendem* Kerim, who can know? Our Mooktar is like Harun Al-Rashid in the days of his glory, out among the people, every place in every disguise. Sometimes he is on display to attract the complainers, seekers of favors, pleaders, the needy, the radical, as well as the rich and powerful. Our mooktar is a magnet that holds our people together. He is tolerant of bare faces and religious differences of the minorities. You'll like him."

"Discontent was riotous on the upper Syr River, why are they more subject to rebellion?" Kerim asked. They had started with a morning gallop. This put the town, Khiva, far behind them. Now, they enjoyed a brisk walk. Kerim had left Leyla just behind them with the packhorse.

"The people here are kin to the Persians, and have worked the soil for generations. There, on the Syr River, they are disrupted by incursions from the steppes and migrations. Here, deserts and distance protect us. We have only a few practicing Zoroastrians and Christians left among us. We think unity of religion makes us stronger."

"It will if it incorporates the right truths to keep an open mind as to where truth truly lies."

Adem looked puzzled, "Mohammad, may he rest in peace, gave us the Koran with all the truth any people need to become great. We conquer the world. We enjoy Allah's appointed rulers and the legal use of many women - as many as we can support. Who needs greater truth than this?"

Kerim nodded thoughtfully, "But what of the issue of sin, and salvation from its presence, control and dominance? Yesu offers us a way out of guilt, self-contempt and God's condemnation."

Again, Adem looks puzzled and annoyed, "All power is with Allah. He writes our destiny on our forehead. How can anything be present, but what He desires? Allah allows our mistakes, for we are only slaves, but He is merciful. Allah states through the Koran, interpreted by our Imams, how to live our daily lives. It is all prescribed, easy and prosperous. You should consider it." Adem trotted a few lengths away, ahead of Kerim. It was a clear indication that the subject was closed.

Kerim dropped back to ride beside Leyla. They were moving at a walk now. He smiled and leaned close to say, "How fortunate we are to be Christians, to know Yesu's power to help us in our crises and problems in life. Personal transformation is needed and not just conformity to rules and regulations."

Leyla glanced up, annoyed, "You've been talking to the guard again about religion? Why would you even bother? You know what they always say: 'You must be like us, we are right, but you are misled, wrong because your scriptures were changed.'"

He bowed a salaam, laughed and said, "Beware of ladies who know a reply before it's spoken. They will steal your heart and put words in your mouth."

She smiled condescendingly, "Words are like food in the mouth: they nourish and they give strength if they are absorbed. As for hearts, they should not be left lying around loose; they must be guarded from harm."

He whispered, "So mine must be truly safe."

She tucked her face in and turned, "As long as it's with me alone." A long silence followed as they watched the scenery. Desert and thorn bush hemmed in their left, western side. The irrigated valley was on the east as the sun rose over the river and fields. Winter was coming and the bite of the air and brown and yellow of the land below underlined the fact that travel would be painful and short as daylight retreated.

"We need a place of refuge to stay the worst of winter. Escape is not our first priority now, safety now has first place."

She nodded, "It must be our prayer for these days - safety and rest." They passed a goods caravan of Bactrian camels moving north. One of the men leading a loaded animal gave them a piercing glance. Leyla felt a sudden warning shock of recognition: it was Umer. She spurred her Fergana mare into a gallop. Kerim joined her, thinking it was a diversion from serious talk.

The guard, Adem, let them go by, but trotted his horse not to lose sight of them. It might take a week or more to get to the Mooktar of the district, but it was better than barracks life and the Christian had strange ideas he had never thought on before. His wives could wait with their quarrels and complaints. He was enjoying his outing.

> - - - - - >ARMY SUPPLY CARTS > - - - - - >

"Look Sergeant, that's what we've been waiting for." The fort and village nestled on the plain, where the River Chu emerged from protective mountains, was coming into view now. The cheering of their men was heard over the squeak of the cart's axles.

Traveling they had seen the havoc of enemy action wherever they passed empty villages. They saw goods scattered, remnants living in the woods, mountains and desert places until one side won. Then conditions of peace would be established. Each war band had exacted its part of goods in the destruction and many villagers cared nothing for which side won, only that peace would come before winter's worst.

"It's been a hard trip, Sir, in every way," admitted the sergeant.

"But Tanra, Allah, God, whatever you call the Creator has let us through without suffering what others have faced. I'll deliver our goods intact. I'll have done something right, as I hoped."

"I'm glad for you Sir; we'll still have to return to the army base."

"I wouldn't return at all if it weren't for the possibility of finding my wife, Nooryouz, in the mountains. I'm sure she has escaped out of Uigur territory and the base, too. She could be wandering with the villagers in the mountains."

The sergeant considered his words. "You were doing labor supervision of prisoners, Sir. You may not have heard that the

28

Village was burned because of the harem woman's death in the mountains. There is suspicion that others escaped over the passes."

Sanjak's expression changed to sharp interest as he replied. "One of the smuggler's boys got a message to a prison boy named Manish, a shepherd. It made him very happy. It seemed like good news of safety or success."

"Who was the boy, Sir? I know them all."

Sanjak thought, "I'm not sure I remember, it was something like a negative: with --*maz*, on the end," he paused.

"*Korkmaz*, Fearless: the pride of his family. His mother's dead, but Aziz bey, his grandfather is one of the richest men in town. If anything is going on in the district they know about it."

"I talked to Manish before he was repatriated, the day we left, and I know she is here and well, with our baby and other refugees from Chang'an in Tang, China. Two were captured and sent off with that new corporal, Tash, who was hurt by his own tongue."

"Yes, Sir, sent off to Baghdad, the girl has a rich father. Tash made enemies and is safer elsewhere."

Sanjak waved to the fort, a sentry waved back. "Once we are in there we'll think of some plan to contact Aziz."

"Welcome, Sir," shouted the sentry. "We was worried about winter supplies. Did you have trouble getting through? The Captain and Lieutenant are out leading forays into the villages for goods and any other things - valuables, that is. The Master Sergeant is left in charge"

"Tend to your duty sentry. I'll do the welcome bit," a rough voice proclaimed as the gates creaked on their hinges. He came out as the gates opened wide.

"Welcome, you be the senior officer now, Sir. How was the trip?"

"Nobody intercepted us. How many able-bodied men remain here now, Sergeant?"

The man smiled happily, "With your men we be almost fifty Sir, a few are wounded or sick, but most are good men ready to hold the fort for our Caliph."

"I, as a foreigner, hesitate to say the Caliph deserves, or doesn't deserve such men and their devotion. So I say: *beri ket ole'son*, bless you."

"Troopers coming from the eastern hills, Serge," called a sentry from a corner tower, "riding hell for leather, not ours for sure." A cymbal clashed and a kettledrum started pounding.

Sanjak yelled to his men entering the fort, "Get the last of those carts inside and close the gate." The kettledrums, empty cooking vats with skin stretched over the mouths, were pounding a warning to all those in the fort. Men were arming and running to their posts. Archers moved up into the towers, as the gates closed.

Outside there was a rush of cavalry, then a pause beyond arrow range and angry words were heard, berating a scout. It seems the attack was to be staged when the carts were still outside the fort. They probably intended to intimidate the defenders and perhaps draw them out in an attempted rescue. Then a mass of mounted soldiers appeared from the western hills. The fort was caught between two horns, one small, the other large; a hammer and anvil made of armed men. The arriving party rode up to the arguing circle and hushed them. A truce party formed and rode toward the gate. A giant officer in bright armour, adorned with bronze, and leather strips and a large iron helmet, moved forward and commanded attention.

"I'm Mangore, Captain of the western frontier. Your forts have been mistakenly built in our territory. We have rectified the mistake made in using the old Tang fort on the Illi River. This place must be abandoned, too. We allowed you to remain to defend the few Muslim villages from the Turkish tribes and nomads, but you haven't paid the tribute traditionally expected." His grin was derisive, "Your rent is due. We're here to collect it."

> - - - - - >CARAVAN TO BAGHDAD > - - - - - >

"I thought a camel train would be riding on top of camels, not walking with them." Maril laughed, as Yeet, Tayze and Jon found themselves continuing on foot between groaning, complaining, towering beasts loaded with the best merchandise of trade. The shaggy creatures towered over them and they were glad to walk on the windward side of their shuffling, smelly line.

"You only ride if you're ill, otherwise you just keep out of their way." Yeet was bright with newly acquired information.

"The thought of being up on that beast makes me sick and hardens me to stay well," Maril added. They all agreed heartily. Tayze brought out some dried nuts and fruit to suck and enjoy. The round faced attendants led the beasts, a man to each guide rope, although a few were linked to each other. Each camel weighed four times more than any guide did. They were not docile, obedient animals. They would kick and bite when frustrated. Angry shouts brought other attendants and passengers to watch, help and always, comment. These journeys are full of such events.

"It's like learning to walk, you're never as steady as you'd like. How are you doing on this sand Sevman?"

Sevman smiled at Jon, and lied to Kardesh as he limped along with difficulty. "I don't mind it too much. It'll be easier later when we are used to it. I don't want to tire Kardesh."

Kardesh laughed gently, he knew his friend. He jibed, "A dark emanation, eh?"

Jon chuckled now, he liked his new friends and a Manichee who could take a joke. Such boys were not to be encountered every day. The stiffly religious are serious.

Sevman and Jon guided Kardesh to one side of the long stride of the camels. Out of the Amu Valley, the sand of the Kara Kum was already under foot, black sand flowing out under each footfall leaving deep tracks; scars on the desert floor where the traces of their passing would exist for days. The pace seemed slow, but they ate up the distance and would continue until an hour before dark. Blow hot or cold it was the pattern and rule of travel, no stops for lunch or breaks for rest, dune followed dune, a mind numbing process. When walking exhausted them Tayze and Maril were willing to share a ride on a camel.

Tash sought knowledge, "The captain said you've come in from thorn country with some important people, Derk bey. Who are they?"

Derk answered stiffly, "They are here. I made friends of my assignments. Among these friends is a Manichean from the last vestige of monasticism that we expelled. They existed before we conquered the Fergana Valley, in the time of Tang tributary states. There is a Muslim, the son of the last important Christian leader in the valley. The Gray Wolf Society is active there. We need to know why they killed her and what relation the son has to it. Something is different about the child. Then, there is the son, of the late heir to the Khan-ship and control of the Chipchak Nation. It is one of the large Turkish tribes to our north. He escaped death in the quarry. We have just gotten rid of the Toozlu sept. They came down to follow the heir. They have converted to Islam and been contracted as royal guards in Samara. Only a few are returning home."

31

Tash walked beside Derk, the person for whom the caravan had delayed. Special, powerful agents to the Caliph held Tash's complete devotion. He wanted to impress him.

"I had a Toozlu prisoner that I brought to Khiva yesterday from the Mooktar of the Upper Syr Valley. We had to quiet riots and fights all along the way. We had to use civilian help because we had so few soldiers. Now, I have to escort these two to Yusuf bey in Baghdad."

"The rich Christian from Changan? The refugees came through some time ago."

Tash agreed happily, he had the agent's attention and he had information to share. "The girl, Maril, was detained by the Uigur Emperor's orders. The servant helped her escape the harem and four of them got away. Only one was caught by the Uigurs at the border pass where our base is located. She was taken to the village dead. The authorities burned the village. We had refugees running away and had to round them up to send back. We caught this girl and a shepherd boy guide. So we know the other two are in the base area. Jon tried to help her escape again and we caught them." Tash thought that Derk bey was not listening closely and came to a halt.

The man had a bemused look. "Sanjak bey is an officer there?" He asked softly,

"I had a run in with that Turk the day I arrived. A gang of cronies beat me up. He was just off detention when we caught the girl here and Jon. The shepherd boy went back with the refugees and I came on this assignment."

Derk nodded understandingly. "What was Sanjak doing when you left?"

Tash thought carefully. "I think he had to take supplies to the frontier forts on the rivers Chu, Almati and the Illi."

Derk bey's face twisted in agony. "I thought I was getting him away from it all, and I put him in the big fat middle of everything that's going on. Blood counts even in angry families. He will help them and they he." Derk bey walked away angry and Tash wondered why.

"Move or stay we must have meat to pass the winter. The grass here by the Chu is already in use by local people, we add to the burden. Many refugees have already slaughtered their animals to reach here. We must decide that all animals not being milked or expecting to be soon, must be slaughtered. Even with that we'll have hungry days." Twozan explained.

Erly had listened patiently to the latest orders. "It must be dried and redistributed so that all will have a portion. Taking from the prudent and well off to give to the needy or those who suffer will not go down easily."

Mookades added, "They'll complain, but won't dare turn back. We need additional supplies, and after what the Abbasid lieutenant said; I think we should go to the nearest fort to apply for it."

Twozan smiled grimly, "We serve a God of miracles. What could be further from the normal than that our persecutors should aid us in any way?"

"Then, lets get an armed group," Mookades said. "Put on a nice military look. We're asking for help, but we won't go as beggars,"

"Right," Erly responded. "We have to look strong, even if needy. We want their respect, as well as their goods for wintering here."

Twozan decided, "We'll take two hundred men. That should make an impression."

**CARAVAN TO BAGHDAD**

33

## PEOPLE, PLOTS & PLACES IN CHAPTER 3

Adem: the corporal who guides and guards visitors.
Derk: is caught in a confusion of cross-purposes.
Erly: must lead the troops to the Abbasid fort.
Jon: tries to understand his fellow travelers.
Kerim: gets a new assignment toward freedom.
Leyla: sees an old danger and a new hope.
Nooryouz: suffers attention and neglect at the same time.
Mooktar of Lower Amu: finds agents for his work.
Sergeant: works closely with Sanjak his captain.
Sanjak: defends a fort from an enemy.
Sevman: finds the going difficult until a friend helps.
Setchkin: finds reasons to rejoice.
Twozan: chooses duty over excitement.
Tash: finds things happening too fast to follow.
Yavuz: confidently counts his gold before it arrives.


GLOSSARY:
*Allah shu kure*: God be praised.
de'kot: attention; alert; be careful.
*dough roo*: that's right; correct.
*hahm dolsun*: praises be; may God be praised.
*tah-bee*: naturally; of course.

A MESSENGER'S END

"I know I saw him with the camel caravan we passed an hour out of the city," Leyla insisted. "Umer is here in the Amu Valley. He's going the same direction we are."

Kerim slowed, "I'll go back and check it out. If it's him I'll know what to do."

She reached out a hand to check him, shuddering in her fear, "Please don't. He may not have seen me. He could have no way of knowing we would go north from Khiva. We didn't know it till just yesterday. Maybe he's just had to find any work possible, since he can't go home."

Adem bey, the guard, had taken the lead, but slowed. "What's wrong? You dropped back. You have to keep pace."

"Sorry corporal, we'll be along, my wife thought she saw someone she knew."

The onbasha shook his head in disgust. "This comes of having barefaced women who can be recognized and recognize friends on the street. Custom is wiser; women should not be talking or visiting on the streets. Don't slack your pace." He rode ahead and, it was clear, would resent any challenge to his orders.

"We must keep up." Leyla agreed and Kerim shrugged and followed. They were in another village now, It had a prosperous look and the congestion grew as they neared the center. Soldiers blocked their approach. Adem bey, however, rode to the troopers to talk.

"Allah has favored your visit," he shouted. "The Mooktar is returning. He is here. Come, you may pass." A path opened between troops and they were able to ride to the village center where important people ringed the governor. They made the salaam to him, as Onbasha Adem bey made the introduction.

"Honorable Lord, these people are sent to you by the Captain of Khiva. They are obviously outsiders in transit with this pass through your territory." He passed the letter from the Mooktar of Upper Syr to the *Efende*. The Mooktar scanned the document.

"*Allah shu kure*, Praises to God, You people are just whom I need. Come inside we must talk. Onbasha, remain here until I return." He led the way, his adjutant ran ahead to open the doors. "I have correspondence that must urgently be delivered to a --, a friend and very important business connection. My people are occupied here with suppressing insurrection and other serious problems in the north, all are under my responsibility. Would you be willing to carry the packet and deliver it to my friend?"

Kerim cocked his head, "Where do I take it to? If it is urgent, it means winter travel. How are we to do that?"

The Mooktar smiled grandly, "There is a line of caravansaries on the commercial road that links the Aral Sea and the Caspian. At the Mother of Rivers in the Capital City, you will find my friend. It is, of course, confidential, but we will give you a pass, food and lodging will be taken care of. I'm offering an expense free trip in winter that has some hardships, but warm food and lodging is guaranteed."

Kerim smiled confidently, "We too, have an urgency to arrive in my country which is north-east of the Khazar capital. I couldn't consider such a detour without some additional form of help, -- remuneration." Leyla stared in amazement, but the Mooktar only looked at his adjutant and raised his eyebrow.

"We have the sum readied, *Efendem*," he hastened to say. "We prepared a pack for a horse. It contains all that you indicated. We will place it on their pack animal in the corporal's care outside."

"In a place secure from prying eyes," the Mooktar indicated.

"You have chosen wisely, Sir, a sum will be given you on your departure and another on arrival. You will inspect the pack. Be sure it is unopened. You must deliver it intact. It is your passport home to safety. You will be rewarded when it is received intact. That word will be your password and sign for recognition and delivery."

"I will do all in my power to arrive intact, Mooktar, *Efendem*."

"See that you do, many lives depend on it." The man's eyes were cold now and dismissive. Kerim knew that their lives were among those depending on it.

Outside the wind blew cold and the corporal made them wait. Leyla mounted her Fergana mare and Kerim the black when a line of loaded camels passed, just beside the line of soldiers. At that moment, their packhorse was led to them. Leyla took the halter. One of the camel drivers screamed shrilly and plunged past the guards to thrust his sharpened staff up to Leyla's face. The mare shied, reared and the lead jerked the packhorse against the mare's haunches. They fell back hooves thrashing. Leyla managed to leap clear. The horses struggled to recover, separating the attacker from his goal. A soldier caught the intruder with a slash of his sword on the neck and the staff with its iron point fell with the man to the cobblestones. The adjutant came running, the Mooktar followed.

"I recognize this man *Efendem*, Umer is a murderer sought by Tewfik bey," explained Kerim as he helped Leyla up. "I served in his pursuit, but he escaped."

The Mooktar scrutinized Kerim carefully and nodded. He spoke to the adjutant. "Reward and promote the soldier. Bury the body and advise Tewfik bey of the event: credit Kerim of the East Bulgars, with the sure identification of the culprit. Let him forward all pertinent information concerning both men. I think we may have chosen well for our agent. Corporal, see them to the Aral border post and return. Now, ride!"

> - - - - - > CARAVAN TO BAGHDAD >- - - - - - - >

"The man you came with keeps to himself and seems very angry. Our corporal seems to avoid him and looks worried." Jon ventured to Sevman, who agreed with his new travel companion.

"We still have questions and even reservations about our brave leader. He always seems to appear at a time of need and knows too much about what is happening. He is an agent or emissary of the Sultan. Yeet swears by him and is full of awe and admiration for everything he says or does. I am now more skeptical."

Jon agreed. Looking over at Yeet and Maril he observed: "I suppose I should be jealous, Yeet has taken a great liking to Maril and they talk and laugh almost all day now."

Sevman nodded, "He's hardly more than a child. He doesn't even have peach fuzz on his face yet. He's a pretty boy who needs friends. Derk snubs him, so he seeks Maril who loves to talk. It's amusing to listen to them, but it doesn't cheer Derk bey. He is sunk in gloom, walking ahead of them. Listen to them chatter."

"For a whole two weeks I envied the Princess Leyla her Fergana mare; I could picture myself riding into Baghdad on such a prize." Laughter followed Maril's outburst and the Tayze, who walked behind, joined them in laughter. Derk who led the camel before the pair stopped and turned to face the two. His face was pale, mouth tight.

"Where did you travel with that princess?" He snapped in steely voice, "You were sent from Commander Onat's base."

Maril started, "*Efendem*, pardon My Lord, to Khiva," she stuttered, "from the Mooktar of Upper Syr River District. She was sent with us from there."

"Was she alone?" He pushed his face into hers, glaring furiously.

"Jon and I came from the base with Corporal Tash and ten troopers. The Mooktar sent Princess Leyla with us. Three of his wounded men were forced to turn back."

Jon joined the group and interrupted. "When our forces were diminished by the demands of the Mooktar, he assigned four wounded men back from fighting to join us. A friend of his, going to Khiva, joined us for protection."

Derk whirled on him. "What's his name?"

Jon shrugged and smiled at Maril. "Kerim of the East Bulgars, on a black, and a dun pack animal."

Derk backhanded Jon across the face and took him by the shoulders to shake him savagely.

Sevman laid restraining hands on Derk bey. "They tell you the truth. I met the man in the caravansary. There's no need for violence. What do you want to know?"

Derk shook free. He was panting and wild-eyed. He now grabbed Sevman's arm. "They were both there in Khiva? At the place where I met you?"

"*Tah-bee*, of course, Kerim bey had food sent in and Leyla talked to all of us, from her room's door-way. Maril and Tayze slept in the room with her."

Maril continued the report of the party. "Kerim and Jon had become good friends on the trip from the Syr River and he didn't know that they were married. It was a secret, so the guard wouldn't let him talk to Leyla when the others did. We laughed about that later. They were the first to leave the inn the next morning."

Derk bey had stopped listening to them. He ran back to his camel and led it out of the caravan. He turned and started back on the trail from Khiva without a word of explanation.

"*Efendem*, sir, where are you going?" inquired Tash, who left his beast to run after the man who was responsible for the caravan's departure.

"I have urgent business in Khiva. They are waiting for you in Baghdad. Yours is the responsibility now. Get them there." Jon and the others stopped and observed the action with astonishment.

"Jon, Sevman, what did we say to upset him?" Maril asked.

"Perhaps our old friend has newer and more important interests than travel to Baghdad. He may be in trouble with his own authorities in dealing with the Toozlu." Yeet stated dryly, "Information is his trade and he has evidently missed some important events." Still they stood.

As the end of the caravan passed, Derk sat down in the sand and started writing on a small strip of paper. He attached it to the leg of a pigeon he removed from a covered cage on the camel's pack. He tossed it into the air. He started again, with a curse, almost running back the way they had come for three days. The bird soared high in mounting circles until it took its flight toward home. It flew north and east with a message that could change the course of life to death.

> - - - - - >A MESSENGER'S END> - - - - - >

High over the fringes of the Amu Valley, where the desert touches the irrigated orchard and farmland, a big peregrine falcon flew. It moved in seemingly effortless glides and spirals in patrol of its hunting territory. Its usual prey was becoming dormant in the winter cold. Others were in change of color and habit in their obedience to the season. Autumn fatness was in the process of diminishing. Hunger produced extra vigilance on the part of all who would survive the change. The swift flight of an incoming bird was noted; size, course and velocity registered in the brain of the raptor. A prey worthy of interception, a week's rations approached. The peregrine made the necessary corrections of course and velocity. It began a swift descent gathering speed to the point of interception.

A bird pressed by time and the setting of the sun flies straight to the cote where friends and neighbors will be congregating with bows and coos to exchange food gathered, stored in their crop with spouse and even summer's fledglings, now young adults. A steady, rapid flight without variation of pulse eats up distance, but exposes the messenger to ambush. Unexpectedly, the lightning stroke that broke the neck came severing the head. The victor followed the trajectory of the body, breaking with out stretched wings, the impact of its fall. He landed on the warm body to begin the feast in a shower of descending feathers.

The next nesting season the messenger's mate will seek another. Message and messenger are lost, and the needs of other servants of nature's God are satisfied. Beyond the plans and needs of those who acclaim themselves masters, a higher will has set all pretensions aside for its own conclusion; an action to silence reactions.

> - - - - - > A FORT UNDER SIEGE> - - - - - >

"Are the remaining supplies packed Sergeant?" Sanjak inquired.

"All are packed and the men in place lieutenant." he answered.

"Good, the men will take the mid-morning duty roster, stand down for now and we will call them up again mid-afternoon to try our luck again on a late departure."

The sergeant smiled sardonically and agreed. "Four hours guard duty will be good for us Sir, the warmest time of day and all."

Sanjak looked at his sergeant knowingly and spoke, "Have them eat a hearty breakfast but warn them against sleeping on the job. Otherwise they might wake with an arrow in their throat."

The sergeant's order rang from the center to the circumference of the besieged fort. The men moved grumbling to the mess hall.

"I suppose you will be praying about this situation, Sir?"

"I always do Sergeant. Do you have any special requests?"

"Just to leave with a whole skin, Sir. You could throw in a request for a good wife, Sir, one I can afford." Sanjak nodded approval.

The siege had continued for a week now, each side doing its routine: breakfast, inspection, guard duty rosters were announced. Hours were spent watching the other side and then rest with meals, maintenance of weapons, games of chance and gossip, occupied them, just as in most of their days of army life. The difference lay in the fact that either side could start hostilities at any moment and men would die at their posts.

"Look, Lieutenant," called Master Sergeant on the wall, "They've got a villager there with Mangore. Ain't he the man from the army Base? Hey, Abu Bahker, you know that man?" he called.

"Yeah, works with Yavuz bey. He's got a letter! They're interested. He's pointing toward the base or something south-east of here."

"*Dough rue*, right, I recognize him now. That is Manson, the Uigur sidekick of Yavuz, The smuggler. Does all his dirty work."

Sanjak stood beside him watching. "Look, Master Sergeant, twenty troopers are taking off with Manson. He acts like he doesn't want to go. They're threatening him."

"Well that leaves only about eighty men here with a few irregulars. There are likely more troopers at Almati fort so we have most of the force tied down watching us. Makes you feel important, doesn't it Sir? Tying up the enemy!"

Sanjak was looking west. "Look toward the river, what do you see?"

"Troops by the look of them," the sergeant swore. "The enemy can't see them. The fort blocks the view. It must be the Captain returning."

Sanjak shouted, "Master Sergeant prepare a sortie, we must distract them so they get caught by a surprise. We'll hit the command tent for information and to draw them toward the fort." Twenty-five men quickly assembled behind the main gate.

"Be silent until we hit the tent. I'll enter and when I come out burn it and yell as loud as you can. Beat the drums in the fort to warn the Captain."

The men were happy to agree, they were bored by the inaction of the last days. The gate swung open, the horses poured through. The Uigur troopers were dispersed and off guard, but the shout went up as the horses pounded across the parade grounds to the command tent where the squad's arrows diminished the guards.

Sanjak hastily entered and came running out with his hands full of letters and papers and they mounted to hurry back under an increasing shower of enemy arrows. They lost one man outside the walls and had three wounded that arrived to safety. They counted seven dead and more wounded enemies. The roar of the drums continued. The Uigur troopers on horse and on foot had followed the retreating men to the fort gate. Suddenly, around both sides of the fort came a stream of horsemen. Their arrows sent the enemy running from the parade grounds and into the woods and hills behind. Relief had come and won the day.

"*Dee'kot*, attention, the squad will now resume the attack. We'll join our rescuers in sending the enemy back to Almati." With shouts of enthusiasm, they again raced through the gate to pursue the last of the retreating enemy forces.

> - - - - - > CHU RIVER ENCAMPMENT> - - - - - >

"*Hah'md olsun*, praises be; you've come. I thought you would be tempted to go to the fort with the warriors," Setchkin shout was jubilant as Twozan rode up to the Khan's yurt and *ordu evi*, command center.

"I was, and started out with them, but we met the young Abbasid lieutenant riding to the rescue of the fort from besieging Uigurs. So, we joined forces and I let Erly command our group. There was too much work here to leave it for long."

She appraised him carefully, "You let another take the glory of the fight and left the critical negotiations to Erly bey? That took real

42

maturity, my love."

"I'm glad you like it. You've been showing some maturity too."

"We've a people to rescue, their lives and ours depend on it."

"We haven't enough food to go or stay. We'll starve either way. Even if we had ample supplies, the question remains. Do we cross the salt steppes in the worst cold or in the spring when we've used our supplies and are weak or in summer when it is furnace hot and dry?"

"We lose people any way we choose," Setchkin said sadly, "Yesu must supply our needs for us, we must wait for His timing."

"Yes," Twozan agreed, "Mookades is holding a vesper service. New families are arriving with hard news of wholesale murder for goods and politics in the valley. In Allah's name they slaughter thousands."

She shivered and whispered, "Let's go now, I need to pray. The songs give me courage." They left the Yurt for a near by sandy field where groups of families and friends stood listening. A well-known song of praise was starting.

A SONG OF PRAISE

1. Lord, let us thank you now for your great sal – va – tion.
2. Your chil – dren praise your name for Mes – si – ah's com – ing.

Giv – en lib – ral – ly by re – deem – ing love.
His great sac – ri – fice fills our hearts with praise.

Praise Ye – su for your great com – pa – sion

in all our weak – ness we glad – ly give you

all our ad – o – ra – tion! Praise Ye –su. Praise!

| 1 | Lord, let us thank you now, |
|---|---|
| | For your great salvation. |
| | Given liberally by redeeming love. |
| | Your children praise your name, |
| | For Messiah's coming. |
| | His great sacrifice fills our hearts with love. |

Women's coda:

Praise, Yesu for your great compassion,
In all our weakness, we gladly give you
All our adoration. Praise Yesu. Praise!

"Friends and newly arrived brothers and sisters in affliction." The voice of Mookades boomed out in penetrating vigor. "We come together in sorrow for your sufferings past and present. For Yesu has told us, 'In the world you will have tribulation.' but he also tells us 'Be of good cheer, I have overcome the world.' The God who provides salvation, provides all we need to arrive at His assigned destination. At journey's end, some of you will be alive in a land of freedom and others in heaven. You must prepare for either place through faith and trustful obedience to His Spirit. Tanra, the Creator God of our ancestors, has designed this world as a place to develop character. He gives us faith to endure. He did not intend life to be all ease and pleasure, but that the people of God might demonstrate themselves His children in all circumstances.  The truth shows in its practice by the life we live. Tanra redeems us to share with us His presence and blessing: spiritual and material. If we seek our own way, we will find no help in our tribulations. However, you my brothers and sisters are not without faith. You have come this far, therefore, 'Trust in the Lord with all your hearts and lean not to your own understanding. In all your ways acknowledge Him and He will direct your path'. This is a promise made by a faithful God. We will trust Him. Let us pray." The people knelt in prayer and many were crying.

> - - - - - >IN A MOUNTAIN CABIN> - - - - - >

"You get in there and stay quiet. I'm your best guarantee of safety and good treatment, so don't get me riled," Yavuz insisted. The hillside was cold and windy. It fluttered the light blanket around her.

"I'm cold and it's dark inside," protested Nooryouz. Standing before the small, mud and twig, wattle hut. "I didn't have time to put on anything warm. This thing you gave me is flimsy.

"It's wool. I'm on the run. How could I plan to bring all I need?"

44

"You could have left me with my baby. I need him."

"I don't care what you need. You are money in our pockets. Now, get in that hut and stay until I call you. There's a bear in the woods here and if you get outside he could eat you." He chuckled and rode away, secure in his knowledge that she would not dare roam. He knew how to handle women. He had been doing it for years. He was proud of his long experience. They were his commodities to trade, if not enjoy. "Within four hours, the boys should make contact and be here," he whispered to himself. "They'll bring the money soon." He was looking over the field of contact from a hill of brush and small trees. The meadow spread out broadly below him.

When the little man rode off, he didn't see the movement in the bushes behind the house. He could not feel the eyes that watched his going. He did not hear the faint growl of anger.

### >- - - - - > ON THE CARAVAN WEST > - - - - - >

"I wonder why we must go on while Derk Bey returns to the Amu Valley?" Sevman asked Kardesh as they plodded on.

"He gave instructions to Tash when we started and he didn't change anything when he left." Kardesh answered.

"Tash pretends he doesn't know us." Yeet stated laughing.

"The past holds painful memories for many of us." Kardesh observed sadly. "It's better to forgot it."

"All money gained without honest labor brings shame." Sevman pontificated smugly. Yeet made a disgusted sound of protest, but his friend continued. "I know of no circumstances where such money works for good." He stared at Yeet reproachfully.

"It got you hospital care and healing that summer." Yeet retorted with heat. They trudged along silently for a long moment.

"I always wondered where you got the money from, Yeet," said Kardesh kindly.

"The goldsmith I worked for paid me with the food I ate, nothing more, because he was stingy. He even complained about how much I ate. He made me clean my fingernails after the work to be sure there was no gold or gems stolen. He watched everything, but gave me no commission when an article I made sold. I counted the profit he made on my work, but he was never generous. When the shop burned, I collected my earnings and later spent it on you."

"Your master died in the fire, didn't he?" Kardesh inquired.

"He upset a melted pot of silver ore. It caught the wall. He was badly burned. We rescued all his treasures from the building. His wounds infected. I lost my job, but quietly collected my wages."

"And spent them on friends," Kardesh concluded.

"A waste of money, to preserve flesh," Sevman interjected.

1.

45

## PEOPLE, PLOTS & PLACES IN CHAPTER 4

Adem: hears a new view of Allah's forgiveness.
Baja: again is required to travel away from her home.
Bolben: although dead still has a part to play.
Captain: faces the problem of sending a corpse home.
Erly: finds that victory can be profitable for everyone.
Harun el Ari: is the younger brother of Mansur.
Kaya: a Christian refugee is required to return a corpse.
Kerim: enjoys challenges to his ways and beliefs.
Leyla: worries about delays leaving the Amu Valley.
Manly: supervises the frontier for the Uigurs.
Nooryouz: is harassed, tired of narrow escapes.
Onat: must face a problem of returning Bolben.
Sergeant Major: must keep discipline in the army post.
Sesli: hopes for a change for the better in life.
Umer: his reported death lacks needed details.
Yusuf: finds his old manager embezzled property.


GLOSSARY:
*Allah is-mar-la-dik*: Good by, I'm leaving.
*Chador*: a robe covering a woman's face and body.
*Choke Yashar*: long live -----; hurray for our man.
*Gelip geldin*: the conqueror comes; he won & came.
*Musaferim*: my winner; my victorious one: my hero.
*Soos*: quiet; hush.

ARGUMENTS TRAVEL

The men argued as they rode. Had they been in a village  a crowd  would have followed, but they were in the country. Ardent arguments attract listeners.

"One man's death, however good he may have been, cannot bring innocence and pardon for another human. Not even a prophet's life can purchase pardon for more than himself. Furthermore, the honor of Allah is involved in the death of a prophet. The death reserved for criminals on a cross is not a way for a prophet to die. Allah would not allow such a crime. The Koran says another was substituted for Isa." Adem's voice betrayed his agitation.

Kerim, riding beside him, replied, "Yesu is the Messiah, sent to free all Tanra's creation from the guilt and penalty of sin. It was and still is God's plan to redeem the human race. All blood sacrifices involve the innocent dying for the guilty. The Jews used to make sacrifices in their temple. Flawless animals, that do not sin, were sacrificed for people who do sin against God. Even in Islam you sacrifice innocent animals each year," Kerim insisted.

Adem protested again, "Yes, but not for sin, it is in commemoration of the act of Abraham. He is the source of our faith, not Isa, though Isa was a prophet of miracles. We Muslims have a garden promised if we surrender to Allah and obey. These are the words of the Koran. You are an unbeliever. Muhammad, may he rest in peace, is not your prophet. We accept your prophet why can't you accept ours?" Adem was confused and frustrated by Kerim's arguments.

Kerim answered gently, "You don't know anything about our messiah, He is a prophet, a priest, a king, and he will come back to set things right. He is Emanuel, 'God with us'. God lived among us in Yesu's person: a perfect man. For that reason, there is salvation only in him."

Adem spurred his horse ahead and was ready when Kerim came up to him. Adem spoke angrily and with emphasis, "We have talked enough. It is obvious that we agree about a few things, like Isa's return and the garden of Allah, but the differences, in practical daily life and in teaching are obvious. You can legally have only one wife in your country. I can have four, plus others if I can afford it. You let your women go barefaced and bold, doing many things only men should do. You make men worse than they are by saying they cannot be saved through obeying Allah, our prophet, the Koran and doing good." He reflected sadly and continued more evenly, "I think we need guidance to find the right path; right choices, not salvation. Men need direction as slaves of Allah. The Koran is my guide." Adem was emphatic, so was Kerim.

The men rode silently for a few minutes, and then Kerim spoke again. "Your mistake is in thinking that men are good enough to please Allah without repentance, reconciliation and transformation. Our race and our hearts rebel against God and his laws. We fear him because of our sins. Our terror of His power drives us farther away. He will redeem us if we permit it. He has sacrificed his beloved, perfect son for us."

"You name him Son, believing that God or the angel Gabriel procreated with the Virgin. This is an insult to Allah." Adem was firm.                                              "It would be if I said or believed it, but Allah spoke the Word into her body and that created Yesu. Like the first man, Adam, a son of God, but in a different way and for a different purpose from the first man."

"Isa is a great prophet. He ranks with the last prophet, Muhammad, peace be to them. Isa is among the most influential, but you misunderstand him. Allah took him directly to heaven; saved him from the cross. Roman hands crucified someone who deserved such a death. I don't need to be saved from my useful, respectable life. Our talks are ended." He rode off.

Kerim looked after him sadly. The last few days always ended this way.

"Each of you thinks himself right," Leyla laughed. "So, each will end up living by his own rules."

Kerim looked up to smile at his bride. "Tanra's rules, not mine, must be obeyed. I'm sure time will prove which one of us is right. However, they are self-righteous, aggressive and insistent on imposing their beliefs. That means more wars and insurrections."

"As long as men will force their own opinions on others," she stated quietly. "Nevertheless, I prefer the one wife and companion rule even though I'm not much on theology."

They rode in silence. Then he spoke, "Perhaps sin is a bigger issue where more choices are available and we know how often we have chosen wrong. Where everything is imposed they only see others' transgressions, never their own."

She changed the subject, her tone was anxious. "Is there no way to hurry this trip? I live in dread of another day."

"Tomorrow, by Lake Aral's shore, we can leave the agricultural land. We'll ride west to the mother of rivers, the great Volga and its city."

She shivered and spoke impatiently, "You are going through with this foolish quest and do the Mooktar's bidding. You may be caught and killed as a spy."

He shrugged, "I can be killed as an escaped prisoner of war. It's better to go along on these little plots and be useful. Service is the disciple's badge."

"To obey and follow Yesu is admirable, but to die because of Him is not something I wish to share."

Kerim chuckled softly, "To be a martyr is considered a holy calling. Little girls might pray to Saint Leyla to protect them from Muslim raiders some day."

She sniffed, "He has not saved me from such a fate. Why would God hear them in my name? I'm no example."

"Tanra's ways are often unexpected, but there is purpose in all. You will understand this better when our travels end."

She shrugged, "As long as the end of this trip is pleasant and at home."

> - - - - - >YUSUF IN SAMARA> - - - - - >

Yusuf stared at the parchment in his hand. It was another mortgage concerning a lien on his farm property. His old manager, Sorba, had certainly been free to put his property in danger for the advancement of funds for his own personal needs. A property had been purchased near Samara where prices were high for the nearness of the Caliph. However, the land and houses were now in his foreman's name, without reference to the source of his funds. Only a court action could return the funds or indemnify with the property itself. Yet the courts were unreliable. How easy it was for Muslims to forget the instructions of their prophet that the older groups who followed God, Jews and Christians, were to be respected in the exercise of their faith. Allah wanted justice to be equal and impartial for all. How quickly majorities forget all such calls for justice. He knew that the manager had professed conversion to Islam. He did so in order to be in agreement with his partners in the swindle of his master. Yusuf feared that the crimes would be forgotten in the heat of religious debate and accusations. He braced himself for another confrontation with Sorba. The only comfort in the midst of the threats to his economic stability was the news of his daughter's rescue and probable arrival in the spring. He could thank Yesu, his Savior, for encouragement in the midst of troubles.

> - - - - - >BY LAKE ISSYK KOOL> - - - - - >

"Who could be out at this time of the night? Put down the lamp, perhaps they will just ride on past." Baja's voice was soft and timid.

"Could it be Yavuz bey?" Sesli picked up and strung her bow. At that moment, the baby woke to complain of his lack of mother's food and comforts. His cry was angry and indignant. He spit out the sweet rag Baja hastened to place in his mouth. The sound of horses, now running in a short dash to the house, sounded outside.

"I'm coming darling," a voice called, "I'm here now, don't cry." At the sound of Nooryouz' voice the baby's volume increased. The door slammed open and a frantic mother grabbed a frantic baby. There were no nuzzling preliminaries; each needed the other, and the baby's cries ceased immediately. A sob of contentment filled the silence. Then Baja spoke as Sesli brought out the lamp from its hiding place. "Thanks to the Yesu of Light, you've come, we don't have to wean the baby another day."

From outside came the voice of Korkmaz, "She was in the meadow cabin over Ridge Valley. Yavuz just left her there in the mountains. He sent away his bullyboys and then rode off. She said he tried to scare her with stories about bears in the woods."

Kadir now stood at the door for permission to enter. "*Gear*, enter, welcome back, you wonderful boys were successful. What a trial we have had here to keep the child fed."

"We followed and stayed out of sight and then he just left her there, He was too short-handed to do everything with only two helpers."

Baja went to the crying Nooryouz and dried her wet face, "There, there, sweet little mother, dry your tears. You are safe and the baby will be well now. Life will be easier for both of you. It will certainly be easier for Sesli and me."

Korkmaz entered now, "The horses are put away, but we need weapons, the pitchfork won't do very much against arrows."

Sesli rose and gave her bow, "Here, I'm so glad some one else will use it. Aziz bey rode north with troops for Almati fort."

The men nodded agreement, "There are big things happening there now and if there is a set back in the fighting it will come this direction. We can't take the girls back to the base. We need to move toward the Chu River Fort west of here. The Toozlu are on the Chu River further west and any chance for Nooryouz to find Sanjak will probably be through them."

Baja agreed heartily, "We need to get out before Yavuz finds her gone and comes rushing back. He knows she'll run back to the baby first, but you're all tired and hungry now. We'll eat and sleep to dawn and get out then. Yavuz is only human he has to eat and sleep too."

So they agreed, "We become refugees tomorrow and join the exodus."

> - - - - - > WHITE MARBLE QUARRY> - - - - - >

"I know this report is a lie, Umer is safe in the Black Mountain Quarry and is now a married man. He and his friend Hussein are both married and working like the men they were meant to be." The father shouted, under the weight of conflicting reports and rumors. The mother and younger siblings defiantly nodded their support.

The quarry village was a hot bed of gossip, speculation and open lies. The news was on everybody's lips:

51

"Umer has been executed, killed for murder."

"Umer is safe in the mountain quarry and another has died in his place."

"Umer is still free and another has been his substitute to die in his name." All the things people say when uncertainty rules. The killings too occupied them:

"Umer killed ten people!

"Umer only killed in self defense."

"Umer never killed anyone. He is persecuted by the nomad family who's boy they disfigured in a village fight."

A desire to involve politics and mystery entered.

"The Gray Wolf Society had marked the lad for revenge."

"The Gray Wolf had put the youth to kill political victims in the secret society's exercise of power."

"The nomad chief had revenged himself on the boy for his damage of the heir."

"Umer had taken the bare-faced daughter and suffered retaliation."

"Umer had served the Merv Arabs to avenge their quarrel against the Sultan."

"Umer was crazy!"

No one could confirm more than their personal understanding of the known facts. Where reports are unclear, confusion divides the people.

Nevertheless, the arduous work continued at the quarries. Workers were busy, as the rich have always to build bigger and better than their competitors and rivals. Government projects: fortresses, bridges, administrative palaces and municipalities were in need of stone for works of utility, pleasure and public display. Some workers had pleasure in their skill and kept a keen, critical eye on the quality of the stone and its uses. Others worked for the money or the necessity of occupation, but the work continues even until this day.

To be human, and to claim civilization, is to build. In making structures, magnificence and durability are the sought-after qualities. In the building of a life, you need the same qualities. Such work brings pleasure to those who understand its uses. Admiration follows a job well done

52

whether an architect, laborer, specialist, furnisher, builder or owner. We are born to build something: a life, if not an edifice or idea.

> - - - - - >ARMY BASE>- - - - - - - >

"We have a small group of Christians living in the village. They were expelled from the Uigur village some years ago in a conversion drive by the official Manichee church. We gave them refuge, they will do the job for a price."

The captain made a face. Christians, although tolerated under law, were not favored because of their poverty and differences with the statutes of Islam. Then he shrugged and spoke thoughtfully. "I suppose it's the only solution, no one else will touch it,"

"We will make an offer of money for their getting us information from the village. Our sources have been silent lately." Onat bey affirmed, "If local authorities are severe with them we lose nothing. There are always new refugees."

"*Dough rue*, right on," exclaimed the captain, "That's it."

"Make arrangements for an early departure with eight men, two teams to take turns and help on climbs. Pay each man in advance to leave with his wife, for none of us knows how the Uigur authorities will view their return. The risk factor is great, but their need for money is greater. They came destitute and without goods. They will get all the facts we want, and perhaps even more, poor souls."

The captain was puzzled. "Why should you feel sorry for such wretches?" he asked.

"Perhaps because that's what they are, through no one's fault."

"If they were Islam, surrendered to Allah, they would have privilege and place."

"You mean like we Seljuks have done?" Onat bey smiled gently.

"Of course, it's so simple to escape persecution and gain merit with God and men."

"I had a Christian grandmother whom I remember. The gain may be less than you think. The loss could weigh down the soul."

> - - - - - >CHU RIVER FORT > - - - - - >

53

"Send them to hell, Allah, Allah," screamed the fort troopers. Only the master Sergeant's discipline, and a locked gate, kept them inside the fort. They watched avidly as the troopers under their lieutenant swept through the besieger's camp. "Yuzbasha, Harun el Ari, *choke yashar*," they screamed as he cleared the enemies' camp and continued the drive against the retreating Uigurs.

"I'll kill the first man who tries to open the gate without my order," yelled the sergeant major. "The goods will be divided after the troopers return." Fortunately, the chase continued for only a little while and the victorious men, Toozlu and troopers, returned. They opened the gate for the men's pickings of the abandoned camp. The leader rode to the sergeant and dismounted laughing heartily. "I've lost over half my troop, not to the enemy, but to folly. They are continuing the pursuit. Some will be ambushed; they'll be slaughtered by the retreating enemy. Unruly fools! They are great fighters, but no discipline. The enemy is moving east they must have surrounded Almaty. They will need relief. We'll march today!"

Sanjak walked to the dismounted warrior to introduce himself. After the formalities, he asked for instructions.

"I'm your supply officer and we have restocked your fort for winter. The Illi River fort is abandoned. Shall I give their supplies to the refugees or take it back to the fort?"

The Yuzbasha was distracted, "Where's my wife, Sergeant Major?" he asked. "She promised hummus with dried egg plant and peppers for my return."

"Here she comes now sir. She has something for you to carry with you in the pursuit."

"*Gelip geldin Musaferim*, You return victorious my hero," she said as she walked toward them dressed in a chador that covered her completely. The voice and walk were feminine and attractive. Every one watched and listened. The lieutenant wore a charmed smile.

"This is the reason for my exile here, Sanjak bey. She was not my father's choice and I want no others. I have perfection here."

"I am honored," Sanjak bowed with hand on heart. Stepping back, he allowed the couple to talk out of his hearing.

"She sends treats for the troops and teaches the wives of the men," the fort sergeant major said. "She even tends the wounded!" This was a whisper in awe. Sanjak's supply sergeant was approaching now to ask permission.

"Sanjak bey, we are ready to depart now. Shall we proceed?"

"Sanjak bey, the Toozlu need your help." Erly bey had ridden into the fort in time to see the fort Lieutenant take a package from a veiled woman and mount his horse. Then, he called, "What's for the refugees, Sir?"

"Give them anything they want, Sergeant Major," Harun el Ari commanded, "anything at all: food, money, anything on the day of victory. My brother Mansur rides with father's blessing to pursue the Toozlu whom the Sultan called. I'll protect the returning Toozlu and the refugees whom the Uigurs raid. We'll see who serves the family honor best." He galloped off with the few men who had entered the fort. The woman retired to her quarters, she did not need to talk to strangers. She would get all the day's news from the other wives.

"Sergeant Major, We need to include the money in today's shipment to the Toozlu. It must go with the food supplies," Sanjak commanded. "Your Lieutenant has spoken. Let it be done."

> - - - - - >CHU RIVER FORT > - - - - - >

"The Uigur money will be put to good use" exclaimed Erly.

"You'll have to escort my sergeant out to your camp, Erly, with the food and money." Sanjak ordered, "I have other business south of here and I have to go alone." He turned to the fort's sergeant.

"Count me out a hundred in gold, Master Sergeant, I must ransom some people." Sanjak looked again at the letter he had found in the command tent of the enemy. Erly drew near as the sergeant left.

"They must not have heard about the news from the West. Mansur is dead, the army defeated. They claim the Toozlu did it."

"*Soos*, hush, Erly, our lives depend on it. We have not heard it here."

55

Sanjak turned to his supply sergeant working on depositing leather bags of coins in the supply carts. "The Toozlu will be your guard to get you to the refugees. Deliver the supplies and money to the Khan Twozan. Give my compliments to them for a safe journey. Return to the fort here with the carts we borrowed from the village. I'll try to be back with the people I hope to ransom. If I'm not here, return to the base."

The sergeant major came with the last bag of gold coins. He watched worriedly as it was divided into saddlebags and Sanjak prepared to leave. Erly was with the carts as they pulled through the gate.

"I should go with you sir. The carts have a guard, but even so it's dangerous out there, especially alone."

Sanjak smiled at him, "I agree, but the terms in the letter are clear. The contact will not be made if I'm accompanied. The ones held for ransom are of such value that I must obey exactly. Besides, who will care for the fort and the Yuzbasha's special treasure?"

"*Allah is-mar-la-dik*, God wills it, goodbye," agreed the sergeant major, as Sanjak rode out the Chu River fort's gate to seek his bride.

> - - - - - >AT THE UIGUR VILLAGE> - - - - - >

"What are you doing here Kaya bey? I thought you were over the line, out of harm, to stay." It was Manly who spoke, "You know our present emperor doesn't want two kinds of Christians in his kingdom."

"We have fallen from the bonfire to the icy waters. In Islam, we are unwelcome unless we convert. Refugees of any religion have small possibilities of prosperity. Besides which there was only one kind of Christian here when we lived here. Your own prophet did not consider himself a Christian any more, and he divided churches for disciples with his doctrines." Manly, while listening, stood considering the burial party, which bore on a stretcher the cloth wrapped body of the smuggler, Bolben. "Commander Onat bey has dispatched us to return the remains of Bolben to his village with the promise to find and punish the killer." Kaya's explanation was greeted with a shrug of disbelief.

"He would not risk his own people, so he dispatched the corpse with those neither nation esteems. Silver buys unworthy service: the return of clay to its place of origin." He motioned toward the village ruins. "There is no homestead place to deposit the body or mourners of the family to receive it. Take it to the cemetery and it will be safe from the army or local curiosity. Let me call someone who knew him and confirm the identity." He turned to a scribe. "Send for Manish or a village elder, immediately." He turned again to the burial party. "I'll let you bury it after it's identification. But remember the laws still

56

stands; you can't stay. Get back over the border as quickly as possible. I'll look the other way."                                    Kaya the spokesman nodded his understanding, "Mercy and generosity bring sure rewards from the Most High." He left carrying the stretcher with his men.

One, however, lingered behind. Manley noticed and impatiently motioned him to speak. "For silver I have information about activity at the base."

For a beating and persuasion I could have it free," Manly quipped, "but money is easier to bear for both of us. Let's hear it. We'll see what its worth." The man remained a long time and Manly paid him well.

THE CAPTAIN'S LADY

## PEOPLE, PLOTS & PLACES IN CHAPTER 5

Adem: finds that Allah is a complex subject.
Adjutant: has little sympathy for a distraught man.
Bolben: causes much trouble to many, although dead.
Erden: the homeland Khan sees new problems looming.
Erly: voices his opposition to a mistaken project.
Derk bey: the agent arrives unannounced and suffers for it.
Gerchin: now in the Caliph's capital, buys property.
Harun El Ari: finds a group of refugees seeking the fort.
Kadir: the smuggler must remain at the army post.
Kardesh: carries his cripple friend on the journey.
Kaya: has a useful yet dangerous role that minorities fill.
Kerim: has no guide to argue with so he tries elsewhere.
Leyla: wants to avoid everything that she fears or despises.
Manish: gains status in his faith, but loses perspective.
Tash: ignores a harsh past and faces a harsh present.
Sergeant: carries supplies to the Toozlu Turks and refugees.
Setchkin: fears, yet defends her father to everyone.
*Sevman*: the cripple acts as a guide for his blind friend.
Sorba: is the former manager of the Bozhun family estates.
Twozan: must travel ahead of the Syr Valley refugees.

### GLOSSARY
*amin*: amen; God grant it.
*bismillah*: in the name of God. A blessing for the meal.
*Kardeshler*: the brothers, the name of the Kokand gang.
*Kelime Allah*: the Word of God; Isa/Jesus.
*Neyo?:* What's that? What do you mean?
*Neyse?*: What's that? What's this?
*Ozur dilerim*: I beg your pardon. I'm sorry.

**A SANDY TRAIL**

"Did the East Bulgar leave with the lady on the Fergana horse?" Derk bey inquired breathlessly. He was dirty, unkempt with beard and hair uncombed and his mood was unhappy in his state of ignorance. His return of two days on the trail had left its marks. His treatment at the office of the Mooktar was one of cold disdain.

"The Mooktar has just returned from his travels down the Amu River Valley and has much important business to attend to. He mentioned seeing such a person and his identifying a criminal that was killed in an attack on the Mooktar's person. Any further information must be sought from himself." The secretary sniffed through his perfumed beard. At that moment, the Mooktar's attendant walked through the office. Derk bey quickly blocked his passage to repeat his question. The man was open-mouthed at the change in appearance.

"Derk bey? I scarcely recognize you.  What happened?"

"I sent a priority message by pigeon, didn't you get it?"

"You've sent nothing. Besides we have an insurrection and disorder in the north and fighting on the east borders."

"But what of the man and woman?" Derk bey insisted.

"I saw them when the murderer attacked my master. They went on their way after identifying the man. I'll try to get you an appointment tomorrow. Why don't you get cleaned up and rested."

**He pushed past the stunned Derk and was gone. The secretary motioned to the guard at the door and Derk was escorted out.**

> - - - - - >IN THEBURNED VILLAGE> - - - - - >

"You have brought back my friend Bolben. He will ride with the horse herds no more." Manish said reverently, "He changed a lot in the last weeks. Sorrow and compassion touched him. He was being prepared to leave us." He bowed his head, "Yesu, his sorrow- filled suffering confirms his love. He became like you. Take him now, in compassion, to yourself; forgiving his sins, *amin.*" The porters listened respectfully.

Kaya spoke, "Show us where his family burial place is please. We have to get finished as soon as possible and get home."

"What's the rush? You have just arrived."

"We're not welcome here and need to leave."

"Too many people have died here lately for people to get riled easily." Manish murmured, dissenting, as he started to lead them.

"Our experience is different," the Christian leader objected. "When disaster strikes, people look for someone to blame, anyone who is markedly different is ferreted out, hurt or killed by zealots. By general agreement the true culprits are let off."

The graves were stone covered and marked by a small stone spike at the head and foot.

"You discredit our justice system," exclaimed Manish, "We would never permit such things under law."

Kaya disagreed. "It makes people feel better and explains the problem away by taking away feelings of guilt or culpability that people feel about the triggering disaster. People know they are guilty but accuse someone else."                    They placed the body beside a clear space in the family plot.

The pallbearers turned to leave. Manish held up his hands for them to stop. "You besmirch the nobility of our people. Now you want to dump the corpse, which is your duty to bury. You leave this dirty clay here, unburied, to contaminate us." Manish was angry.

"We've no tools to work with, we are bearers only. We've been paid by the Muslims to bring the body to the home village. Who will pay us for the burial?" Several villagers were attracted by now.

"The body is evil and must return to the earth." Manish insisted, "You can't leave it to bring sickness and death to the village. We've suffered enough."

"How can we bury it without tools? Give us something."

"We don't have tools here and no money, but you'd better bury him anyway. You have knives and hands. The ground here is sandy." More villagers had arrived and formed a circle about the bearers. Several picked up stones.

60

Kaya spoke to Manish in a quiet voice. "Control your people and we will do the work for food."

"They've agreed folks. Move back and give them room. Someone bring a basket to pass up the earth. Aren't there some shovels in your houses? It's faster with tools. The plants will transform his body into something higher and cleaner. He was a good neighbor and deserves our consideration." The bystanders thinned somewhat   as people became interested in speeding the work and getting tools.

"Kept some beautiful horses, Bolben did," remarked one.

"He really wasn't that good a neighbor," stated another sourly, "He cheated my cousin when they were smuggling liquor to the soldiers. Left him in the lurch when they got fined. Gelmani never has forgiven him that." Heads nodded in agreement.

A young man spoke, "He was bragging lately about a harem girl he got to, called her a princess." He looked about the group, "He was obviously lying." Some agreed, others disagreed, and a few looked curious or envious.

"With all the stir over the escaped girls, it was silly to talk the way he did. He drew attention to our village." Others spoke up. "The authorities burned our village because of a dead girl."

"You can't tell me he knew nothing about it," they agreed.

"Be sure your sins will find you out," another pontificated.

"Got what he deserved, damn him." There was general assent.

"We're not to judge," objected Manish, "he's on the wheel of life and fate, just like we all are." Silence greeted this statement. The wheel of life had come from Buddhism, but was mixed with Mani's teachings. It reminded them that a failed life resulted in another cycle; the need to pass another life. Rebirth was not a pleasant thought. They knew one life was trial enough. Yesu of light! just to get a man buried in a destroyed village was difficult enough.

> - - - - - >CARAVAN TO BAGHDAD> - - - - - >

The wind whipped sand in their faces as they trudged along. Kardesh continued to carry Sevman on his back and they walked in the lee of a camel to cut the force of the wind. They had rigged a kind of sling that put the weight on his shoulders like a backpack and Sevman served as eyes for his big friend. There was the promise of staying a long season on the other side of the desert, but they still managed to travel from dark to dark. The desert stretched on endlessly. They begged Tash to stay out the winter in some caravansary, but he resisted and became abusive and angry. There was no relief from the relentless cold and irate caravan manager. Strangely enough Tash chose to ignore his previous knowledge of Sevman and Kardesh back in Kokand when the *Kardeshler* gang prospered, but was crushed by police. His leading the take over and the violent consequences may have changed his mind about revenge. His anger seemed to focus on Derk's desertion and his responsibility for their safety. Onward they marched pausing only for a day of seeking camel replacements or accidents. Men were injured while attending camels. Cinches broke, cargoes spilled, and time was lost in repairs. Tediously, each day stretched and blended painfully into another.

> - - - - - >THE ROAD TO GECHET CITY> - - - - - >

"Well, the Muhtar of the upper Syr was correct. The lower Amu valley is prosperous and orderly, but many here are still Christian. The nature of the land would produce abundance under any orderly ruler. I don't see that Islam can take the credit for its condition." Kerim stopped his horse to look back at the distant valley behind him.

Leyla did not stop but forged ahead saying, "I never want to see any of those places again. It's a crowded land of wild wolves and thieves."

He laughed as he followed her. "So we return to the land where the wolf is our totem and ancestor."

She shook her head in disgust at his stupidity. "You know what I mean. It's a land where women are not respected or protected and there is no freedom for them."

He caught up to her. "They would say that a woman's best protection is to live confined in her home and unobserved when outside it. She must always have a protector present."

Her scornful glance swept over him. "I have known both freedom and protection in the homeland."

"Then you are blaming the cities which we lack, for the sin of lust. You forget the sudden raids and attacks of enemies and enslavement."

A troubled frown creased her forehead. "I mean, we are Christian and don't do such things."

"May I remind you that not all are Christian who pretend to be so. Such things happen in every land. It's proof of our fall away from a state of grace."

62

She shook impatiently and spoke scornfully, "Next you will condemn us for being guilty of sins."

He smiled, "No, I offer good news that God took our guilt and paid the penalty by the sacrifice of a perfect man, His lamb. To prove the yielded gift of life was accepted, Tanra raised his Messiah, Yesu, from the dead. So we are not only free of guilt and sin, but to be united with Yesu before God forever. We are being changed into his likeness now in life, and transformed completely after death."

She relaxed, "You make it sound so good. How can we be sure it's all true?"

"That's where the element of faith comes in. We can't prove it. We have to believe it and put it into practice. We will have the kind of internal proof that convinces the individual, but which the world distrusts because it can't be proved; only demonstrated."

She shrugged and responded thoughtfully, "As a little girl I obeyed because it was right and I loved Yesu and the virgin, his mother. I wanted to please them and do what people liked. It kept me out of trouble and made life fun. All that stopped when we moved to the city." She paused. "I learned to lie and keep secrets from my father. I started to fear."

He listened carefully, "Faith is replaced by fear. Belief is shaken by reality. Trust leaves us in the face of danger to ourselves or those we love. This is where the battle is gained or lost. Will we trust God and go on?"

He continued, "We are trusting God and living on the Sultan's bounty now. Tanra elects curious providers as well as unusual circumstances for our salvation from this land we are leaving."

She made a face and pulled her hood closer over her face, against the wind. "Next you'll say we're beyond trouble."

He laughed and quipped, "Saint Paul writes 'We are endangered among Pagans and Jews.' But our contacts and paymasters will still be Muslims. Our world holds many kinds of people, customs and opinions. They are the onions and garlic to spice our lives."

"By the time we get back to the tribe you'll be too good for horse meat and bulgur," she sniffed; "a spoiled outlander always complaining about local food or lack of it."
He laughed so hard that he cried.

"I married an idiot" she stormed. "I like a real world where you get what you see, not what you don't see." She spurred her horse into a gallop.

He stayed with the pack animals and let her go.

> - - - - - >IN THE CHIPCHAK HOMELAND > - - - - - >

The council was whispering, the serious faces of those gathered were in contrast to the relaxed exchange of information and jokes that were the usual prelude to debate and decisions from the Chipchak Khan.

They averted their faces from Kaplan, whose great bulk filled one corner of the greater yurt. All knew of his son's death at the hands of a Bulgar. The royal niece had chosen the marriage gladly. Everyone had expressed their condolences in the proper words, but the marriage of the old Khan's widow to the father of Sanjak and leader of the Toozlu clan had placed local opinion and power into a new balance. The latest news was seriously upsetting. Tribal democracy was at work creating new alliances and parties in view of the latest occurrences.

Khan Erden's mild voice filled the yurt. "All here are aware of the insurrection in the Syr Daria valley. Most of you will be aware of the abandoning of farms and villages and many joining forces with the Toozlu to return to the freedom of the steppes and grasslands. We must decide how we are going to meet this host of men and families. They will be costly to fight or equally costly to receive and feed. I understand there are relatives of some present who are returning. I think it fair that we should hear them first. Then, we can consider the cost and response."

➤ - - - - - >NEAR THE CHU RIVER FORT> - - - - - >

"There are tents and yurts here, almost in sight of the fort, Erly bey. I hadn't realized you were so close," the supply sergeant declared.

These must have come yesterday and today. Our camp is still two hours away. The refugees extend a day's ride down the Chu River; at least as far as the water goes."

The sergeant rode listening, taking in the extent of the tragedy. "Many of these families started moving into the Syr valley during the civil war when the founding race was divided and careless of the borders. Local residents resented them. Only when safety is assured can zeal return to

64

make the border people conform and obey Sharia Law. Now politics and enmity rule to complete the ruin."

"The first step in recovery is to feed the hungry and give them a place to rest safely. Then we can talk of God's will, future plans and possible agreements and moves," Erly responded.

"At least I can help distribute the food," the sergeant concluded, cracking his whip over the cart animals.

>- - - - - - - DERK IN KHIVA> - - - - - >

"Are you the Adem bey that took two foreigners to the northern border?" Derk bey demanded of the soldier riding alone, southward. The soldier stopped to stare in contempt at the demanding civilian on the expensive horse.

"Why is that your concern sir?" he answered roughly. "This is the Mooktar's business," he asserted, "You have no authority here." He shook his quirt, but used it on his horse.

"*Ozur delerim*, forgive me, he called after the man. "I'm here on official business. I must know where they are."

"Gone back to the land of war. They go to abominable Kazar country and will need their Messiah's protection." He shrugged his shoulders as he gave the ungracious reply, scarcely pausing in his departure.

Derk bey stretched around to stare after him. The pair were now beyond reach, but their guide had the facts necessary to continue pursuit. There were contacted agents with plans already made to return the escapees to the Caliph's will. Since the Mooktar had explained the reason for the mission that Kerim of the East Bulgars had undertaken. He, Derk, was not to interfere. However, after the completion of the task -- the delivery intact – Things change . Then, the special position of the agents would be finished. Derk would have to wait for an opportunity to act. He thought a moment more and decided to ride after Adem bey. The sun was over the south in its highest winter position. The policeman was obviously hungry and tired, ready for lunch and a rest. Derk turned and set his horse into a gallop after him.

> - - - - - >SAMARA GUARDS> - - - - - >

"These are the quarters your people will occupy while in Samara. There are enough Turks and other barbarians scattered among the population that you will have little trouble with market or other wants." The guide's words were kindly condescending as he led the officers-to-be among the beautiful structures built to a Sultan's high taste. The guide carefully pointed out the new edifices for the new security force. The caliphs who came after the civil wars and disturbances tended to keep the Arab factions at a distance. These caliphs promoted minorities into positions of importance. Keeping the source of their prosperity safe from his enemies would be their only preoccupation.

Gochen chuckled with satisfaction. His eye picked up the bits of information important to trackers and herdsmen hunters. Automatically he divided the various peoples into groups of like kinds. In his mind, each herd had its value and uses. Though he was accounted an uncouth soldier-slave of the Shadow of Allah, he knew which herds would be useful. Also, he knew which would be an obstacle to his rise in power and control. Even in his homeland, he had heard of a subversive power at work in favor of his people. The secret society would give power to those who would be in positions of influence over the life of the Caliph. Those who would be palace guards would come to control admit ion of any touching the life of the one who controlled an empire.

> - - - - - >CHU RIVER CAMP> - - - - - >

"*Neyse*, what? You're returning to the homeland with a few hundred followers in three days?" exclaimed Erly bey the second in command. "Take one or two thousand. How can you trust the Kaynaklar? They will yoke you and sit you on stakes!  They control the Khan. You can't expect mercy from them."

Setchkin hanum reacted fiercely by retorting. "*Neyo*, what's that? You know the Khan always favored his brother, resisting all good advice."

"*Esenlik*, peace dear ones," ordered Twozan. "We have received an offer of peace and reconciliation and I will accept it.  We will take all families who are eager to travel and leave."

Erly shook his head and held in his anger. "No offence intended, but we have suffered at the hands of the Tiger before this. I can't believe he has softened or changed."

Setchken paused, and thought before saying, "We can only hope as we pray for him."

> - - - - - >KHIVA DISCUSSION> - - - - - >

"Our journey to the Aral Lake was different from any other assignment given by my commander," Adem bey explained.

66

"The man is a Christian who likes to talk about his faith. I learned many things and though he frequently angered me when talking about such matters it was thought provoking. Allah's manner of treating Jews and Christians is a clear indication of his nature and power."

"*Dough roo*, truly," Derk bey agreed, "Allah is the largest subject in the universe, yet so few study the sources to try to understand Him." The dinner had turned into a lengthy, lavish affair and both men were relaxed and content.

"I, like most of my people, had assumed that my ways were those approved by Allah, and the best in the world. I had never thought of the reasons for their existence, except that the Prophet, peace be upon him, had demanded willing compliance. It is supported by law and custom. Suddenly this stranger demanded that I give heed to reasons and sources I had not thought about. Abraham was a friend of Allah, but I had not thought of what such a friendship would involve. They interacted all the time; he alone in all the world seemed to serve Allah. Allah promised him things, and he obeyed Allah in everything. They liked and depended on each other, Allah kept difficult or impossible promises, even when it took time. Abraham was willing to give his son in the test Allah put him to. We should be willing to go to the same extent of sacrifice."

Derk bey listened to the explanations, he grew tired and said, "Fortunately Allah does not require such a test of us now. However, this man must have mentioned his plans and destination. Talked of his home?"

Adem shrugged, "The woman was anxious to get home and was against his trip to the Great River. Nevertheless, they were newly married and she was deeply in love. He didn't seem to mind where he went or shun any task, as long as he could talk about his Tanra and Yesu. That means Isa, our prophet, in his language. He said that the prophet Isa came to fill the inside of our faith, while the last one defines the outside. Like *bulashuk*: dirty dishes, the inside is as important as the outside. I had never thought of it in that way. He had stories of Isa I had never heard before."    Derk

67

bey interrupted, "So, he persuaded you to become like him: to believe that Isa is Emanuel, Allah with us?"

Adem answered calmly, "Isa is called *Kelime Allah*, by Muslims, the Word of God. He was a living Koran. The imams argue about the Koran, was it created or is it uncreated… eternal? We can use the same arguments of the *Kelime Allah*, Isa. It would seem to be an open subject. We are called to be like Abraham. To be a friend of Allah requires all the help we can get.

"I learned that no teaching of any prophet, peace be upon them, may be neglected. Allah never changes, all truth is eternal."

Derk grimaced, "What is truth?" he murmured. "But he never spoke of plans or mentioned other persons?"

Adem rose, said the *h* prayer, for the end of the meal and said finally, "He left the future where it should be left by friends of Allah. His obedience will be correct and timely. His Messiah will see him through any suffering encountered. I thank you for the meal and commend you to Allah who rewards the generous." He left the astonished Derk bey to ride away.

Derk bey grimly proceeded to buy the equipment necessary for the trip to the Khanate of Kazars. He could not allow a war prisoner to escape. Turks in the empire would flaunt it over all authorities. It would be munitions for the Gray Wolf Society. His duty was clear.

> - - - - - >SAMARA GUARDHOUSE> - - - - - >

"You will be doing the Caliph a favor by keeping a valuable property out of the ruthless, scheming Christian's hands. My master had me buy it in my name with my money to fool the authorities. Now he intends to take possession and claim I swindled the money. I need money for the judge and to stay clear of his law suits." the speaker paused to appraise the effect of his words. He smiled, and hurried on.

"You'll need a place for a residence and center outside the barracks. All the important commanders have palaces and hunting grounds to invite important people to share for some special occasion."

The old steward of Yusuf bey spun a large and fantastic story to gain a fantastic sum from the recently paid Toozlu chief, Gerchin; now captain of a new guard in training for the security of the Caliph's fabulous palaces and royal hunting grounds.

Gerchin listened carefully, nodding agreeably, he corrected him. "You are about to lose the property to the true owner, and you want me to pay twice the price and stand the chance of losing it. You use the funds for other special projects you plan. Now hear what I am willing to do for you.

"I'll give you a quarter of the price you quoted. I'll be a character witness for your trial and will hide you on the property so no one will ever take you away. You can help me get servants; girls to do the work. The property will be safe with me. The Sultan favors me."

Sorba objected. "I must have a third of the price. I can't let it go for less. Be reasonable, the expenses won't allow it."

"Agreed, we will meet to sign over the property before the judge. Be there this afternoon after the *Ikindi* prayers, understand? Don't be late."

### > - - - - - >A MOUNTAIN MEADOW> - - - - - >

Mangore the captain snarled at the angry man riding beside him. "Well, here's the meadow where's your boss with the girl?"

Manson shrugged disdainfully and gazed in contempt at his captors. "I told you the instructions were to come alone. You have not listened. They could be anywhere up there." He indicated the vast mountain and woods. "You have weapons. I have none, but you brought a troop. They won't come unless you send them away."

Mangore swore in frustration. Then he remembered the reward. "You know it's not safe here without troops. I'll send them down to the river to rest and eat. I'll stay to receive the harem fugitive."

"The boss is foxy, you better have them far enough to be clear of pursuit. Otherwise he'll leave us to wait." Mangore shouted the orders and the troop under their Onbasha retired to rest by the river. "You'd better be telling me the truth about this," he growled.

"You'd better take the thongs off my hands. I'm no prisoner. I'll build a fire and he'll see we're here, just three of us." The captain obliged, but stayed mounted while the man dismounted to set a fire. As the blaze flared out its presence, another light caught their eyes. Far in the distance on the other side of the field, a blaze rose from a fire. One man, Sanjak, could be distinguished there standing by the fire, awaiting contact to buy a treasure.

## PEOPLE, PLOTS & PLACES IN CHAPTER 5

Baja: must travel away from her homes to remain safe.
Chavush: This sergeant must keep order and move his men.
Kadir: has to assure the safety of the people at the lake.
Kerim: enjoys his honeymoon, but wants to travel faster.
Leyla: wants to go north home, not westward.
Mangore: loses both gold and treasure.
Manson: gets the gold for his boss, Yavuz.
Maril: longs for her home in Baghdad.
Sanjak: follows the trail of the pursuers.
Sesli: sings of her needs and fright.
Setchkin: foresees problems in the homeland.
Tayze: helps a friend during difficult times.
Twozan: risks his life to return in peace to his home.
Yavuz: loses his treasure, but wins the gold.
Yeet: must make important decisions in the spring.


## GLOSSARY:
*bash ooze to nay*: as you command; I'll obey.
*bulashuk*: dirty dishes.
*dough roo*: right; correct; exactly.
*evit*: yes; affirmitive.
*ikindi: afternoon prayers at 2:00P.M.*
*neherlerin anasi*: The Mother of Rivers; the Volga River.
*Ney'se*: What's this? What do you mean?
*orley namaz*: noon prayer time.
*Ozur dilerim*: I ask your pardon; Pardon me.
*kalk*: get up; arise; on your feet.
*uyan*: wake up; awake.
*zeeng'in de-eel'em*: rich I'm not! I'm not rich!

MOUNTAIN CABIN

Sanjak saw the starting fire, but the distance was too great to recognize the leader there with the troops. He was sure that the Uigurs were waiting for some contact. The troop might be coming for him. Since the fire was going well he withdrew. He faded into the background where stands of pine or brush stood against the mountainside. Rather than wait, he rode where he could observe the enemy fire and see if there was any contact with the sender of the message. He was waiting on the wrong side when the small figure of Yavuz rode up to two waiting men, but he could hear the shouts of their confrontation.

"You've brought the money then? It's not with the troop you sent off?"

Mangore stood appraising the little man. 'Border trash,' he thought, 'believing nothing', honoring nothing but money, full of lust and cunning. He smiled confidently and spoke curtly. "Would I come without the ransom? Why come without the girl?"

"She's in a cabin in the mountains, bring the money and we'll go there." The men moved toward their horses.

"Two against one? I'll bring my sergeant," he affirmed. "He raised his voice to a shout, "Chavush come. How do I know that you don't have men waiting there?"

Yavuz saw that he was facing a bully. "You are warriors and have government gold. I have only my man here." The sound of a running horse gave them pause.

The sergeant appeared, without slowing he rode his animal up to the astonished Yavuz and pulled his beast into a rearing halt. Its hooves narrowly missing the dodging Yavuz, who mounted, circled, and cursed the group.

71

"Easy Chavush," grinned the commander, "you've frightened our procurer."

Yavuz was already riding across the meadow up the nearest hill passing a stone's throw from Sanjak, who watched in silence as the three others followed riding swiftly. He rose to find his horse. He must get her away before the men returned to the troops. He too, rode like the wind.

"She's here in the cabin, but I want the money before you get there. " Yavuz placed his horse across the path to the woods, The horses were thoroughly winded and strung out behind the commander and Yavuz. The commander of the troop spat, "Why should I give anything before I see the girl? Here, I place the money here on the stump where our two men can guard it. *Git*, go to the door and call the lady. She will make both of us wealthy."

> - - - - - > CARAVAN TO BAGHDAD > - - - - - >

The desert sand felt cold underfoot and the wind cut through all the coats and wraps beneath it; Cold found spots near the face and neck to chill. The daily march was a marathon and the nights too cold for repose or true rest. All the travelers slept fully clothed. Jon, Kardesh, Sevman and Yeet under camel-hair covers, Tayze and Maril bundled near by under another. Days lost coherence and the weeks passed unnumbered except by the caravan master and the young corporal Tash. The food was as monotonous and tasteless as the scenery.

"What will you do when you reach home Maril?" Tayze inquired each night and the girl would begin to explain the pleasures of garden and bath. She only remembered the home as it was when she was a little girl. Then years passed during their long trip and stay in China. She would make up the parts she scarcely recalled. They were as real to her as the easily remembered places. Tayze was sometimes asleep early and she would plan the wedding she hoped to realize on arrival. She never remembered that weddings were the domain of fathers and mothers in her country; as was the selection of the groom. She knew where her heart lay. In the morning she would see his solicitous face and hear him inquire as to her condition and wants. Then they would march together up and down the dunes and around the dry hills and gravel washes. They would enjoy the one constant pleasure of being together: the joy of enjoying each other.

72

God filled their excursions with constant conversation. They knew more of each other than many persons years married.

Only Yeet seemed at times distant or preoccupied. He often marched alone and was solitary in his habits. He resisted invitations to go off with others for a call of nature and the teasing and bragging that men sometimes indulge in with reference to their sexual development.

Once, when he left late at night, Tayze offered him a burning sage stem for light, taken from the campfire. She held up the blazing stem expectantly.

"I don't need light for this Tayze," he protested indignantly.

"Put out the blaze when you get ready," she retorted, "But put it behind you. It will warm your bottom and ease you." He took the stem reluctantly and headed out a long way from camp to dig his hole and finish his business. Returning, he tossed the smoldering stub on the fire and smiled his thanks to Tayze. "I'm glad you suggested that, it does make you feel better."

"I know," Tayze replied, "We will be done with this travel by spring. Then there will be some decisions to make about our futures." Yeet nodded and went to his place to sleep. Sevman was already hunched up to Kardesh and Yeet got in beside him at the end of the line. They faced another long night.

> - - - - - >BY A MOUNTAIN CABIN> - - - - - >

"There's no one here." Mangore stepped inside the rough cabin to look behind the door. Yavuz stuck his head in far enough to confirm the fact.

"She was here. Look again." He shouted. Manson picked up a piece of wood and hit the Chavush on the head. He seized the moneybag and quickly mounted his horse. He led Yavuz's horse to the door. Yavuz pushed the commander violently pulled the door shut and mounted. Both were dashing away as Mangore slammed open the door with his sword drawn. He screamed in rage, and ignoring his stunned guard, ran to chase down his mount that had pulled loose from the lead in the hands of Manson.

At a distance, Sanjak could see the three horses escaping up the mountainside. The commander was now on their trail, while the Chavush stood without his horse, shouting for his men by the river. A string of men came in ones and twos from the river camp. Several set out after their commander while others chased down the Chavush's horse. Eventually the plain seemed empty.

Sanjak watched the search by Mangore's squad in the valley below. He sat on a boulder beneath the skyline of the mountain resting and sharing his ayran drink with his horse. He drank from the bag and the horse from his master's stiff leather hat with earflaps worn against fall and winter winds. Both were tired from the long trail. Yavuz, the messenger and the pursuing Uigurs vanished. Sanjak talked to his horse; something most herders do for company. Naturally, such intimate conversations are satisfying; you rarely get an argument on any statement. However, if the master intends it, objections can seem to flow from the horse's mouth.

"We have joined fools on a fool's errand. They will never lead them to the valued prize. Remember the words of our hero, Boldar, the East Hun. A retreat when the odds are against you is the height of prudence and wisdom, to continue, the greatest of follies. To expect the unexpected is a denial of logic; the word itself declares you must not expect it. It comes only on Heaven's orders."

The horse, finishing her refreshment of sour, salty milk, licked her lips and nodded her head.

Sanjak brought his horse up to the boulder and mounted to ride thoughtfully away. He moved on their trail. He was reluctant to give up now when they were so close. Yavuz would not go to a hiding place. He might go to the place where he had captured her. He would not return to the base. Unless Mangore caught him, they would go to the place where she might be. He was tempted to play the fox following the wolves: with great caution. However, Boldar's words calmed him. The odds were against a rescue. He could go back to the fort for reinforcements. However, the Toozlu camp would be better.

> - - - - - > BAJA'S DEPARTURE > - - - - - >

"*Kalk uyan*, get up, wake, morning is here. There is no time to linger." Only Baja was up before light. She had prepared food for the trip and was carrying it out to a cart. "Kadir, get the horses ready. Korkmaz, bring one of the nanny goats with the kid, tie her to the cart. Nooryouz get the baby's things into the cart now, you can feed him on the road. Sesli, help me in the kitchen." From the quiet that existed when she arose to pray and prepare, all was now energy and action. The loaded cart and baggage with Kadir leading was soon on the ruts that served as the road going north. Korkmaz was sent out as scout to watch for and avoid Yavuz bey. The extra horses were tied to the cart and the nanny had been allowed to ride behind Sesli and Nooryouz. They took the road to the Chu fort since the fighting against the Uigurs was at Almati further east. People whose lives depended on smuggled goods, develop a sensitivity, even an affinity, for areas neglected, but accessible to those wishing to escape notice by authorities. That instinct served them now.

> - - - - - >ROADSIDE CARAVANSERAI> - - - - - >

"At the rate we're going we won't make the Mother of Rivers before spring," Kerim complained sitting back.

"I don't mind," said Leyla between bites, "Getting full satisfaction from a husband requires the long winter nights and time spent together. Besides, I have to work through all that theology you keep throwing out at anyone who will listen. We don't have Adem bey to respond to you now, and you spread it around more."

He smiled indulgently and stretched, "I rather think he enjoyed it between tantrums. They always think simplicity in theology is superiority."

She stretched and looked over the food tray to pick at a few neglected bits. She sighed as she left it bare of anything useful. "I'll declare! This winter travel has picked up my appetite tremendously."

He laughed and gave her a quick glance. "You're not feeling queasy in the mornings?"

She sniffed, "I'm the first ready to travel in the morning. I'm not stretching, dragging and yawning."

He grinned good naturedly, "You're not expected to do the same kind of work I have to do to please you."

She sniffed again, "You seemed to enjoy it and no doubt about that."

"I'll admit it, but it does demand extra effort on my part."

"And I love you for it. That is why I enjoy this travel together; riding to the next caravansary, spending the hours talking and playing. I never knew the Kaynaklar to be good at anything except raids and politics."

He sighed, "I'm demeaned by Toozlu prejudice: the old families against the new successful upstarts. I'll have to learn to live with it."

She leaned over to press his head close to her.

"I'll make it as easy as possible as long as you keep your performance up to my expectations."

He objected, "We need to spend more time on the road."

She moved toward the veiled bed and stopped to shrug, "We should be at the Kazar capital by spring. Why rush? There's nothing more to eat, we can go to bed."

"*Bash ooze to nay*, as you command," he replied tenderly. He moved to her side, arm around her shoulder.

> - - - - - > BAJA'S CAMPING > - - - - - >

"I think we should go on toward the old fort on the Illi River. After all, the area above is largely grazing. Only a few people live there. It is only in the low ground that you find villages." Baja explained ready as always to direct the lives of others.

Kadir disagreed, "You would pass too close to Uigur territory and there are irregulars that raid the herds. We'll go to the Chu River above the fort. I have friends I can count on. Besides the army will be distracted with the fighting and we can pass near them to hide until things settle down."

Nooryouz was walking beside the cart. Her life as a shepherdess had accustomed her to the pace of walking. She was not used to horse-back riding. She was afraid of the horses, to the amusement of the villagers.

"Sanjak will be going north eventually. He always told me about life in the tribe. Oh, how he loved it! If this is the main route north, he will pass this way."

Every one guarded silence considering the options. Only Sesli couldn't keep silent long. She started to sing quietly as she rode beside Kadir.

| | |
|---|---|
| 1. | I thought he was a quiet man, |
| | With stern and piercing eye, |
| | Yet gentle and protecting hands. |
| | Come to take away my lonesome sighs. |
| | |
| Chorus: | The long and chilling nights, |
| | Full of fright, hold no hope or light. |
| | One longs for warm love bright, end of night, |
| | Truth and right saved by light, |
| | Face the dawn's new delights while seeking you. |
| | |
| 2. | I thought he was a keen man, |
| | With warm and yearning eye, |
| | Yet cool mind and persuading ways. |
| | Come to show me where true safety lies. |
| Chorus: | |

76

3.
I thought he was a silent man,
With heart of flaming fire,
With strong but happy faith in God,
Come to teach me songs that lift me high.

Chorus:

**A QUIET MAN**

"I'm with you, Kadir bey," she said, smiling demurely, "Where you go I'll gladly go."

He appraised her coolly, then smiled. You couldn't do better," he assured her. "But my money is going for land purchases for now. How could I have a bride price for your family?

She thought of several possible answers, but finally said, "Part of the property could be made over into my families name and that would suffice them for you are paying it all off aren't you?"

"You must have a good head for business, I think." He laughed, "Such a woman is valued by my people."

Baja was riding close enough to be following the conversation. She now intervened for match making was her delight.
She rode closer and said, "I'm her sponsor for she's as dear to me as a daughter. We've passed many difficult moments together, so you'll have to treat her well for my sake."

The women laughed and he shook his head. "Don't get too greedy Baja, *zeeng'in de-eel'em*, I'm not rich," he pleaded.

She reacted scornfully, "Aziz Is giving you his business, Yavuz is on his own and deep in trouble. You have the most to gain from all that's going on."

"I have enough to start getting property and a reasonably affordable wife, no more." He affirmed seriously. "If she's pretty and smart that's all within the limits I've set. Don't overcharge me."

"You're getting a bargain at any price." Baja insisted.

"I'm not staying for these remarks. " Sesli blushed, racing ahead. She rode up beside Nooryouz, who walked behind the cart. "How's the baby doing on his old diet?" She called cheerfully.

"Vigorously, he can't get enough right now," was the response. "What's happening back there? I thought he was interested in you, Now he and Baja hanum are talking up a storm."

Sesli agreed., "It's about the bride price, the value of the woman and the urgency and wealth of the man. I hate it, but everyone thinks it's the only way. At least it isn't a political arrangement. I like the man and I can tell he wants me. It's almost like getting your own choice. we'll get along great."

"Choose carefully and prayerfully. No one knows what the future will bring. Happiness is elusive. It cannot be held or caged. It can come and go in an instant."

"I know, but the view from where I am looks great."

> - - - - - >BACK AT ISSIK KOOL LAKE> - - - - - >
"Yavuz bey, why are we going back to the Issik Kool Lake? Baja and the girls won't stay there. They'll run," Manson stated.

"Because it is the first place Baja will come to when she is tired of hiding. She can't be happy any other place. Here or

78

the base for sure and she won't show the girls at the base so this is where we wait."

Manson looked uneasy. It sounded good, because he was tired of hiding, too. He knew that Uigur trackers were searching the woods and meadows for them. He doubted that the lake was beyond their reach. He wished he had never touched their bag of money. Yavuz was in possession of it now and would never part with it.

"Yavuz bey," Manson began, "Wouldn't it be better for someone to get back to the base and see what's happening there?"

"You'll stay with me. I don't want any loose talk about our activities around the base. They might tempt you to tell too much. Besides I want your help with those two. The boy's gotten strong this year and Kadir is dangerous. Aziz may try to stick his nose in again. He's set on taking over my line of work for the base. But I'll stop him, whatever the cost."

Manson shrugged; the boss was past reasoning with now. He would have to break with the man as soon as an opportunity arose.

> - - - - - >AT ALMATI FORT> - - - - - >

"Aziz bey, Thank you for your help here at Almati. The irregulars have withdrawn and the regulars must have retreated beyond the recognized border. Harun will be back at his fort, now. You are free to go about your business and may Allah reward your fervor and time."

Aziz bowed a salaam and stroked his beard. "I have a sister at the Issik Kool. So I'll stop by on the way home."

"If you return to the base I can send some dispatches with you and keep my force here up to strength. It will take the morning to ready them."

Aziz agreed, "You have until the *orley namaz*. We'll break bread together and I'll leave."

"Go with Allah and watch the hills, there are desperate refugees about."

"You worry about the dispatches and I'll worry about my back," Aziz grinned.

> - - - - - >NEARING GETCHET CITY> - - - - - >

They sat for a time on the high eastern bank of the Volga, *Neherinlerin Ahnesi*, the mother of rivers, and watched the steady high flow while their horses cropped the new grass on the hill. At last she spoke, "I thought all the rivers flowed north; even the dry land rivers like the Amu and Syr flow north-west."

"Tanra makes different rules for different areas of His worlds. Only the spiritual rules are universal. They are the same everywhere," he answered happily.

"How do you know that?" She queried sharply, "You haven't been everywhere to prove that it's so."

"Scripture assumes it to be true. Tanra applies his rule everywhere. He is aware of every creature in every corner of his creation."

She spurred her horse to move toward the ferry. "Why should He crowd us so? Do we need constant watching?" she complained petulantly.

"Are you trying to find a place free of him?" inquired Kerim, kindly, "What have you to hide?"

"When I was a little girl I could take my problems and complaints to the Virgin and feel like She understood. That helped me. Now, I'm embarrassed to tell her things, and the idea of Tanra watching me... us, shames me! I like what we do. It isn't wrong."

"God makes it to be what we need to start a family. If we had been impatient and done it without God's blessing you would hate it and not feel this joy. The Virgin serves as a confident for the innocent: those married need stronger council to match the new delights."

She rode unheeding down to the water's edge and paused to watch the ferry poled into its site for loading the waiting crowd of animals and people.

"Well, you were the impatient one as I remember it, but we are married and blessed. I hope Getchet, the crossing, will have better beds and food than the last two stops."

> - - - - - >TWOZAN GOING HOME> - - - - - >

"Stop now, and set a fire. We're strung out for miles and we don't have an accurate count of how many have decided to travel north with us." Twozan declared to his adjutants. Setchkin sought out a dried stream bed for a kitchen and the helpers used a bag of water to start a broth boiling. Outriders were sent to bring others into line with the campsites stretched along the trail, so none would wander off, lost in the dark. Some would camp where they were at dark and try to find the travelers in the morning. The late starts on short days were a trial, but they were assured that there would be no danger to them now.

Nevertheless, Twozan had night patrols just in case. He trusted the word of the Khan his old master's twin brother. However, there were others in the home world that would not look on their safe arrival as a joyful occasion. He counted his new father-in-law as one of the chief objectors. He had probably pursued the claims of the baby left in his power rather than the one Setchken held. The death of Erben would have seemed to clear the path to power in the proclaimed heir. Khan Erden would have to watch his back, lest the temptation to enjoy a long regency tempt the ambitious. While the heir in his minority, would hope to take power from those who long had enjoyed it, he would also be in danger. The tribe was aware of all this and would be a hornet's nest of angry suspicion and distrust.

Was there some way to relieve their fears? He would have to support Setchken and her claims for her child. He could lose her if he were reluctant in support.

Unfortunately, the loss of the Princess Leyla and her marriage to Kerim of the East Bulgars was an unknown factor. It would be too complicated to explain. It had best be forgotten by those who knew. When he faced his Khan, how much would he dare to relate? How much dare he hide? It was against his nature to hide things. How could he explain it all and be believed? He pondered these things as they traveled.

A MATCHMAKER LEADS

## PEOPLE, PLOTS & PLACES IN CHAPTER 7

Abdullah: finds a new, dangerous assignment.
Aziz: goes home with dispatches from Almati.
Deborah: a generous gift saves her from slavery.
Chavush: believes a criminal's blood poisons ground.
Gerchin: finds more resources and power for himself.
Kaplan: sees his plans in tatters and forms new plots.
Karga: gets the blame when things go wrong.
Kaya: returns to the army base, but moves on.
Kerim: arrives late and must act decisively.
Kurnaz: breaks rules to get the one who defrauded him.
Leyla: has trouble understanding life and God.
Magazi: realizes that their exile or death is eminent.
Mangore: commands Uigur Army Regulars to win land.
Nooryouz: despairs of finding her husband.
Sesli: is happy about her marriage negotiations.
Thomas: finds the favor of a loan turned against him.
Yavuz: is filled with hate and suspicion.
Yusuf: finds his foreman is still a cheat and deceiver.
Sorba: still takes advantage of people for gain.


GLOSSARY:
*Ah'jah le et*: Hurry; Be quick!
*Bu ra 'dai sin*:  Here you are!
*efendi*: Lord.
*efendim*: my Lord.
*El betty*: Of course; naturally; certainly.
*gelden*: they came; they've arrived.
*ha ki ki*: true.
*Isa*: Muslem name for Jesus.
*Neredeysin?*: Where are you?
*Ol maz*: It can't be; not that.
*Ordu var*: There's an army.
*Shabat*: Hebrew name for the Sabbath.
*yav room*: my baby.
 *Yok*: Nothing; negative.

**SORBA PLOTS**

"You don't sound very enthusiastic about my marriage, Noor."

Nooryouz smiled gently, "There come hard moments in any marriage, there are misunderstandings and separations. So be committed in your soul. Otherwise it might end in bitterness and failure."

Sesli looked carefully at her, "Would that be the results of your separation; a sense of defeat? You never seemed angry."

Nooryouz smiled faintly. "I'm tired of hiding and running. I'm forgetting what it is to have a husband. I'm wondering if Yesu is the Savior he taught me to pray to. Why does he take so long?"

Sesli stared in shock: mouth open. "But you seem so quiet and trusting. I didn't know you felt this way. Why didn't you say so?"

Nooryouz shrugged and sighed. "What good would that have done? I'm tired of adventures. I want my husband and a place to live; steadiness, not change."

Sesli said, "We know Sanjak will be trying to find you now," She assured her, "He will be moving toward us scouring the border area to find you. You have been hidden up to now."

Nooryouz nodded her head, "Yes, but if I take a chance and become better known the Uigur spies will try to take me back to the Khan."

Sesli giggled, "If the letters got to the authorities you will be known about by both sides and perhaps Sanjack as well. You'll know very soon.

"Yes, and that's why I pray to Allah through the prophet Isa. It gives me confidence, and I have some good things happening to me."

"I pray too, but I've found little in the way of answers that I like until now. I'm feeling a change coming on. It's exciting."

"I'm glad for you. Sanjak says that prayer requires persistence and some answers to big things coming slowly. I guess I need more persistence. I must be happy in waiting for God's will to show up."

Sesli disagreed and turned her horse to go back to the marriage negotiations. "I don't have the patience for it. Some things happen too fast," she laughed and raced away.

Nooryouz trudged on wearily. Softly she started to sing her complaint. With her friends happiness she felt her condition more acutely. She was waiting alone.

I AM ALONE

I wait for him, on-ly, Time goes by,
I am a-lone. I wait in vain for him.
How I love him! He loves me too. Oh, my love,
What will I do, if I don't find you?

1.      I wait for him only.
Time goes by, I am alone.
I wait in vain for him.
How I love him. He loves me, too.
Oh, my love, what will I do
If I don't find you?

2.        I count the days slowly,
           They slip by without a change.
           My hope grows cold and thin.
           Yet, I love him. Does he love me?
           Oh, my soul, how can I live
            if I can't find you?

> - - - - - >BAGHDAD COURTYARD> - - - - - >

"I've been waiting for you Thomas. You remember the three gold pieces you borrowed?" Old Thomas faced Sorba his old taskmaster, with a start and seeing the two police with him quailed and knelt, begging, "Please, let me talk to my master. I will get the money somehow."

The old boss laughed, "I have the paper and your sign. I give you a choice, pay it all today or give me your granddaughter, Deborah. The parents are dead. By law she should be Muslim. I can use her to advantage and will cancel all your debt to me. I will even guarantee a life in a rich household for her. You might even get the privilege of seeing her sometimes. What more can you get for an eight year old child? The captain of the new guard will be generous, so I'm being generous to an old fellow worker."

"Please, my master waits the completion of my errand. I'll come to the court before vespers."

"Get there and bring the girl with you. You can't expect any man to wait for his money forever."

> - - - - - >CHIPCHAK KHAN'S YURT> - - - - - >

"Here they come, it looks to be about fifty men and women, families even. I see a woman and child riding before them. It looks like Setchkin and the heir," reported Karga to the vast tiger seated on a large mare. Both looked very uncomfortable.

"They should have been dead several months ago, according to our orders from the head," Kaplan snarled at his skinny associate. "I trust our archers are in position and ready for our command?"

"Wait," the Crow injected, "there is a large mob of men on the horizon. *Ordu var*, it's an army!"

85

"*Ol maz*, not that," cursed Kaplan, "Why were we not warned?," He turned to his awed associate, "Cancel the planned attack. We are forced to treat with this diplomatic party before us or be destroyed. We must trust in talks to gain our aims and the Wolf's purposes."

They watched the horizon fill with thousands of armed men. Carts and wagons appeared carrying families and goods. It was a tribal incursion. Appearing from the desert the Toozlu minority had grown, yet the Brotherhood of Chipchaks had not been alerted and called in for defense. The core of the nation lay exposed with only several hundred fighting men present.

"The Khan rides out to meet them, councilors follow. They are going to trust them."

"We will join them, I must eat quince and greet a Toozlu son-in-law. I pray the spirits that she is not pregnant. I will deal with your pitiful failures later." The giant whipped his horse into a run.

> - - - - - >SAMARA COURTHOUSE> - - - - >

"Thomas has failed to show with the child I promised," Sorba growled, "but I'll have the police with me when I get the girl tomorrow morning."

Gerchin cocked his head and agreed, "Yes, come to the property tonight If you like, I'll have my men guard it."

"In the morning," Sorba promised, "I have important accounts and titles to bring with me. I'll wait a bit more."

"Stay well," Gerchin said on departing.

"Go well," was the prompt response.

"*Buradaysin*, you're here, so I won't go looking for you." The voice of Yusuf *efendi* came from behind the man watching his promised defender fade from sight. "I have filed a case against you for the full recovery of all I've lost through your mishandling of my father's estate. I've left the evidence and the denunciation before the judge and the trial will be announced soon. Thomas has told me about your demands. Why should I forgive you what you won't forgive others?"

"But, sir" stuttered Sorba, "I need money. I have his papers and sign. It's only three gold pieces, nothing huge."

"That's all the more reason to show mercy and forgive or agree on a plan of payment. You offer nothing."

"I want the money or the girl. You pardoned me! You didn't say I had to quit being a good business man." Sorba waved the paper recording the debt.

"Here, I give you three gold coins and I will take the debt." Yusuf removed the paper from Sorba's hand and crushed it. He walked to the nearest light, being lighted in the courtyard and astonished all those listening to the argument. As it burned, he said, "*Isa*, the Messiah and Savior, has pardoned me. It isn't bad business to pardon those who show a contrite and thankful spirit."

> - - - - - >YUSUF'S SAMARA MANSION> - - - - - >

An excited Deborah answered the door at the Bowzhun town house. The eight-year-old child shouted the news in the astonished faces of her father, Thomas and Yusuf bey. "*Gelden*, they've arrived." Then she disappeared and the two men went to a room where the volume and cheer indicated the presence of some unusual activity.

The whole household staff and family were scattered around three or four individuals. Koolair and Deborah were animatedly talking to a young man-child of smooth face and neat turban. His young servant, the Hun, was talking to the guard and several men servants. Two, no, three strangers sat quietly and occasionally conversed together. His daughter, Maril was hugging her mother, surrounded by the women of the house. Almost everyone in that circle seemed to be crying. Yusuf joined them with loud cries of joy. On the masters arrival several of the women took their tears to the kitchen to ready something special for the occasion.

Everyone got bits and pieces of the story told by different lips. They heard very little in historical sequence, but every listener treasured the jumble of information. Each hoped for another occasion to hear more and to get the correct chronology in their minds. A few even ventured to talk to the tall blind man and his little crippled friend. The corporal, Tash, talked little, but was delighted with the foods, drinks and tidbits sent out from the kitchen.

87

"We've been expecting you for two months now," laughed the *sarai* keeper in Getchet. They've come by every week to ask about you. Even the stable cats know to watch for a black and a Fergana mare with a couple who are important to someone."

"We're glad to have waiting friends. I hope they're not tired of waiting and ceased to be friends." Kerim quipped. "Where are they waiting?"

"Not here," explained the agreeable master, "They were by yesterday. They worried that you would miss the opening of the theater program. Starts tomorrow after *Shabat*, the Saturday is over."

"But tomorrow is Saturday," protested Leyla.

"*Shabat* starts tonight," explained the keeper," and ends at sunset tomorrow. Jewish days start from dark to dark, not many people know that."

"So, after dark we go to the theater tomorrow. Is it safe and how do you get in?" Inquired a curious Kerim.

"They left the admission to the side box just in case you came. They wouldn't be permitted to come here on *Shabat*. Kazars are strict about things like that. You're free to believe what you like, but the rules follow the Torah and no other's rules. Do you understand? It sounds hard, but it isn't." That did not reassure Leyla as much as the smells coming from the kitchen and the lovely room whose door he was opening for them. "Good, we have tonight to rest up."

> - - - - - >A BAGHDAD HOUSE> - - - - - >

"I tell you there was somebody in our house. I can tell when things are moved around. You may not notice, but I know exactly where I left everything." Abdullah listened with the bored patience of a man who is acquainted, and unimpressed, with each statement of his beloved.

"My dear fellow you are imagining things. We are not being watched nor are there snoopers around the house."

"There you go blaming me for others actions… making me at fault. I don't accept that." He was near tears and Abdullah patted his arm solicitously, his voice tender.

"Now, now let's not get upset and distressed over this. I'll put out tracer patterns and we'll see if someone scars them. The traces will show. Tracks will prove you right."

The small man took a deep sigh of relief. "Oh, I thought you would be reasonable. Yes, that will be the proof we need. I don't want to move, but if it's really necessary." He did not finish the statement. Abdullah shrugged and moved about the house looking in each room. His annoyed voice returned brusquely.

"I see no difference in anything. It's just the way we left it. We will take all the precautions."

Magazi agreed worriedly, "We can't be too careful where the Gray Wolf is concerned."

> - - - - - >ABBASSID ARMY BASE> - - - - - >

Kaya, the Nestorian Christian, arrived home after his report to the base commander Onat bey. They reported the burial of Bolben. He noticed one of the men had stayed behind to report what he observed in the Uigur camp.

Kaya told his friends to prepare to continue the travels with family and valuables. The Syr valley was a logical destination for land would lie idle with the departure of the occupants. Those desperate for new opportunities could not ignore this possibility and would flock to the area in spite of the present dangers. A chance for a new start moves the desperate. They agreed not to include the spy; for once a profitable behavior is acquired it is seldom abandoned. He could not be trusted.

> - - - - - >ISSYK KOOL HOUSE> - - - - - >

"Baja, *neredeysin*? Where are you?" Aziz bey bellowed his inquire to the sky. There was no answer as he drew near the house by the shore. When he stooped to shout once again the door opened and Yavuz stood with a knife pointed at Aziz throat.

"I've gotcha, you big hypocrite: all your brag about being an honest smuggler. You're in the flesh and dream trade just like the rest of us."

"Yavuz bey what are you up to now? Why the knife? I'm not here for the police."

89

"Don't play the innocent with me, I've seen the evidence, the girls were here. Where have you hid them? I want my part in their value. I knew you were up to some dirty trick on our last trip over."

"What have you done with Baja? I want my sister."

"What has she done with the girls? Where has she hid them? They were here," Yavuz screamed.

"There was a relative from the valley village with her here and Baja promised to return to the base."

"I don't believe you. You're helping her. You got them."

"I think I do believe him," a deep male voice cut in. "But if either of you move you'll die." Yuzbasha Mangore stepped around the corner of the house and stared in contempt at the feisty Yavuz. "Drop the knife you little cheat." An archer stood ready on both ends of the building and a squad of mounted men poured into the space before the house.

Yavuz dropped his knife. "I'm glad you're here," he shouted. "This man is the one who stole the girls and has hidden them. He was going to tell me."

"That's not what I heard, but wait… you tell me where you've been big man."

"I was at Almati and coming home, I stopped to see my sister here. This wild man jumped out to wave a knife in my face and accuse me of things I've never done." Conviction and anger underlined his voice.

"How did things go at Almati?" inquired Mangore with sincere interest.

"They were hard pressed by the irregulars, but the fort held and the Chu fort sent reinforcements and cleared them out."

"Had we been at either place, the whole affair could have been significantly different."

"Allah knows, I don't," shrugged Aziz.

"You serve a God who accepts no efforts, but His own; exactly like the Jehovah of the Jews and Christians. Why try if human effort accomplishes nothing? How petty and illogical you are. God crowns effort and strategy." Mangore was angry now. He stood, his fists on his hips, measuring with contempt his captives.

Aziz murmured, "If you say so."

Yavuz snarled, "You agree with anyone who looks your way. Claptrap, excuses for failure that's all I hear from you." His face was now in Aziz's face. He'd forgotten his danger.

"I found the money in the house," Chavush reported, "but I didn't find the big guy who hit me on the head to take it." He brought the bag to Mangore. "What do we do with the prisoners?"

"One man cheated us and either lost or never had the woman we were hoping to find. Either way he deserves to die. The honorable man fought against us and helped defeat our irregulars. He is an enemy. We can take no prisoners nor leave eyewitnesses."

"Commander, it will pollute the earth to shed criminal blood here. If it were in combat that would be honorable," Chavush, the sergeant protested.

"*Haki'ki*, true," Mangore stated firmly. "Look for leather bags or covers in the house and sheds."

"Here are some grain bags," a trooper shouted. The men knew what to do. Yavuz was thrust bodily into a bag, with blows and kicks, and they closed the top with a rope tied tightly around his throat. Aziz was too tall to stand and was beaten down, forced to sit. They tightened the rope to create difficulty breathing. Then, they laid them out side by side in front of the house.

The troop enjoyed giving more kicks, blows and stomps on the helpless victims. Then mounting, they rode their horses over the bags.

"Curse you Aziz," Yavuz strained to shout, "I knew partnership with you would kill me some day. You never listened to me and now you've fallen asleep while I suffer."

> - - - - - > SAMARA ROYAL PALACE> - - - - - >

A flustered secretary burst into the office of Kurnaz bey to cry out in frustration "*Efendim*, that street dog has sold the Samara estate. Sorba is before the judge now: cashing in on money we advanced him to buy it."

"What?" roared the Royal Advisor. "That property was to be given over to me when the Royal Eye was elsewhere.

91

I need that land for my palace and hunting grounds. Can it be stopped?"

A slight lift of the chin preceded a brief explanation. "It was being signed over and the money paid, when I arrived. I protested to Sorba, but he pretended ignorance and the Turkish commander said I should be temperate with my words, 'lest heat come to fire in the courthouse'. I could do nothing because of the situation."

Kurnaz stood eyes narrowed in concentration. "Perhaps we should terminate 'a varmint that steals calves from the herd'," he quoted. "We have two hiding perpetrators of the concluded Khorasan Shame Project. We can include a third assignment, as if it were a first for our daring duo, before terminating them. What do you think?"

"*Efendim*," the assistant's voice quavered, "You have never used the Society's agents for personal vendetta. The head's own rules, Sir. Would he approve such an action?"

"*El betty*, of course, the best procedure is to get the head's approval, but here we have a natural. The two agents will go outside the boundary of Dar al Islam. They can stay out or return for a fitting termination to their useful career for the Society." Kurnaz licked his lips. "I'll clear it with the head. You will rewrite the instructions," he continued, "to our newly discovered agents. Have them destroy Sorba's account books. I'm sure they'll accommodate us promptly. Yusuf bey will owe me for the elimination of a nuisance he was too weak to prosecute and put away for his crimes."

"You're sure the Head will comply, Sir?"

The vizier glanced slyly at his assistant, "We both know that it is death to know too much about our Society's head. However, we in the upper echelon know his purposes. I'm sure of his willingness to finish the targets chosen."

> - - - - - ->BAGHDAD HOUSE>- - - - - - ->

"Abdullah, *gel, ah'jah lc et*, come, quick!" the panic in Magazi's voice sent his friend running to his side.
They stared at the bundle sitting inside the barred door. A message bundle had arrived during the night. The gray-brown dog hairs inside confirmed what they already knew from experience. The Wolf was at their door. Three numbered

bundles waited inside the packet. The first had a city sketch with a street and house marked out. Mud brick and cane indicated the type of structure and a drop of lead solder (the kind used by a tin-smithy located nearby). A pomegranate bloom gave a clue, a bit of charcoal indicated a fire and a hanjir marked the death of the house's resident.

"It's an assassination and I expect our lives depend on doing it promptly," Abdullah indicated, sweating.

"I know that house," Magazi exclaimed. "The bushes show over the wall. I got supplies there. It's rented to the estate manager by the owner; some kind of obligation."

"I wonder why the Wolf would get interested in some one like that," Abdullah growled.

"What's in the second set of instructions?" Magazi inquired nervously.

"There's a tiny model ship, the name of a southern port on the Caspian Sea, a metal star of David!" They exchanged looks of astonishment. Abdullah continued. "We have to go to the Kazar Kingdom, to Getchit. We must kill a government agent. Here is a copy of his number."

"I memorized the list," Magazi said, "Let me see it. It's Derk bey, what can he have done?"

"He may have gotten too close to the truth about the Society." Again, they stood facing each other.

"He's giving us the chance to escape outside Dar al Islam." There was a long pause.

"Perhaps for the same reason: death or exile!"

"Let's take exile and life," affirmed Abdullah. "The third bundle must have the money."

"Right," Magazi affirmed. "With the name of another victim; a high agent of the Gray Wolf Society; they're cleaning house!"

"Who?" Abdullah demanded hoarsely.

"Seerlee bey, himself! I once thought he was the head." Magazi found himself whispering again. "We may be offered a choice, but I wouldn't count on it," both fully agreed.

Abdullah concluded, "We must out-fox the Wolf."

## PEOPLE, PLOTS & PLACES IN CHAPTER 8

Baja: is guest of the fort commander's wife.
Gazellim: holds the hearts of many Getchet citizens.
Harun El Ari: patrols his territory and discovers refugees.
Jon: receives a promotion and new duties.
Kadir: is caught and taken to the fort for protection.
Kerim: Enjoys the Kazar theater performance.
Leyla: meets insults and artists at the theater.
Maril: loves to talk about their trials and her helper.
Nooryouz: finds herself captive with a lovely hostess.
Setchkin: explains her brother's death to her people.
Yasmin: the commander's wife entertains guests.
Yav room: my baby.
Yusuf: enjoys the return of his daughter and servant.

## GLOSSARY:

*Abbasid*: name of the family of the uncle Mohammed.
*Bach onlar'a*: Look at them.
*hanum*: My lady; a term of respect used after the name.
*hich*: never; not at all.
*Kim gelir*: Who comes; Who's there.
*ko'jam*: my husband.
*sept*: (English) indicates subdivisions of a tribe or nation.
*sutlach*: a special dish of rice pudding, milk and spices.

**SATURDAY NIGHT**

"I knew I had to jump, it was the only way out of the harem.
I wanted to go home, but the mattress and floats were so small
looking. Then I saw Jon down below motioning to us, so I closed my
eyes and jumped to him." The breathtaking escapes held everyone's
attention. She portrayed Jon's leadership and valor. It was clear to
everyone that one person held her attention and admiration after her
forced separation from her family. She was obviously in love and
told of his exploits with attention to details that embarrassed him at
times.

The celebrations at the Bowzhun town house went on all night.
Some of the travelers dozed off, but enough were awake so someone
was always available for questions and explanations. This way
almost everyone got to tell of some part of the journey. The story of
Tayze and the boys was listened to with less urgency than the trip
from Chang'an and escape from the harem. The fact that she had
lived as a shepherdess produced laughter and admiration. People ate,
drank, came and went as the night wore on.

"I've been waiting for a chance to talk to you," Yusuf bey
announced as Jon came back into the room. "I need a man to take the
job my new steward used to do. I need someone to manage the flour-
mill. His old assistant does the grinding fine, but can't keep the
accounts straight. Can you do that?"

"I'd like to try," Jon replied. "Nooryouz and Maril taught me
writing and some of your language, but I'm going to need help
starting."

95

"You'll get it. He's especially sensitive about his customers and flowers."

Jon laughed, "After the deserts we've crossed I can promise daily water for all."

"There's another matter of concern to us. We have introduced Koolair as our daughter. Our old manager suspects otherwise, because we did not advise father. We say it was because of health, we didn't want to disappoint hopes, and later because of the expulsion turmoil. You know they will take her if they know she's an Umayyad Ambassador's daughter. Please support us in this."

"I can truthfully say I remember Maril playing with Koolair when I went to work for you in Chang'an."

> - - - - - >WITH THE CHIPCHAK KHAN> - - - - - >

"I request permission to address the royal court and the excellent Khan of the Chipchak nation and brotherhoods on the valiant yet regrettable death of my brother, Kynan of the Kynaklar."

Setchkin bowed to Khan Erden before the council and assembly. The preliminaries had not gone smoothly. Each sept was suspicious of the motives of the others. The mild Khan was tired of the complaints and welcomed the opportunity for diversion.

"We welcome the wife of my father, the Khan Erdash, and her child to court. Speak Mother, we are listening." Curiosity brought quiet and a new interest to the assembly. What would the child bride of the old Khan say? Wouldn't anything she could say fan anger?

"As a little girl, I adored my big brother. He teased, yet carried me on his horse to adventure, taught me what he had learned and showed me the curious wonders of the steppes. When he went away to the Bulgar court, I was lonesome. I became a friend of the Twozan family and others to fill my time. When my brother returned he was changed and pursued other interests, ignoring me. When I caught the Khan's attention, I felt excited and honored. The following events brought responsibilities."

"I confess that I was not a worthy companion and I had much to learn to fulfill my duties. I apologize to all of you who suffered, in word or deed, indignities by my callous and unfortunate behavior. I have asked of Yesu His forgiveness and power to change; which I so needed. Tanra has blessed me and granted my requests. I have found peace and joy in serving where my heart has led." The beautiful voice and appeal ended for a moment and the crowd exchanged glances. This indeed was a radical change. They wanted to hear more.

96

"My brother made an earnest attempt to rescue me from the Toozlu, who had taken me for security in their attempt to contact the younger twin, Erben. Kynan's attack, using mercenaries was to avoid a blood feud. He was defeated in the Muslim Army attack. He was captured and imprisoned in Kokand."

The crowd exchanged anxious glances and nods of recognition. They already knew these things were true.

"Meanwhile, the Toozlu fought a series of battles that impressed the Seljuk commander and led to the contracting of Gerchin's band to serve the Sultan."

Here listeners whispered their proud agreement around the crowd. "Kynan escaped from the garrison and made his way north following us. I met him the morning after my joyful marriage. I was surprised at the strength of his character. He was strong and firm like the heroes of Kaya's time. He decided to make peace between the Toozlu and Kaynak by marrying Leyla, the daughter of Erben.

"He rode ahead to guide and to guard our crossing of the Syr River Ford. There he met Kerim, who had rescued and restored Leyla to our band. They met in a thorn thicket near the river and fought for her hand. Kerim won and Kynan died. According to the agreement, Kerim married Leyla that night in spite of his wounds. Our priest spoke the words of eulogy for Kynan." These words she repeated by memory to all.

'We bring to your remembrance, *Tanram*, our fallen fellow tribesman, Kynan, a brother of Setchkin hanum, son of Kaplan of the Kynaklar clan, friend and protector of the high Khan of the Chipchaks. The youth was hostage to the East Bulgars, later captive of the black banner of the Abbassids whom he defied. He escaped out of their lands. Here, on the border of his freedom, he has met his end honorably; admired by all. He was a credit to his family, and trusting in Yesu did all that is right and necessary for the good of the tribe. May his memory be treasured, Amen.'"

A hush had filled the assembly. Here was sacrifice for the blessing of the nation. She, herself, had married to reconcile the two hostile groups. Reconciliation was now complete. They understood and celebrated!

> - - - - - >THE KAZAR THEATER > - - - - - >

"Who are these strange people with the curls down the sides of their heads?" inquired Leyla.

"Jewish men always cover their heads and their women wear scarves to hide their shortcut hair or shaved heads," Kerim explained. "The sarai keeper told me about them."

"They wear lots of gold and look at those jewels. I've never seen so much in one place! Just look at the cloth they wear in their turbans; see the sheer quality of the women's robes. Could you get me some clothes like that?"

"It sounds like I will have to." Kerim laughed, "We are going to be a plain contrast to their opulence. But look, the orchestra is coming in." Several men with the same side curls and turbans brought instruments of string, wood and metal with them. They sat beside the stage in an area not covered by a curtain. After some preliminary tootling, they broke into a lively melody accompanied by drums, bells, gourds and other sound makers. Then a man appeared to talk and provoke laughter with jokes that were spoken in the Kazar language, only a part of which they understood. Strange Hebrew words were interspersed with the familiar and the people laughed in outbursts that indicated great enjoyment. They clapped their hands to indicate pleasure.

*"Bach onlara*, Look at them," Leyla said, "those men are pointing at us and laughing. Why are they so rude?"

"We are out of style, dress and place, here in travelers' clothes and in a special box tonight. It seems ludicrous to them," Kerim replied. "Probably they're curious too, but are using the occasion to show how smug and right they are."

"Well, I don't like it and I'm not coming here again," Leyla replied crossly. "I'd like to go now."

*"Hich*! No!" Kerim hissed. "Our orders are to see it though. Let boys be boys for now." The noise increased when they announced the next number. Everyone had comments to whisper: "She's my favorite."

"She does something new tonight,"

"Gazellim has a new song."

"Don't you just love her?"

"I love what she does with her hair."

"They have some new girls."

"Watch!"

A voluptuous, tall woman with shining black eyes and hair appeared on stage. She was expensively dressed in fashionable clothes. The orchestra obligingly swung into a bright minor melody. Her arms held a water jar on her bare shoulder. She smiled modestly as she started to sing. The stage behind her gradually filled with girls of different sizes and dresses, all with jars or buckets to join the refrain.

#1

I carry my water jar
 perched on my shoulder bare
 to the well each day.
(All the big girls do it!)
The boys will be waiting there
 anxious to talk to us,
 but we will pay them no mind.
(though we laugh about it!)
One will be waiting:
 kind, strong and handsome.
(He makes my heart sing!)

Refrain:

Yes, he loves; He loves me!
Yes he does.

Chorus:

Then at night I dream he is kissing me.
 Softly and tenderly, head on my shoulder.
 Lord, I know that love will rule over me,
 Guarding me, blessing me,
 Making my family.

Refrain:

Yes, he loves; he loves me!
Yes he does.

GAZELLIM SNGS

99

# AT THE WELL

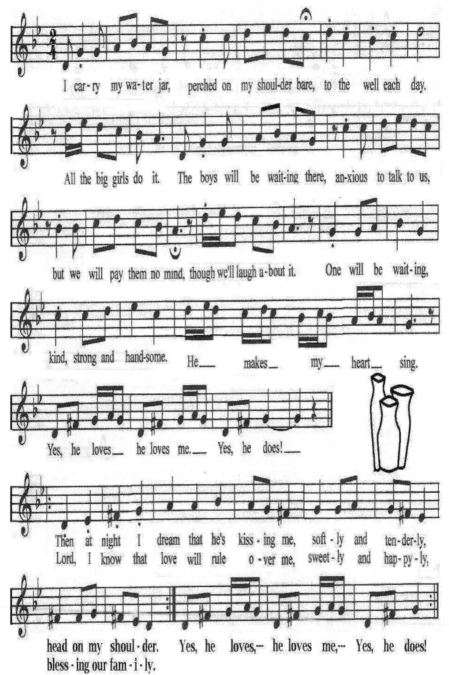

I car-ry my wa-ter jar, perched on my shoul-der bare, to the well each day.

All the big girls do it. The boys will be wait-ing there, an-xious to talk to us,

but we will pay them no mind, though we'll laugh a-bout it. One will be wait-ing,

kind, strong and hand-some. He__ makes__ my__ heart__ sing.

Yes, he loves__ he loves me.__ Yes, he does!__

Then at night I dream that he's kiss-ing me, soft-ly and ten-der-ly,
Lord, I know that love will rule o-ver me, sweet-ly and hap-py-ly,

head on my shoul-der. Yes, he loves,-- he loves me,-- Yes, he does!
bless-ing our fam-i-ly.

100

#2
We walk to the water source,
  morning and evening too,
  for our needs each day.
  (every family has to.)
The boys all find chores to do
  so they can see us there
  but we pretend they're not here.
  (While we look them over)
There's one I favor,
  keen, wise and prosperous
  he's the one I chose,

Refrain:
Yes, he loves, he loves me!
Yes, he does.

Chorus & Refrain:

   The actress and chorus moved in advancing and
retreating lines and pairs in smooth enticing moves and
flourishes of arms and skirts before the second verse began.
The Gazelle leaned forward both confiding and showing
cleavage to all. The audience watched with open eyes and
mouths, fascinated by the display.
   The audience was in a frenzy of applause as the Gazellim
finished her number. Men in black suits and turbans stood
on stools or benches to throw kisses, or money at her feet.
Some made gestures offering their hearts or lives to her. A
smile of triumph showed briefly on her face. It was soon
replaced by sweet acknowledgement. The audience hoped
for an encore, but a belly dancer came instead and the
audience soon abandoned their hopes for a shimmering
presentation.
   Erotic dancing, dating from women's earliest needs and
men's delights, has been polished for many emperors and
pharaohs to arouse the flesh and spirit to the delights they
falsely seem to offer. The artistic adornments and additions
serve to increase enticement.
   Leyla noticed with concern Kerim's fascination with it.
However, she soon became interested in the combination of
moves, music and costume. Art became real!

Yuzbasha Harun el Ari left a few top men at the Almati Fort until he could get reinforcements. The Uigur irregulars had scattered and the regulars seemed occupied elsewhere. Ahead he could see a group of refugees moving through the hills in a north-west direction. He needed to investigate for he had to know everything that was happening in his territory. He divided his forces and sent one troop behind to stop any retreat and he rode ahead to cut them off. People on the road were skittish and fled on approach, but he needed to know what they had seen on the road. The missing regulars of Mangore's command worried him.

"Halt there, we need to know your names and places. keep your hands in view, but rest easy. We mean you no harm."

"I am Kadir, partner of Aziz bey the importer. Here with me are family, Aunt Baja, the boy Korkmaz, my promised bride and a lieutenant's wife and baby. Aziz bey went to join you at Almati three days ago. We came this way because the Syr Daria is still in chaos. We seek safety."

"We are returning to our fort, you will be safe there. My wife will take care of the ladies. Aziz bey will likely come after us if he has men for protection."

Kadir nodded happily. "He's with his men. We're buying land on the Issyk Kool, but it's not safe with the fighting going on around us. We decided to seek the safety of the fort."

The officer frowned, "You will have to provide your food. We can use your help at the fort, but our supplies are short. Because of the many refugees we must stretch them." The rear guard had ridden up and the entire body moved on toward the fort.

The commander asked, "What news at the base. How is our new Binbasha dealing with the emergency?" The conversation went on. "You say the baby belongs to a lieutenant?" el Ari asked.

"*Evit*, yes, Sanjak bey has been on the base without her and she has come seeking him."

El Ari laughed loudly, "Yes, he was our supply officer and has gone out to supply the refugees with the Toozlu people.

I didn't know he was looking for her to come. He never mentioned that he was a father. When my wife has her child everyone will know it."

"There is the fort," Harun el Ari stated, as they entered the parade grounds before the stone walled structure. "When we enter the gate you men will surrender your weapons and the women go immediately to the house near the hamom where my wife will meet them. The men will have to give a statement of origin and intent at the *ordugar*, headquarters."

"We will want to return to the Issik Kool when there is no more danger," Baja stated anxiously.

Kadir agreed pleasantly, "When the irregulars go back to their base and the country settles down. I have properties to care for, and my wedding to celebrate."

The lieutenant smiled broadly, "Pleasant duties must wait their time. This activity by the insurgents will die down and we'll get control of the Syr valley again. You'll be home before winter has passed. Markets were starting to open this week and you'll get all you can use there."

"How fortunate you are to have such a good, sweet baby." Yasmin declared to the new women travelers as she dandled baby Nevrim on her lap.

"Yes, he's learning to drink from a cup now," declared Nooryouz with pride, "but only sweetened water." The women laughed.

Baja commented wryly: "And you've no idea how much trouble that was."

Sesli nodded agreement, adding. "I chewed and spit bulgur until I can't face it in a meal now."

"Then you will starve if you go north to the tribes," Yasmin commented. "They haven't the variety of food you find in Dar al Islam."

"I'm marrying property on the Issyk Kool Lake, near Baja. We'll be neighbors. I'll let her wean all my babies." Sesli said. This brought on gales of laughter from all.

103

"I've been two years at the fort and I'm still waiting," she complained. "I do everything Allah requires and yet, still no blessing." All made sympathetic sounds patting her hand.

"These matters require time," Baja stated authoritatively as the eldest. "Pleasure in marriage is required before the pain and responsibility of birth and nurture of children. The youthful longing and anticipation should be fully satisfied for stability and nurture of a family. Men are practically useless in all but the pleasure. They become more helpful as the child becomes mobile and inquisitive. It falls to the woman to keep both happy. Not an easy task."

They sat with scarves thrown back revealing their hair. All listened with respect and care as the bowls of *sutlach*; rice pudding mixed with milk and honey was served in celebration of their reception and hospitality. Yasmin had invited in the Sergeant Major's lady and some enlisted men's wives. Naturally, there were no men present although a few of the boys were getting tall and would soon be out training in the soldiering they already played at. Older girls talked of current activities, dress, and older boys already being trained. They knew their fathers would choose their future husbands in political or personal family deals, but boys were still a popular topic of conversation.

"I've not heard your story, Nooryouz," declared Yasmin. "Tell us about your man and how you got such a perfect baby." All agreed with anticipation.

"Sanjak is a Chipchak assigned to guide the expelled minorities out of Tang China." Nooryouz began, not sure of how much should be revealed to her new hostess. "They were generous to include people of many nations. So, I accompanied a neighboring family, the Bowzhuns of Baghdad. My parents are dead. We met under unusual circumstances. I loved him from the moment of our meeting. He had the same feeling. We were married on caravan and lived in a tent. He was out, gone from dawn to late night. It was a harsh life, but love made it passable. Here you have the proof that Allah's blessings come to those who suffer injustice and expulsion."

"Were Muslims not exempt from such drastic action by treaty?" inquired Yasmin.

"I, obviously, was not; though I know others were allowed to stay. You could say I left for love, for Sanjak was my life," she concluded. "Now he is!" The baby giggled to the delight of all.

"Children are the supreme delight of all marriages, well worth waiting and suffering for," Baja stated. They agreed.

"My husband, Harun el Ari was surprised that Yuzbasha Sanjak did not mention having a baby. He is so desirous of one, he would have told the whole fort." Yasmen said, laughing sadly.

"Sanjak was here? Where has he gone?"

"He took a bag of gold and left a week ago," said the Sergeant Major's wife. "He had to ransom someone important. He'll be back, his sergeant is still out with the refugees."

"I ought to go there too. He'll be helping them."

"*Kojam*, my husband, won't allow it! There are dangerous, subversive things going on among them. Some practice the heavenly procession and whirl about in the way of the ancestors. Those Turks worship with oboe, cymbals, shrilling pipes, drums and dances. It's an offence to Islam and our prophet. They must submit and surrender to Allah or move out of our territory."

"How do I get together with my husband then?"

"He is an officer of the army of Islam and Allah. He will return to the fort. You must wait for him here."

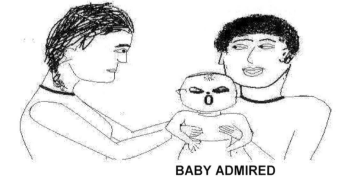 

BABY ADMIRED

105

## PEOPLE, PLOTS & PLACES IN CHAPTER 9

Abdullah: must urgently obey his new commands.
Army Adjutant: is worried about rations for the troops.
Atilla: always does the unexpected wherever he goes.
Erly: gets new supplies from the sergeant.
Gazellim: accepts message and messenger at face value.
Kerim: endeavors to deliver a secret (with the password).
Kurnaz: as royal vizier, hears a confession.
Leyla: finds she married a man she does not understand.
Magazi: feels the hot breath of the Gray Wolf on his neck.
Onat bey: makes emergency provisions for the troops.
Sanjak: arrives at the Toozlu camp without his treasure.
Seerlee bey: reveals his illegal activities to an enemy.
Sergeant: admires nomadic life, but prefers civilization.
Sorba: has many confident plans for a safe future.
Tash: finds trouble because he followed orders.
Tayze: recognizes a friend at the door.
Vizier's Assistant: tries to keep two contrary commitments.
Yusuf: is visited by a troublesome man from his past.


GLOSSARY:
*ah-chuck'ter*: it is open.
*Bozkurt*: Turkish for gray wolf.
*Efendim*: My Lord.
*inshallah*: may God permit it; God willing.
*kafir*: not a Muslim; unbeliever.
*Kim gelir?*: Who's there? Who has come?

**A PARTY'S END**

"The door's not barred," Abdullah whispered. He pushed gently. *Ahchuckter*, it's open!" They stood before the house indicated by their feared employer, the Gray Wolf.

"Go in, don't just stand here, where we can be seen." Magazi scolded, pushing past big Abdullah into the house.

"*Kim gelir*? Who's there?" roared a drunken voice from further inside the building. They followed the sound to its source.

"I'm a tin smith," replied Magazi. "I have to leave town and take a boat north on the Caspian Sea. I wanted to sell some of my tin supplies."

"A tinker? Come back tomorrow and the dealer will be here. I'll be gone to build a bigger, better house."

"You're leaving the city too?" Abdullah asked. " I have a new and better protector to shelter me from my ungrateful employers. I'm celebrating. Come, have a drink." Sorba indicated seats.

"You're generous. Thanks indeed. Refreshments speed our work. Let's get a fire going and warm things up."

"Who's your new patron?" Inquired Magazi kindly, "He must be important to defend you."

"Chief of the new guards, but I don't need him for my defense. I've got records and receipts to show where the money has gone: a paper trail back to the highest officials of the Sultan."

"Big game indeed," marveled Abdullah as he sampled the brew. "You must keep the papers safe. Surely they will be coming after them."

"They have no idea they exist. I have them ready to go with me tomorrow to safety." With an air of triumph he indicated with his chin a large packet near the door.

Magazi nodded to Abdullah, whose teeth gleamed in the fire light, showing his smiling agreement. "May we can help you deliver that heavy bundle to a place of safety?"

"No, I'm celebrating now. At dawn I'll get a porter and go." Sorba growled uneasily, wondering if he had revealed too much to strangers.

"A dawn you'll never see," proclaimed Abdullah, as he reached for his knife.

> - - - - - >SULTAN'S PALACE IN SAMARA> - - - - - >

"The officer of the guard said I was to report here on the completion of my duties," Onbasha Tash nervously stated to the assistant of the Vizier.

"You arrived this morning Corporal?" he inquired.

"Yes Sir, my mission is completed," Tash replied.

"Another reason to celebrate, Kurnaz *Efendim*," the assistant called out in a happy voice. "The dispatch from Derk bey has arrived."

"We are enriched as well as rid of a slimy leach; a double victory," the Vizier agreed as he entered the room. "Our emissaries will be on their way north on their next mission." He looked at the young soldier. "Well, where are your charges?"

"Safely delivered to their home, Sir," Tash stated.

"What! You let them go home?"

"I was assigned as escort, Sir. They were not to be treated as prisoners -- Derk bey's orders."

"But there are expenses to be considered."

"Yusuf bey paid the caravan master his fee," Tash explained wondering if he should explain his own gift and the party that delayed his appearance until afternoon. An oppressive silence descended on the room as the two officials considered the situation.

"Let this fool go," suggested the assistant, "Our friends will deal with Derk bey, his instructor."

"Go then, rest and get ready for new assignments." Kurnaz ordered. The perplexed Tash was happy to leave.

"We have lost the hoped for rewards for the girl's return to Yusuf. But the incriminating evidence and the witness we feared were eliminated! All evidence against us burned up with that shop." Kurnaz growled.

> - - - - - >KAZAR THEATER> - - - - - >

"You've brought some important dispatches for me?" asked Gazellim, seated in her dressing room. "You've been slow getting it here. The other couriers were more prompt."

"We were celebrating and didn't realize there were time limitations on our delivery," Kerim replied.

The Gazelle made a disagreeable face and sound. She made no effort to be cordial or attractive now. An arrogant, abrupt manner characterized her. "Well, where is it? -- the dispatch?" she demanded.

"I didn't bring it -- too risky. Also, you haven't given the pass word. So, I understand nothing you are hinting about and bid you good night."

"Stay, by Abu Baker's beard, you are not the simpleton they have made you out to be, if it's intact." She was smiling her approval.

"By the sword of the holy prophet you are not the charmer you appear to be on stage, but it is intact." he replied, careful to use the key word for identity.

She laughed, "Right, who is the mouse behind you?" She indicated the awed Leyla.

109

"A princess in disguise, I'm trying to smuggle her back to her home. Now that we are both clear coded lets get down to business."

"Where did you hide the bundle?"

"Under the mattress at the wall in our inn which I presume you already know and arranged for us."

She nodded, saying, "It will be gone before you get there. So our business is finished. I have no time for royalty in disguise. You may go."

"First you will tell me why you, a Jewess, work for the Sultan? He is an enemy of you and your nation."

"For money, they pay well, as do all who love secrets." She paused, then, continued. "You, a Christian carried the dispatches for similar reasons, but since you show concern for me I'll share a secret with you. An agent, Derk bey, is only three caravanserai stops behind you. I believe he is to terminate your escape; an affair of national pride."

"May the Messiah and Redeemer of Israel: guard, guide and bless you," Kerim declared earnestly.

Surprise showed on her cold, beautiful face. "And you as well," she finished, turning to her bronze mirror.

> - - - - - >WITH THE MIGRANTS> - - - - - >

"You have saved our lives, Sergeant! May the Christ show you mercy. When you finish the distribution of foods, some of us are ready and will depart immediately for the north."

The Sergeant disagreed, "You won't find stores or food available, beyond the desert, Erly. It's all tribes and subsistence from the margins of 'Dar al Islam'". He shrugged; it would be beyond civilization. He could not imagine life elsewhere. He could disagree with home policies and politics of a caliph, but life outside could only be disaster and death.

"You have not lived there so you don't understand tribal custom and interdependence. We will survive now with your help."

"We have tea ready, Sergeant, a treat for you and us if you will accept it." He smiled engagingly and moved toward the yurt.

"I find the ways of the nomads attractive already, and I do like to see the faces of beautiful women around me." They all laughed.

"You would like our freedom to choose and move as need arises. We learn how to handle both feast and famine."

The sergeant surveyed the food trays and the meat dishes resulting from the slaughter and drying of jerky for the trip. He smiled again patting his stomach, "I can see the feast before me, but I'll go back to the fort to face the famine." They took it as a joke, and laughed.

> - - - - - >ARMY BASE HEADQUARTERS> - - - - - >

"Only half the squad made it through with one wagon, sir. The rioting in the valley is general and looting has turned to banditry." The harassed army lieutenant reported.

"Assign half rations for the fort and send out two more squads to the wagon road. I'll fly out a message to the Mooktar of the lower Amu for additional food and troops on the next shipment." Onat bey commanded the adjutant. "I'll see if Aziz or some of the smugglers can pick up Uigur-land food for us as well. They have the contacts east-ward."

The adjutant made a grimace of disgust. "I should hesitate to eat food improperly slaughtered or unapproved by the imams."

Onan smiled knowingly, "The majority here are Turks by origin they can handle the food and the rest will have to go hungry."

The adjutant looked resentful, "Shouldn't we withdraw our northern troops from the outposts?"

"To what end? Rioting always descends to misery. I don't want the Uigurs to make gains on the Syr or Chu Rivers to turn our flank."

"The Toozlu have brought this on us, we should have wiped them out or harried them out of the land."

Onat looked down sternly, "You've no idea how difficult that would have been. We can't win the friendship of the tribes, if we arouse nothing but hatred. They can be needed reinforcements for our armies rather than wolves on our flanks. Our future could depend on it."

The adjutant disagreed, "The tribes are *kafir*! They bring us nothing but disgust and disorder."

> - - - - - >ATILLA IN SAMARA> - - - - - >

"Yusuf bey, I don't know if you remember me? I came from Chang'an with the refugees and exiles. I'm Attila bey from the Amu River district in the Fergana Valley. My farm is near Kokand."

111

"Yes, I know you. You were rather notorious in our caravan. What do you want?"

"I've heard that your daughter has happily arrived from the east and several others with her. I want to know if they know about some friends who were coming this way: a blind boy and family."

"Tanra preserve us, is that you Attila bey?" Tayze called from the patio of the house. She came to the door and greeted him effusively. Attracted by the commotion, Kardesh, Sevman and Yeet came to the door.

"We left you chasing a criminal on the upper Amu," Tayze commented, "did you catch him?"

"Those searching lacked good leadership and refused to come help me. I gave up and came here," he shrugged in disgust.

"Someone stole food from us all the way to Khiva."

"It was Umer," Kardesh reported. "He got to Khiva."

"Why didn't you tell us before?" Yeet inquired.

"He was repentant and sorry for his crimes."

"He is still guilty and should die for his crimes," Atilla insisted. "Sorrow does not undo damage."

"But it may change the damager and present opportunities to do good," Kardesh insisted.

"I don't know any criminals who have done that," Atilla replied.

"It is a change that only faith in Yesu's death and resurrection can make in a human soul," Tayze said. "For this we come to the week of His passion: Easter. It is the Christian's celebration. Atilla, you must come with us to church and be thankful."

"I've gone with you to so many places, why not to church, too."

"Yusuf bey, Will you allow our friend to stay a few days?"

"He can spend the Easter holiday with us, if he wishes."

> - - - - - > ON THE CASPIAN SEA > - - - - - >

"Away at last," Magazi exclaimed, "What joy to be free of the dictates of the Sultan and his agents!"

"Don't be rash, he has a long reach. We are leaving Dar al Islam to destroy one of his agents."

"But we can make a break for freedom, can't we?" He looked at his partner, Abdullah, pleading and expectantly.

The big man sighed and looked away. They felt the pull of the waves and cold wind on the boat as it moved north. "Ice will be moving down the river and we can't make port at Getchet. We'll have to get out at a port on the west side to avoid wind blown ice floes and other problems," he declared. Then he went on "We'll have to study the situation

112

carefully. I don't know if such a place exists in this world of hate and prejudice." He reached out to pat a hand.

"If there is, we'll find it." Magazi affirmed.

"*Inshallah*!" Abdullah whispered.

> - - - - - >ERLY'S CAMP-> - - - - >

"I'm looking for the supply sergeant. Has he been here?" Sanjak inquired at the hut made with a cart and draped felt. It was in a ditch on the north side of the Chu River. He was to deliver here just a few days ago." They motioned him on westward, so he continued asking his way to the *ordugar*. There he found his sergeant and Erly in a dispute.

"You'll get no more supplies regardless of any agreements you can cite. There aren't any in the whole northeast. The riots destroyed the stored crops. The whole area may go hungry this winter."

"We have less than a month's supply since one group left yesterday. Did you save our lives just to make the starvation take more time?"

"Wait, Erly *Efendi*," Sanjak said. "You don't have to starve. Get the different tribes to travel together then they'll share better. Relatives will feed them when they get close to home. You can move them north now."

"You're full of easy advice. Your dad left with the warriors and most of the remaining Toozlu .I'm left without leaders, money or supplies."

"But when conditions of peace are reached, supplies will be sent. By that time some of the other tribal groups will be home. Get them off under local leaders."

Erly frowned at Sanjak, "Some will have to pay passage rights to get through other's territory."

"I brought gold enough for all of them."

"You found your treasure, Yuzbasha?" asked his sergeant.

"No treasure, just this gold from the fort. I never got a glimpse of her. She could be any where in the northeast."

> - - - - - > GETCHET JEWELRY STORE > - - - - - >

"This is the jeweler favored by the Gazelle," Kerim reported with satisfaction, "We have to get our money into other items of value. The Sultan's money must go." He indicated a store with a rich display.

She nodded eagerly, eyeing the jewelry longingly. "I want a necklace and one of those jeweled girdles, like the dancer wore last night."

113

"Where would you wear a hip belt?" he queried.

"It certainly held your interest last night. Why should others get the attention I deserve?"

"In church this morning they said we should avoid any appearance of evil or worldly lust," he laughed.

"Marriage is sacred and not worldly or evil. It is difficult at times because it needs spice and variety as a reward for faithfulness. If these trinkets hold my husband's attention, I must wear one occasionally."

"I have just the thing," the jeweler, who had caught the interplay, reported. "Here is one Gazelleim ordered, but the maker used a jade stomacher, which she does not favor. You can have it for half the price she would have paid." He displayed it.

"Some have poor taste in stones," she observed tartly, holding it up. Then she turned her back to hold it before her hips. She gave a sigh of deep satisfaction. She restored it to its place saying, "Alright, now, show me your jade necklaces. I must look like a princess when we arrive."

> - - - - - >PALACE INTERVIEW> - - - - - >

The activities of the Gray Wolf Society brought me here to search out the killers of Prince Mansur. Bozkurt, a secret society's head, is a master plotter for his agents are now dead by his own hand. So, he has neatly covered his identity. There are clues however. The society is no threat to the throne. They are concerned to preserve it. A change of rulers, however incompetent that individual may be, brings too great a disruption to the empire. Justice demands a speedy trial and deserved execution of plotters; lest they aim at the throne. I must admit that I have worked for the society, they pay well." Seerlee spoke his mind to the minister as the Wolf had instructed.

Kurnaz bey responded coldly. "The government is not unaware of the activities of the society you describe. We do not smile on any secret society. Their agenda will not have Allah's approval. The Caliph is Allah's shadow on earth. He does not fear the devious ways of plotters. We know of the criminals you describe. Our authorities will catch them first.

You have been very bold to confess your identity as a worker for a proscribed society. Why have you dared say this?"

Seerlee answered proudly, "My master gives precise instructions and I obey my orders."

"So, is this a test of obedience or is it a delivery into the enemy's hands? To obey or disobey, either could mean your death."

"I'm too useful to dispose of for no reason. My directors know better. We both have useful information to share. I await your pleasure."

"I envy your masters, for such a life-risking servant is not easily found. Let us work together that I may test your skills. Then we will see. I have an agent in the Amu valley who has blundered on government business and I must rectify some of his actions. Derk bey has failed me."

Seerlee's eyes narrowed, he spoke quietly, "For such a man to fail is indeed a grave thing."

Kurnaz pondered: 'a grave,' was it a pun? An intentional reference to burial? How much did this man know? If he could be sure, the man could still be useful. Perhaps he can remove the two instruments of death who know too much. We could send this one north to the Khazar tangle to do several critical jobs.

"I have a proposition for you," he began.

HIDDEN MENACE

115

## PEOPLE, PLOTS & PLACES IN CHAPTER 10

Attila: becomes interested in his faith and travels.
Baja: gets her trip out to unexpected excitement.
Erden: arranges for peace between the factions.
Jon: is to become a merchant prince by marriage.
Kardesh: hears the commanding voice to depart.
Kerim: meets his boyhood hero, who threatens him.
Kynan: is resurrected to meet an old patron for lunch.
Leyla: new threats and competition frustrate her.
Peri lee: meets an admired boy from dad's court.
Setchkin: faces difficult choices by the Khan.
Twozan: receives a dangerous post of honor.
 Yasmin: is against attempts to contact refugees.
Yeet: is undecided on where to go in his travels.
Yusuf: decides to honor his daughter's wishes.


GLOSSARY:
*Adoni*: Hebrew for 'The Lord Almighty'.
*ah'lamma*: don't be sad.
*bash ooze too nay*: as you command; on my head.
*binbasham*: my general, head of a thousand.
*bowzkurt*: the Gray Wolf.
*chador*: public dress required of all Muslim women.
*Chavush*: sergeant.
*Eriha*: the Jordan River and the land beyond it.
*Haj*: the duty of one trip to Mecca in a lifetime.
*Kiblah*: the direction in which one is required to pray.
*Kudus*: Holy place; Jerusalem.
*ordu eve*: army headquarters.
*Shalvar*: baggy pants that close on the ankles.
*Sharia*: holy law, observed in Muslim countries.
*Shetiel*: Jewish farming villages in the Ukraine.
*soos*: hush; shush; shh.
*tanom*: okay; I agree.
*yuzbasha*: lieutenant; head of a hundred.

**GIRLS GROW-UP**

"*Binbasham*, the supply train has arrived through the upper Syr Valley road. Goods from the lower Amu are ample and will supply all our needs."     "Excellent, but we'll stay on strict rations for another week. It's had a good effect. Some of the older men can see their feet now. However, increase the ration to the mounts. Our horses have been tiring too soon on the exercise field."

"They discovered a gruesome execution passing the Issyk Kool Lake. Two resident villagers from our base were trampled to death in sacks."

"Not trouble with Buddhists I hope."

"They think not sir, more likely, Uigurs. They use the same style executions, but for different occasions and reasons. Our men buried them at the house. They found dispatches from Almati fort carried by Aziz bey."

"Yes, I remember our honest smuggler. He's dead?"

"Yes, he fought for those defending the fort. They defeated the irregulars and requested two squads for the Spring season. The other man was identified as Yavuz."

"It will save us a trial and execution. However, Aziz bey should receive a commendation of some kind. He was brave and enterprising."

"His sister is Baja hanum; they live in the village."

"I will consider the matter. Meanwhile, prepare two squads for departure to Almati with supplies."

"*Bash ooze to neigh*, as you command."

Onat watched the yuzbasha leave. Then turning, he spoke, "You can come in now, Sergeant. I saw you waiting with news. What have we received?"

"Bowzkurt orders the release of a yuzbasha to return to the tribal area; only that, no explanation."

"Our society's purpose is to increase the internal tensions and divisions of the northern tribes; to bring them into service to our Sultan and provide fighting material for the expansion of Islam. The Arabs are hopelessly divided as demonstrated by the civil wars. The man in question is a potential fracture point with a possible reconciliation now brewing there. We must force him out and away. The Crow feels that only he can disrupt the situation. We received and forwarded frantic messages from him this week."

"But Sir," protested Chavush, "With Tang China backing the Mongols and the Chipchak nation's reinforcement of the east. The Kirgiz could be squeezed south into our area."

"They could destroy the Uigurs and take their place. The Bowzkurt Society is not Allah to know what will happen, but they will work for our own enrichment and rule in the world. In the West, Byzantium is our chief rival for world power. We need troops with the ability to out-fight them. Our success lies in using the people of the north, the Turks. We must bend them to our purpose."

>- - - - - - - >IN THE KHAN'S YURT> - - - - - >

"The nation has agreed through council, Twozan. Since you left in voluntary exile last year, you cannot remain here in your old territory. It has been partitioned between resident clans. Your new place will be in the east, defending the nation against the pressures of the Kirgiz and Mongols," explained Erden, high Khan of the Chipchak nation and brotherhoods. "It's an important post that brings opportunities for enrichment and prestige. The Toozlu descend from Ozkurt the hero of Kaya's wanderings and share always in the promise of a thousand years of greatness."

"We accept the generous allowance and place granted by the council and will obey at first opportunity as weather permits," stated Twozan, humbly. "We welcome the obligation to protect our nation. We thank the Council and Khan for the pardon and reconciliation offered," Twozan bowed.

118

"Thanks be to Yesu for the opportunity to learn through obedience that costly forgiveness brings blessings and healing," Erden concluded.

"Where will you stay, Mother?" inquired the Khan, smiling and turning to Setchkin, sitting beside him.

"Where any dutiful wife should be found. At the assigned place of her husband, beside him always."

"Tanra's blessings abide with you, Mother. I want you here for the birthing of my child. We will have a corral of young princes to deal with."

"The child of promise will have a royal retinue to council and protect him until his maturity."

"After the birthing I will accompany the Toozlu east. I will have an heir for my husband after Summer's departure." Twozan looked surprised.

"Good news indeed, Mother," Erden chuckled.

"It will be difficult to leave Takkan here with the others. He is such a sweet child." Setchkin covered her face with her hands.

"*Ah'lama*! Don't cry, Mother. Take him with you until his ninth year, Mother. We will not send him to any neighboring tribes. He will already know the Kirgiz and Mongols. We will keep him safe with us." Those present smiled, except for the Tiger and the Crow.

> - - - - - >AT CHU RIVER FORT > - - - - - >

"We've news," Yasmin declared to her lady friends. The supply sergeant has returned to the fort. He's talking to my husband in the *ordu eve*."

"Sanjak didn't come with him?" Nooryouz asked.

"Just the troopers," Yasmin declared.

"I'll just go and have a talk with him or the men. I know everyone at the base," declared Baja hanum.

"No, that is not permitted, we keep Sharia law here in the fort," Yasmin protested.

"*Tamom*, okay I'll wear the chador, they know my voice. Some of them have been in my house on business with Aziz." She moved to the door.

"A relative or other man should go with you," Yasmin declared. "You can't just go anywhere."

"I'm sixty years old, who's going to bother me? Rules are made to protect and aid people in doing their business, not to interfere or make things more difficult," Baja left abruptly, forgetting her chador.

"You are without a doubt the most unreasonable man in the world. We get to the city to which you have been urging me to go. You make me move more rapidly to arrive on time. Then you give me one day to shop, go to church, theater and, tour, then want us to urgently move away." Leyla complained bitterly while Kerim continued to pack the spare horse with more than it should have to carry.

"You have spent all our money in that day and two nights. We are no longer under government support and danger increases with our remaining. Just think, we are going home to show off your new clothes, jewels and other pretties." He transferred some packets to his own horse to lighten the load.

"I thought we could go to the theater again. You liked that." Her voice was light and suggestive.

"Not enough to die for it," he exclaimed. "Did it occur to you that the Gazelle knew more than an agent of the Sultan could know about a man's name, purpose and location inside Kazar-land?" He paused, "Unless she works as an agent for this country as well."

"She's an artist, an actress; men love her." Envy and awe showed in her voice.                    "She is playing the double agent and can get us killed, if she doesn't get killed first. Mount up! We are going north. Derk bey is trailing us."

> - - - - ->FRIENDS LEAVE BAGHDAD> - - - - ->

"You won't regret leaving Baghdad and Samara behind," Attila assured his friends. "You saw enough to know how dirty and ugly they are except for the mosques and palaces of the rich."

Yeet, however, voiced his reluctance. "I was hoping that Jon and Maril would be married while we were here. He certainly got the new Turkish guard to use the mill to grind their food."

"He speaks their language and knows how they like it done," laughed Attila bey. "It'll take more than business ability to buy into the Bowzhun family."

120

"It was generous of them to agree to keep Tayze as part of the family," Yeet insisted, riding close.                  "Only after you promised to cook for everyone that's going on the trip," retorted Attila.                  "She insisted on that, I knew she was too tired to go on. She got in contact with Gerchin and part of the tribe she knows. She can cook favorite dishes from home for them. Jon encourages her to sell some in the market," he replied. Yeet was now red faced and loud of voice, he rode ahead to join Kardesh.

"You could have stayed," Kardesh stated gently. "You came in obedience to my guiding voice. I must go to 'Eriha,' and stay in *Kudus*, Jerusalem. You are Muslim. You can go on to Mecca and Medina, make the pilgrimage with him."

"Certainly," agreed Attila. "Join me on the *Haj*. Our prophet promises blessings on all who do what Allah requires. Jerusalem is only the third most holy city in Islam. It was the *Kiblah* and all the faithful prayed toward it until they turned their backs on it for Mecca."

"I haven't decided yet," Yeet stated, still agitated.

"What's to decide? Any Muslim would jump at the chance to visit all three; expenses paid. I count it my act of charity. Consider the merit I gain from Allah in the exchange," Attila smiled proudly.

"I can't decide yet!" Yeet shouted in a strained voice. He spurred his horse and raced ahead. He rode on before the group for a while.

"He finds leaving friends difficult," Sevman said.

> - - - - - >DRESSING-ROOM> - - - - - >

"You're a week short of your target Derk bey. It was clever using a Christian for a messenger. They came as appointed, everything intact. He and the mouse did some shopping and left going north."

"No, I questioned the ferry people; a Ferganga horse has not crossed the river." Derk replied sitting in the actress's dressing room. "That mouse is a Chipchak princess and is quite cute from all accounts. I've missed meeting her narrowly on at least three occasions. I mean to amend that flaw as soon as possible. He's a slick fox."

"Your information is flawed," the Gazelle retorted tartly. "The man is simple and straight forward. He tried to evangelize me in this very room. The mouse is a prude that loves flashy, fleshly things. They didn't cross the river, but went up the west side of our Mother of Rivers. They'll cross up near the Tartar country. He has some kind of relations with the East Bulgars, and will go through their country. Let me add that the B*owzkurt* Society is after them, as well as the Sultan."

Derk bey sat for a moment, taking in all that was said. "Why would the Wolf want him? Most of their efforts are to disrupt and capture the Caliphate. They would stay clear, or even help him escape."

"The order came from the north, I'm told." Her smile was mocking and contemptuous. Her superior attitude was noted, and resented. Yet business was more urgent than correction.

"Fill me in on the latest changes here in Getchet."

"Commerce continues to expand up the rivers, but there is a tall, fierce, northern people who come with amber and sea ivory. They command the forest people and lead them to take over the trading posts. They resist the Kazar forces. Every year they take more posts and they control the portages to the northern seas. Every summer they send fleets of boats and men." Her face showed anxiety.

"How is the royal house handling this threat?"

"They're hiring the Tartars and using them as defense forces for the trading-posts. We are a commercial people and we must keep the rivers open for legitimate trade and free of pillage. There aren't enough wild Kazars for this kind of control."

"Why do you call them wild?" He laughed, amused. "The whole nation is Kazar, isn't it?"

"Yes, but they have taken vast numbers of expelled Jews from Rume. Many proselytes and converts keep Shabat with them. But the old Kazars of the country-side remain as they were; therefore, wild to the citified types, who are used to living among people of different faiths."

122

"I'm always surprised that your people do so well in business and administration of the area. You Jews direct a prosperous country," Derk bey confessed.

"*Adoni* has always promised us prosperity for obedience to His laws," she replied proudly.

"But the Koran says you are a people cursed forever. You killed your prophets and your Messiah."

"Yet we are forgiven and restored on repentance. We have a second Jerusalem here on the Mother of Rivers. I was raised on a *Shetiel* west of here on the Don River. We are many, for Adoni protects and enriches us as His faithful witness to all nations."

"We in Islam have surrendered to Allah and are always prospered and multiplied even more. We obey our prophet and receive the world for our inheritance. You are wise to help us. You would be wiser to join in our worship and guarding of Allah's laws. Our Sultan is the shadow of God on the earth."

"I serve for money and other needs of my own. I must respect what is yours, but I remain a Jewess by preference, in spite of the rabbis' exaggerations of our laws."

"Your children will serve Allah and our prophet; be sure of that. Your religion is racial, restricted to your tribe. Ours is universal and open to all. To obey our Allah's laws is to enter paradise." He was now becoming tense and stood to make his predictions.

She, too, had risen and stood smiling into his face. "Your man will have a week's travel ahead of you. You'll have to hurry if you expect to see more than their dust."

> - - - - - >YUSUF PLANS A WEDDING> - - - - - >

"You have made remarkable progress with the mill, Jon bey," Yusuf bey affirmed happily.

"Yes, father, as I told you: Jon does everything well." Maril joyfully echoed her father's approval.

"Well, God has given me opportunities and a market among the enslaved Turks and northern people here. They want home style food," Jon reported modestly. "We grind our own brands and outsell most of the merchants." All agreed happily.

"Please daddy, we don't want to wait anymore, I want to marry Jon this summer." She took his hand and looked pleadingly into his eyes, "You know I'll never love another as I do him."

"Your mother has been working on the bridal dress that was your grandmother's. We have contracted wine for the banquet and I intend to invite every important man in the sultanate. You see, I have anticipated you. It will be the social occasion of the summer. We'll use our Baghdad palace for the number of guests will be great." Yusuf glowed with excitement. "Some pretend to despise Christians, but anyone who misses this wedding will never buy or sell with me again."

> - - - - - >KERIM BY THE VOLGA> - - - - - >

"There's a fast moving armed group behind us," Kerim warned as they rode beside the vast river.

"Let's hide in this grove," Leyla replied. "We need a rest and some food. I'm starved," she complained.

"You're always hungry now," Kerim commented, "I think you must be feeding two." They entered the woods that hid them from the approaching group.

"Nonsense," she retorted, "I'm still trim and pretty. You'll find no fat or swollen parts on me. So, don't you go looking at that actress or those dancers. I'm available any time you feel up to it."                                    "You make me ashamed," he teased, "Can all of my efforts have been in vain?" They dismounted and he took down the food bundle. She spread a cloth over a large, fallen tree trunk to be off the damp sod.                                    "Tayze said you have to have a time of peace and prosperity to get the new family additions."                              "What kind of additions?" he queried, sitting down.              "Babies or even livestock of any kind, they don't foal on drives; only when they are safe in pasture."

"You mean you won't conceive until we are safely home?" his voice held incredulity.

"We are made in God's image, I've heard you proclaim, but we are also related to the animals; so I believe it's true." She sat facing him on the trunk.

"You expect me to be contrary to that?" he teased and pinched her cheek, "Make me try harder?"

"No... I mean, yes... that is, I expect you to stop complaining when I eat a lot." She finished, blushing in confusion. He laughed loud and long. "*Soos*, hush, you'll wake the dead with that noise."

"They came in and should be close here," boomed a powerful bass voice. Down the trail came a large man, too big for his horse. He came, riding the flagging animal into the clearing, followed by several armed retainers leading a mule loaded with packs. A beautiful woman, dressed in *shalvar* and coat followed with several more retainers.

"Why tarry, father? We're on the edge of Tartar country. We need to reach the ferry to be in our land before night." The lady's voice complained sharply.

"My horse is lame and this beast I ride can't carry me home. I need the horses of the travelers that entered the woods. I must have those horses."

"Look here, Lord Kerim," a warrior called, "The horses are here and the riders eat."

"Take them. Kill the pair if they resist." He swung his weight to the ground and stood a head higher than his horse. The warriors surrounded the eaters.

"Welcome, Lord Kerim, we awaited your arrival. Come and eat with us. I'm Kynan of the Chipchak, whom you may remember. We wait to accompany your guards to Tuzgol of the East Bulgars." He stood slowly, opened his hands in invitation and indicated the spread lunch.

"Kynan," the girl gasped sharply. "How come you here?" She dismounted and stood by her father.

"Perilee" Kynan gasped in shock. "You've grown up." He stared, open mouthed at her. Then, he added hastily, "This is my wife, Leyla of the Chipchak."

"It has been five years," she responded, ignoring Leyla. "I'm of age, now, sixteen," she affirmed proudly as she walked over to stand beside him.

"You have food and horses we need, Kynan," the giant Kerim, a man in his late thirties, stated. "We will accept both." He motioned; the warriors relaxed. "I think the black should better bear my weight," he observed. "Perilee can use the mare until I need a change. Now, on to the ferry!"

# PEOPLE, PLOTS & PLACES IN CHAPTER 11

Attila: prepares to continue on pilgrimage.
Baja: travels to get Sanjak and Nooryouz together.
Derk: finds only bodies and stories to aid his quest.
Gazellim: knows how to find secrets and deals with a spy.
Kerim: the East Bulgar, dies in Kynan's place.
Kurnaz: decides to ignore courtesy and custom.
Kynan: must get home under his own name.
Leyla: must comfort the girl who took her possessions.
Orhan: must lead the daughter of his dead master home.
Peri'lee: looses father, horse, and prized goods.
Seerlee: is identified by a Jewish name from his dark past.
Sevman: knows the subjects that interest Atilla.
Yasmin: tells the story of her courtship by Harun.
Yeet: decides to remain in Jerusalem longer.

GLOSSARY:
*Allah hu Ekber*: God is great.
*Adoni*: Lord, used by Jews instead of God's name.
*Babam*: my father.
*Du' ah ed'e jay'um*: I'll pray; I'm going to pray.
*hoja*: a man who has completed the trip to Mecca.
*Kabba*: the central building in Omar's Mosque.
*kafir*: unbeliever; idolater.
*Kelime Allah*: Word of God.
*Menorah*: a nine branched candelabra.
*Neden*: Why?
*Shabat*: the Jewish day of rest starts Friday night.
*Shatan*: Satan; the devil.
*Shetiel*: Jewish villages or farm settlements in the Ukraine.
*Tanram*: my Lord; my God.
*Umma*: the community; people of Allah.
*Yesu gel*: come Jesus; help me Lord.
 *too'zak*: a trap.

GAZELLIM REPROVED

"Here is the ferry site, but where is the boat?" shrilled the talkative Perilee who rode the Fergana mare beside her father, who rode the black.

"He may be blocked by the ice. It's moving heavy and full today," the father responded.

"We can't stay here over night," she complained.

"Go, call them, Orhan," he ordered the young warrior who rode beside him as a page.

"The Kazars are so unreliable," complained Perilee to Kynan, who rode next to her. "They have their *Shabat*, when they absolutely refuse to work and neglect all duties. I can't understand how they hold their empire together. Their God is Adoni and He requires all kinds of strange behavior from them. I guess you saw it all at the crossing in Getchet. However, they have many useful, interesting things to sell or else I wouldn't set foot in their land. I can't endure their strange hair-dos and clothes. Do you know," she confided, "the married women must shave their heads and other parts and bathe in their temples every month? They think highly of themselves and look down on others," she complained loudly.

"Why go then?" soothed Kynan, playing the Chipchak boy she had known during his time with her tribe as a serving page to her father.

"They sell such beautiful things, all there in one place. The market is fabulous. Father says it should belong to us. We'll take it some day."

The warrior descended to the river and called out. "Kerim the great, of the East Bulgars demands your service." Several people with animals were at the ferry landing and turned to see the travelers on the hill above them. One listener mounted a horse and waved a banner on his lance point, before racing away.

From the woods behind them thundered a band of warriors, bows bent to shower the party with arrows.

"Tartars, run," screamed Perilee in a panic. Beside them the vast bulk of Kerim fell, his body filled with arrows. Kynan's horse fell under him, so he dived for the black and mounted as it struggled free of Kerim's bulk. He saw Leyla and their packhorse go racing for the landing, so, he too followed, running hard. The Tartar attackers killed the Bulgar warriors, whom they left dead. Only Kynan, Leyla, Perilee, and the warrior at the river's bank were left alive. Strangely, the Tartar band pursued no one. They took the head of Kerim bey and left with the loaded mules.

The ferryboat appeared from behind a huge cake of ice, pushing its way through the clogged river. The survivors remained trembling at the riverbank where the ferry eventually arrived.

"*Babam ay neden?* My father, oh why? Why this attack?" Perilee was screaming now as the ferry drew up to the shore. The passengers were now refusing to get off, except for several Tartars who quickly gathered their things and jumped to get out and away. The two men quickly got the horses and the girls onto the boat, while the rowers debated what to do.

"*Yesu gel!* There are dead men, murdered on the hill. We aren't sure why," Kynan shouted.

A reply came from the boatman, "They may be bandits, but they have gone away now."

"They took the portable goods, but did not strip the dead or pursue us. You must decide which is safest," Kynan said.

This announcement quieted them. At last they took all the frightened people back to the other shore where they demanded the return of the passage fee. Shouts and curses were raised in the process of debarking.

Some jumped ship while others watched the rescued girls and listened to their cries of distress.

"My father is a hero in our nation. Who would want to kill him? We're at peace with the Tartars, at least since last summer when they raided us." Perilee stood crying to the audience of passengers.

"We must get her back to her family with the news," Kynan whispered to the young warrior.

"Agreed, but how do we calm her?" he replied.

"*Doo'ah edejay'um*; I'll pray," he said. "*Tanrum*, hear us," he proclaimed. "Friends and family have been snatched from us by evil men. We do not know why, but You understand all things. You know how to punish the guilty. We leave these things in your hands. We pray now for these who were spared the fate of the others. Give us strength to endure and to take back the news. Receive to Yesu's garden the souls of those who are redeemed by His great sacrifice for them. Show them mercy Lord, amen"

Kynan gave money to the boatmen to bury the dead when they were sure it was safe. As he led the horses off the boat he was prompt to place Leyla on the Fergana mare and put Perilee on the horse Leyla had raced to the dock.

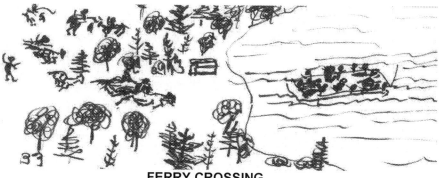

FERRY CROSSING

129

**The youth, Orhan, led the way home, while it fell to Leyla to accompany and comfort the girl. The men had to stay together and do the work of camp and travel.**

## > - - - - - >TOOZLU CAMP> - - - - - >

"How much longer?" Baja asked for the tenth time. The day had stretched painfully since leaving the fort. The sergeant shrugged and made a half gesture forward in way of an answer. More hungry children from carts and hovels had run after them begging bread. The supply man doled out pieces of bread from his bag and the children ate staring after them.

"Why don't they go to the fort?" she inquired.

"Too dangerous," he replied. "The irregulars sometimes appear without warning. Besides they don't have food to spare there."

"Why are they still here if the others have pressed on to the tribal homeland?"

"Some were afraid to go. Others were sick or unable for some reason. They used their travel food waiting," he gestured helplessly.

"Is Sanjak helping these people?"

"That seems to be his idea." He pointed ahead. "There is the headquarters where I left him last week." A large cart held the frame of a yurt. Basins and jars were scattered about the door.

"This place is deserted. Not a soul here," Baja said.

"*Too'zak*! A trap!" exclaimed the sergeant, as five men with drawn bows appeared and held them helpless. They raised their hands in surrender.

"By all the emanations" shouted Baja, "are you blind? This is an old lady and a guide who's been here before. What harm can we do? Where is Sanjak? Someone speak up!"

"We thought the Uigurs had returned," Erly bey chuckled as he came out from behind the yurt that concealed a cave in the riverbank. "Why'd you come?" He shifted his gaze to Sanjak who appeared behind him from the cave. "Look what we got! Straight from the fort I'd guess."

"Yes, and you've got a wife and baby there. They need to be picked up before someone discovers who she is." Baja's eyes sparkled excitedly.

"What are we waiting for?" he inquired joyfully." I'll take all the guards on duty now, and Erly will bring up a second squad later. Uigurs are still around."

## > - - - - - >ATILLA JOINS THE HAJ> - - - - - >

**"How do I look?" Attila bey inquired proudly. "It's the best Egyptian cotton." He was amply clothed in white, the uniform of the Haj.**

130

"You look elegant," Yeet stated with admiration, "sort of richly humble, if you know what I mean."

"Exactly, well put, Yeet, we can not lose our own individuality while showing our common humanity as part of Allah's *Umma*: His People." Atilla smiled confidently, "It is a mark of distinction to know both sides of an issue or argument, fairly presented, and still be able to chose correctly and justify ones choice."

"If you chose wrong, the fruit of that choice would soon be apparent. Results speak loud and clear," Sevman stated.

"You're sure you won't stay and see more of *Kudus*? Jerusalem has so much to explore and meditate on," Kardesh asked earnestly.

"Yes, it reflects so much of your Christians' doctrine of threes: Muslims, Christians and Jews sharing one city. It favors your Alexandrian Trinity as well: Eternal Creator, Living Word and Universal Spirit, one Allah forever," he finished smugly. "Our prophet, peace on him, saw the Creator on the night journey; spoke of *Kelime Allah*; taught that Allah is as close as our neck's artery to all.

"Much would depend on how you define each part of the statements," Kardesh observed.

"Exactly," declared Attila, "that's where we would dialogue. I find traveling with Christians stimulating. It sharpens the mind to think about God's actions and nature."

"Then your Sultan's empire should be at its best for you have Christians forming about a third of the population of all your cities," Sevman observed.

"But not where I'm going now. None but Muslims are permitted in the pure heart of Islam."

"Will the people be different and better there?"

"Perfect obedience should make the difference apparent to the dullest eye," said the figure in white.

"What if they are exactly like men everywhere?" questioned Yeet earnestly.

"Then the Christians' doctrine of universal sin is truer than we Muslims like to think," Attila laughed. "You really are missing a great opportunity to find many answers to your questions, Yeet."

"I must stay with my friends until they are settled and I have seen everything offered here. There is a Trinity of John, the Baptist, Yesu, the Christ and Paul, the Apostle to understand."

"A lifetime of study in itself," Kardesh interposed.

"But with the discipline of body and soul at God's command, we may become useful in His service," Sevman added. "As a cripple I can have no other goal." A silence followed his statement.

"Perhaps I will go to convert the *Kafir*, after I have seen Egypt. To move people who bow down to sticks and stones to the true and final revelation of Allah through the last and greatest prophet. It is a fitting task for a man who has kissed the black stone that fell from heaven and traversed the *Kaba* three times. I will throw rocks at the column of *Shatan* and run on the plains of Arafat. My offerings will be accepted. I will be a *hoja*, honored by all the people wherever I go. *Allah hu Ekber!*" Attila stood looking proud and confident. His decision was final; his dedication complete.

>- - - - - - - ->GETCHET THEATER>- - - - - - - ->

Derk entered the theater unobserved and late, as he was accustomed to doing. All eyes were fixed upon the stage. The audience of men was fascinated by their beloved star.

He sat in his chosen spot and noted with disgust the Yeshiva students. He wondered how long his Sultan would permit the existence of this state whose prosperity was contrary to his prophet's declaration of servitude for all Hebrews.

Gazelle hanum was dutifully performing her onstage religious number. She included one for her Jewish clientele. This assuaged doubts as to her origins and loyalty to the nation. Holding the nine place *menorah* high, lit and flaming with pungent oils, she started her anthem. Her magnificent voice filled the building in the hush of the audience's adoration. Those who came lacking the entrance fee, could hear her from the street.

Praise we all the Great Jehovah,
Source of blessing, hope and joy.
Flooding us with truth and guidance,
Bringing life to everyone.
Sing His praise forever, Great God I love.
Guard his words and precepts
Now and evermore.

PRAISE WE ALL

As she continued, both students and young warriors started to cheer her tribute, when the giant figure of a Chief Rabbi arose and interrupted with clenched fist and angry voice proclaimed in his rage. "Adonai is not to be called by his names. It is not allowed! It is written: 'You shall not use the name of the Lord Your G-d in vain.' Sacred names used frivolously, carelessly in such a place as this! The council will hear of such scandal! You shall not be held blameless for this blasphemous offence!"

Both the audience and actress looked after him in stunned silence as he stalked out. Derk bey wondered how she would handle this public rebuke. She handed the *menorah* to one of her attendants and motioned her offstage. Then she stepped up and proclaimed in a hearty voice, "Pickle face will not allow us to sing praise to Adoni. What else is mighty and worthy of praise in our land?" As if on cue, a voice answered, "The mighty River Volga!"

"Yes," she retorted, "Maestro: raise the music a whole note, and make it a little more lively. Let's see if your boys can handle the fingering." Then she launched into the same melody changing only the object of her praise.

### PRAISE THE RIVER VOLGA

Praise the migh – ty Riv – er Vol – ga,
roar – ing proud – ly through our land.
Flood – ing us with food and trea–sure,
bring – ing life to ev' – ry one.
Sing her praise for – e – ver, Ri - ver
I love. Guard her shores and
wood –lands. now and e – ver – more.

Praise the mighty River Volga,
Roaring proudly through our land.
Flooding us with food and treasure,
Bringing life to everyone.
Sing her praise forever, River I love.
Guard her shores and woodlands,
Now and evermore.

With cheers the audience acclaimed the actress. They insisted that she repeat the altered hymn again and again with patriotic vigor. By the next night, the whole city was singing it; in a week, the nation. By month's end the Kazar army had adopted the song as the hymn of praise for all the forces of the land. 'Praise the Mighty River Volga,' took their allegiance. They would need the resolve it instilled in them to stand against a summer enemy sailing from the north.

Derk immediately recognized the fact that escaped most of the audience. She had taken a visible, impressive reality for the ineffable Allah, and substituted praise of the material world for the sublime. She descended to idolatry with patriotic zeal. He smiled; Israel had shown its true nature and weakness. The Kingdom's fall was only a matter of time. He smiled in grim satisfaction. Ismael's descendant would triumph over the weak and *fallible* Isaac. The promise of Allah's Kingdom was through Abraham's first child.

Derk left for the urgent meeting, for there were other questions to resolve. Allah would give him an alliance with the northern invaders. Victory over the idolatrous Kazars and perfidious Jews was assured. He wondered how much longer his government would find this known double agent useful. He wondered if he would be the agent chosen to terminate her usefulness. He thought he would not like that duty.

> - - - - - >SAMARA PALACE OFFICE>- - - - - - - - >

"The invitation has arrived, Kurnaz, Excellency," the adjutant advised the vizier. "It's a work of art," he showed the elaborate work in gold leaf.

"The merchant prince expects all customers and friends to grace his ceremonies and banquet halls. Why should we who are of the true faith lower ourselves to attend?"

135

"Because Christians pay over half our tax revenue even though they are only a third of our total population. They produce wealth even as do the Jews who live among us. They will not be shy of a Christian wedding and neither should we. Politically they are powerful and they can punish us by refusing to deal with our contract offers and needs."

"Nonsense, they have no right to snub us. I will not go regardless of the consequences. Make a note of that. They can marry themselves to all the Huns in the world and I'll not pay them a thank you or a God bless you. I'll plan a hunting trip for those days. That will be my excuse. Make a note of it, I say. Advise the palace, I'll invite the Sultan and chief men."

"Yes, my Lord."

"We'll show the merchant who the really important men are. Order the preparations."

> - - - - - >DRESSING-ROOM>- - - - - - - - >

"Back so soon, Derk bey?" inquired the Gazelle.

"Another has fulfilled my task. Kerim bey is dead and the woman crossed the river into Bulgar lands. The Tartar kill included all the warriors," he responded perplexed. "They took his head. The body is reported to be bigger and older than I thought it should be. Witnesses say he rode a black. A pretty young woman rode a Fergana mare. It must be them." He shifted uneasily. "Two pages and two women crossed the river and took the two horses with them. But the dead man, identified as Kerim by all present was beheaded."

"So my information about the Bowzkurt Society has been demonstrated correct," she smugly said.

"Why take his head?" he contended.

"Identification, someone wants to see the man dead, but wants to be sure," she stated.

"It is not their way of operating; it's out of normal character. They kill for Islam or to weaken the effective powers of the Caliph. They have a secret agenda."

"Why be perturbed if it promotes Islam?"

"We can't have two governing forces. Allah must rule through the Sultan. We must have Theocracy, the rule of the one God through the commands recited by our prophet in the Koran."

"You have four schools of interpretation of that recited law from the Koran." She smiled provocatively. "They differ, which is correct? Where does the truth lie?"

"We have no time for that one. For us the point of interest is where the head appears."

"Kerim's head or the Wolf's head?" She replied.

"Both, lives may depend on it," he predicted.

> - - - - - >THE CHIPCHAK ROYAL YURT > - - - - - >

"I have readied the soup, my lady. It's cooling now I'll bring it," Peri, the old nurse called to Chichek hanum, the wife of the Khan Erden.

"She has no appetite, the baby hard presses her stomach," a younger helper whispered.

"She must eat for strength to deliver," the old nurse whispered back. "It's cool enough now, get it."

"Oh, no darling, don't eat our lady's lunch!" The mother was appalled at the sight of her four-year-old sitting by the stone-circled yurt fireplace drinking the soup with the help of a kangal puppy. Both faces were stained with the thick gruel prepared for the Khan's wife. Startled, the child dropped the bowl spilling the rest. She started to cry while the pup ran away.

"Now it's spoiled," the old woman shouted angrily. "We will have to make more."

Outside the tent, the child was screaming. She was holding her stomach and doubled over vomiting. Her mother hurried over to hold her.

"Must be something in the soup," the mother complained.

"Nonsense, it doesn't work that fast," the old one replied. "Oh, Tanram," she whispered in anger. Then, "I'll get the shaman," she shouted as she ran away.

"The priest is a better doctor," the mother replied.
Both child and pup were dead within the hour. Mounted men spread out in search of the old nurse.

> - - - - - >CHU FORT HAREM>- - - - - - - - >

"How did you come to marry Harun bey?" asked Nooryouz while she wrapped the baby, Nevrim, in a clean cloth. "I'm told that his family had made other arrangements and chosen a girl."

"Oh, yes, please tell us about it," pleaded Sesli.

137

"My brother was in training in the same regiment in the city of Merv, where we lived." Yasmin replied. "He brought Harun to our house once. Of course, It is not customary to have someone who is not related come to visit, but my brother loved him. They were always together. They lived and played constantly as a team together. We were surprised one day to hear him come in the house and I ran to kiss him. He was a great tease and I always hung about him since we were little babies. So, when I heard his voice I ran and caught him from behind and kissed him on the cheek. However, it was Harun, who turned to look at me while my brother laughed. I stood staring and then ran to my room and stayed without eating three days while my brother tried to persuade me to come out again. He thought that if he told funny stories about Harun it would make me laugh and come out. However, it filled my mind and heart with Harun. Before they left for the war, I saw them once more. I was properly veiled and I could feel his presence even before I saw him. I could not take my eyes away. He looked at me only once and as we looked I saw he knew and felt the same for me."

"What then?" gulped Sesli, breathlessly.

"When the army returned from the Indus River wars we learned of my brother's noble death. Harun came crying, after the days of mourning were over, he asked for and got my parents permission. Father had sympathized with the Kajerites. They believe in equality under Allah, even to the extent of the government. The El Ari clans claim a distant blood relationship to the prophet; 'peace be upon him'. The child of such a man was not acceptable so they refused to attend our wedding. I have never met them. We have been posted to the far frontiers where we find service to Allah to be our reward."

"But Allah has blessed your union with joy and respect by all your people," Nooryouz added.

"But not with children yet," Yasmin finished.

"Waiting is the teacher of patience." Nooryouz said, as she kissed Nevrim. "Trust Allah, He, at least, is always generous."

> - - - - - > GAZELLIM'S BEDROOM > - - - - - >

"*Soos*, quiet, don't call out," Seerlee said. He sat on the bed and looked down at the sleeping beauty. He tossed back the covers and gazed at her figure, now stretching voluptuously before his eyes. "Come, the show ended last night you don't have to perform now."

"Would you come to see me perform?" she asked. She stretched in her long wool nighty.

He caught both her wrists and pulled her from the bed. "Here, sit at the table and leave your knives and tricks in the bed. You know I'd not go see you exhibit your face and body like any harlot to the lusting crowd." He pushed her into a chair.

"They like the belly dancer, just like you do. It's the face and hair you don't want to see; the things that give us personality, character and dignity. The parts below are what you are willing to drool over. Women's proper place and use in your eyes."

"The *Shetiel* Judge's daughter pronounces her judgment," he snarled in her face.

"Simon, impoverished son of Sarah, the adulteress, rejects all justice and logic for the injustices and prejudices of *Sharia*; All the rules being one thing for the submissive and another harsher side for all the resistant and other-minded. Has it brought you peace?" Her impassioned face was flushed.

"Have you no fear then?" he inquired. "You can't know what I intend. Have you no respect even for safety's sake?" He pulled a knife from his sash.

"Let me show you something," she said and reached for a stack of cards on her table. "I count off 21 cards and I offer to show you your secret choice with three questions. Do you accept?" She was calm.

"What are the stakes?" he inquired grimly.

"Put down the knife and let us talk," she replied.

"I wouldn't have used it anyway" he retorted. Sheathing his knife and sitting down beside her.

"Look at the numbers, Simon, and choose one. Then I'll find it for you." He looked sternly as she shuffled.

"One, two, three," she counted, putting three cards face-up. She repeated, continuing row after row to form three files of seven cards each. Finishing she asked: "Which row is your card in?"

"The first," he replied, looking over the numbers and symbols of circles, squares, exes and triangles. "Where did you learn this trick?" he asked.

"From the wagon people, the Gypsies. They migrate regularly and settle only to plant a crop or two. They gain by work or entertainment. The leader owns everything, but gives women and work to those who agree to stay and serve him."

She had placed the first row, now scooped into a mini pack in the center of the other two packs. She repeated the dealing from the top into three lines again: "One, two, three," until the three lines were finished. "Which line is it in now?" she asked.

"The second," he responded. "Why do you deal with that kind of people?" he asked.

"They travel and are a gold mine of information."

"The Rabbi's daughter makes strange friends and acquaintances." His voice held admiration.

She giggled and shrugged "From my childhood, I guess. You remember? Father said it would be the death of me. Now, which row?" she asked as she completed the same process.

"Second," he answered, watching her place that row in the center of the packs and start counting the cards out, face down.

She stopped on number eleven and looked up with a lively face. "Make a little bet? A gold coin?"

"You said three questions, no more. You've ask your three. You eliminated fourteen cards with the first question and then only seven possibilities remained. You eliminated four on the next question. Only three cards remained to sort out. My choice should be in the middle, but you can't be sure which it is. It's still my secret till you turn it over."

"Human life is like the game. Many people hide their secret goals, but by their choices, they eliminate all the false

140

assumptions and advice of other people. Finally the goal, worthy or unworthy, is reached. What is your secret goal, Simon? Will you carry me to someone's harem? Perhaps, you'll keep me secreted for ransom or ravished for your passion? What are your plans now?"

"I admit that I did think of shipping you out wrapped in a rug." He shrugged, "Romantic nonsense, since no bonds will hold you long and I would forfeit my life. Come finish your game. You delay for your maid to come."

"Here is your choice Simon, I reveal it to the world." She turned over the card. "Two circles, what kind of eyes are they?"

"Wolf's" he whispered, "I'll go. Let me kiss your hand." He slid his ring's crown inside his left hand and flicked its head aside to bare the fangs. He took her hand to his lips.

"You are denied to me, I deny you to all others." He brought his left hand up and pressed his ring against her wrist. She gasped and turned her hand to see the two punctures and a black fluid in two drops against white skin. She put the wound to her mouth and sucked the spot, spitting it at him. She did this three times before collapsing on the chair. Cold pride filled her face as she spat again and whispered, "Sarah's bastard has shown his secret goal."

CARDS REVEAL CHOICES

141

Abdullah: is endangered by the Wolf's assignment.
Derk: faces a challenge that threatens his life.
Gabi: named for the Angel Gabriel, is generous.
Harun el Ari: is recalled from the fort by his father.
Kardesh: blind, must now beg for coin and bread.
Karga: shows a heart as black as the crow.
Kynan: comes alive to an old past could die again.
Kerim: killed at the river, will another use the name?
Leyla: learns much she didn't know about her man.
Magazi: knows their danger is real.
Manfredo: the priest faces disappointments in his post.
Melek: is a friend of Kardesh and Sevman in Jerusalem.
Peri: the old nanny seeks help from her employer.
Perilee: her inheritance is guaranteed, but love lost.
Rafi: is no angel in spite of his name, Rafael.
Saida: an Abyssinian Christian girl helps friends.
Sanjak: discovers he has missed his opportunity again.
Seerlee: tries to finish his last task for the Gray Wolf.
Setchkin: attends funerals and prepares to depart.
Sevman: lame, must ride and guide his blind friend.
Twozan: faces the problems of leaving home and security.
Orhan: leads to home, but loses to the Bulgar council.
Yasmin: fears meeting her father-in-law in Merv.
Yeet: regrets promising Tayze to do the cooking.


Glossary
*baba*: father; daddy.
*bash ah noo zah' sa a'luk*: be comforted.
*demmi*: the name used for religious minorities.
*Kadi*: Muslim city official.
*Ne den oily*: Why is that; Why that way?
*ne var ne yoke*: what news; what's new?
*sadakat*: alms, charity required after Ramadan.
*Sorma*: don't ask; out of the question.

HALF A LOAF

Kardesh was off to beg at the Church of the Holy Sepulcher. Sevman rode as usual on his shoulders as he took up the chant: "Alms for the love of Jesus; Show a forgiving Lord your love for the needy; *Sadakat* for the love of Allah." each aimed at the religion of the potential giver. However, in crowded lanes of the old city the litany was treated as ridiculous. The two-in-one figure became a familiar sight in Jerusalem. In the afternoon they would go to St. Helen's Church at the foot of the Mount of Olives. The small copper coins they collected was hardly enough for the next day's rations ordinarily. But the Easter season was ahead with the hope of good collections when the city was filled with pilgrims.

Yeet started for the upper town. It was full to overflowing with refugees from the Armenian rebellion. Their war against the Caliphate was savage. It was rumored that the Kazar Kingdom and the Byzantine Empire were backing the Armenian rebels with weapons and money; both seeking to protect their borders by helping to form an independent allied state. The influx of poor families fleeing the fighting filled the cities in all neighboring areas. The Governors reluctantly subsidized bread for the refugees.

By going to the Armenian district of the city, Yeet could get more bread for the money.

Yeet stopped near the bakery, he could smell it far down the street. He closed his eyes and tasted the flavor in his mouth. The months of travel and little food since Attila left, had sharpened his appetite and appreciation of bread. Yeet had been left with the domestic work: keeping the goods safe, cooking and washing clothes were his portion. He hated picking the stones from the lentils and making the money reach. He sighed and touched his waistband with his last small coin.

"You've come to the wrong shop lad, this bakery is for the refugees; Christians from the Caucasus." A stern young man he had not met before looked at him quizzically.

"My mother is a Christian and we are from the far northeast. The old man here lets me buy." Yeet's head was up, but his chin trembled slightly. The man did not smile and he seemed to see into his mind.

"My Uncle Gabi is named for the angel Gabriel and is tender toward all down-on-their-luck youth. What's your name? Who's your father?" His face was cold and set. Outside the building a loaded cart drew up.

"Yeet, son of Ali of Yemen. Here's my coin give me half a loaf." He slammed his copper coin on the table.

"A Turkish name, for one sired by a soldier occupying your mother's land. We have such among us too." He cut a loaf and pushed the larger part across the table. His words canceled his generosity. "I knew you weren't *demmi*, a Christian or Jew. You've no humility in you, only a mix of pride, fear and anger." He smirked down at the boy.
Yeet shouted his reply, rudely pointing his finger.

"You fear the *Kadi's* anger if you feed a hungry stranger. Your Uncle's generous, but how hard the nephew!"
A crash and rumble announced a load being dumped. The rattle of a cart sounded in the bakery. The baker jumped through the door with a scream waving his arms in vain.

"Bastards, shame of your mothers. You must take the fuel to the side slot. Come back! You'll get no pay from me. Damn you, come back here." The cart rattled on unheeding.

144

"I paid them yesterday, for the week, Rafi. We'll have to stack it." The uncle appeared outside the door. He waggled his head uncertainly, and then shrugged his resignation.

"The owner pleaded his need of money; the slave shirks his duty; we lose." He turned to look into the shop. "Come work, boy. I'll give you two loaves if you'll come help carry the sticks and charcoal. We stack them down the narrow slot to feed the oven. It's your opportunity." Yeet moved forward quickly. Rafi however, ran back into the shop, opened the drawer and scanned the money-box.

Yeet stopped at the door and looked back proudly. "I may be all you say, but I'm honest. Your coin is still on the table. Keep the half-loaf till I'm finished." He joined Uncle Gabi carrying and stacking sacks of charcoal.

> - - - - - >THE CROW'S YURT> - - - - - >

"You must hide me," the old woman whispered vehemently in his ear. "It was your powder." She was greeted by silence. "You can't turn me away, now. I know too much," she said and without permission darted into his yurt.

The Crow stood thinking desperately. Then he followed her inside.

"You returned with Setchkin hanum. You must say she gave the powder. The Bowzkurt will give your family great wealth: what we promised you for the miscarriage, and triple for your death."

"Must I die then" She reached out pleading.

"Willingly or I'll kill you here and now and save the money. I'll say you attacked me," he affirmed.

"Let me see the promised gold," she demanded. He shrugged and pulled a pouch from the bed roll in the corner. As he straightened up, she pulled her knife and struck his back below the shoulder blade, under the heart.

"You've done enough against me and my little Setchkin, you old scavenger." She picked up the pouch, ran to the yurt of a relative, where she hid it. Then she went out and walked to the Khan's yurt to make the confession.

>- - - - - - - >CHU RIVER FORT> - - - - - >

"The message is urgent Harun bey," the commander of the squad called out as the gate of the fort opened wide to receive them. "You are ordered home to Merv. Your father is bereft by the death of his older son, your brother Mansur.

*Bash ah noozah' sa' a luk*, be comforted," he called out, using the traditional words of sympathy. Hearing this, cries of mourning spread through the harem and other buildings.

The custom of letting blood was strong among the Turkish troops, although frowned on by the customs of Islam. Each trooper would make his way to the presence of the yuzbasha to extend his feelings of sympathy and personal grief over the family disaster. Small symbolic cuts appeared on the outside of the hand or little finger. In the women's quarters, the same intense feeling of mourning was expressed with shrieks and cries of anguish. These were done by all and especially by the wife of the commander. Special foods were prepared and served while they urgently completed preparations to depart.

"Our messenger says Onat commands that all the guest ladies resident in the harem must return to the base. Then, they must proceed to Merv. I think you are being called before the Sultan. You are important to him," Yasmin reported to Nooryouz. "You will have to face Onat bey and your fate, just as I will have to face my Harun's father and mother. Not an easy encounter for either of us." She leaned over to pick up the baby. "Oh, if only I had one to take home and show off!" she sighed. "I will take the baby out now. You and Sesli finish packing and come."

>- - - - - >KERIM TRAVELS EAST > - - - - - >

"We've been on the road for a week Perilee, I need to talk to my wife now. You ride ahead with Orhan," Kynan requested, smiling. She brightened immediately; a week of mourning is difficult at sixteen.

"I miss you, but I've learned a lot from Orhan about the local situation in Tuzgol," he reported riding by Leyla's side. "What have you learned from Perilee?"

"A lot about her friend, brother, and crush that lived in her father's house from her fifth to tenth birthday," she looked at him smartly. "I got a lot about Kerim bey. I think you took his name in admiration of the man. He's a big star in the Bulgar sky."

"Yes, he's been pressing north, forcing the Tartars west of the great river. It puts a wet barrier between the two

146

nations, giving more security. She is the only living heir, his sons are dead in battle and Orhan is hopelessly in love with her," he finished.

"It's mutual," she smiled cockily. "For that reason we'll have to continue the present sleeping arrangements. We won't leave them alone long. She's headstrong and well over the shock and mourning." They paced their horses faster to stay up with the laughing couple ahead. "I've been talking to her about Yesu and Tanra's blessings in marriage. She has never thought of such before."

"She will need a father figure to complete the arrangements for marriage and the managing of the estate for a while. I wonder if the present revival of my self as Kynan is only a temporary resurrection."

"So you expect to go to heaven after this?" she teased as they drew closer to the pair.

"If I play this wrong I may go directly and leave you in hell," he warned.

> - - - - - >GETCHET CITY> - - - - - >

"Our arrival is badly timed," Abdullah exclaimed to his beloved. "The actress has been murdered and eyes are searching everywhere," he looked about.

"The head has prepared this to finish us. What can we do?" Magazi's voice trembled.

"We can't run away, it's a confession of guilt. We must go to the crime scene as if we wish to solve it. We will also go to the reported place of Kerim's death."

"Yes, they will be sure that is an act of the *Bowzkurt*. If the Kazars didn't arrange that murder themselves."

"That is possible. It would repay the messengers for the messages they delivered to the moles," Abdullah finished.

"We'll be acting on guess work! Don't we have any inside information sources here?"

"Prisoners are informed of their execution only for revenge or for additional information. That is where we are at this moment. They want us to writhe and despair. I won't give them that satisfaction."

"You're right Abdullah, we'll act confident and do as you suggest."

147

"Welcome again, Kardesh and Sevman. Have you eaten today?" A group of children greeted the two boys as they came to the courtyard. Kardesh laughed happily as he lowered Sevman to the tiles and placed the cart near him.

"God promises us daily bread in the 'Our Father' prayer. So I have eaten well, little friends. And you, have you eaten?" This formula was regularly followed each day.

"Of course," a beautiful black girl answered, "I cooked for my brothers. I have brought a portion so you may sample my work. I'll need recommendations when the matchmakers come to look for brides with great abilities." She threw her head back to laugh with brilliant white teeth lighting her smile. She handed a small bowl to each boy. Bread covered the warm contents. The boys sat and ate with enthusiasm and the children started their games, work or classes. The boys scooped their bread to the bottom, to clean the bowls. The last crumbs disappeared. Sevman sighed and dragged himself to his cart. The girl's younger brother came forward and pushed Sevman out the east gate toward the market. It was deemed prudent that only the Christian, Kardesh, beg for alms at the church.

Kardesh sat near the entrance of the Church of the Holy Sepulchre. He was now a familiar sight to both local clergy and families who served the church. The Abyssinian boy, Melek and his older sister, Saida, children of one of the church guards were his favourites. Saida and Melek would visit him during the morning and he would tell them stories of Kaya, the ancient hero of his homeland.

"*Ne var, ne yoke*, what's new, friends?" Sanjak shouted at the fort sentinel. "I hear my wife finally got here." He rode up to the gate with Baja.

"Came and left with Yuzbasha Harun just this afternoon Yuzbasha," the lookout shouted.

"*Ne den oily*, Why's that?" shouted indignant Baja.

"Ordered back to base, Harun's father wants him home. Our new yuzbasha ordered the lady and baby back too." The new commander appeared beside the sentinel to view the two at the gate and observe the troop drawn up at the outer edge of the parade ground. He sounded the alert that called the garrison to their appointed posts.

"Let us in and we'll talk. I need some answers."

"*Sorma*, don't ask. I've only one bit of information to share." he shouted, "You are relieved of all army responsibilities and free to return to your homeland."

> - - - - - >JERUSALEM CITY> - - - - >

Manfredo looked about him in disgust. He had such dreams of the beauty and blessings expected of living in the home country of the Christ. Yet it was a dry and desolate land with only a smattering of churches dedicated to the memory of the Lord. War and neglect had made the land desolate. The Caliph's decrees and power ruled with an iron fist. Church activities were limited and building was restricted, bells muted. Pilgrims were hassled and sometimes cheated by the unscrupulous of all faiths. Christians were held in contempt. They were part of the *demmi*, those protected by the Sultan; when he cared to make the effort. Life in the Holy Land was unholy and base and all one's zeal and love did not change it. Manfredo came to doubt both his call and his devotion. Something had to be done, his nerves were frayed. His transfer from Nazareth to be secretary to the Monsignor had not turned out to be what he had hoped for in the promotion. There had been some compensating beauty in Galilee with the lake only a day's trip away from Nazareth, but Jerusalem? The only beauty was the raven locks of Saida, visible through the barred window of the secretariat. She was out before the church each morning, her cheerful voice always brightening the day. Thoughts of her shortened the long nights. She was spending much time near the front of the church these last weeks. He should see why she no longer came to the office with flowers for the Monsignor or appeared when he said mass. He missed her.

"I'll step out just a moment Sir. I'll only be an instant." He called to his Lord and hurried out. He caught a glimpse at the door of Saida's departure with her water jar on her head.

The priest stopped by the tall foreign beggar sitting at the Church's gate. He was wiping the water from his face and

149

hair. The man didn't wear the honey-colored square badge that the Caliph had decreed for the Christian *demmi*. His clothes, while worn, were of a different make. Manfredo wondered angrily in what language he would reply.

"Why are you here?" He tried Greek first, then Arabic.

The man looked up and mouthed a memorized Arabic phrase, 'begging'. Again in market argot the priest shouted. "Who are you? Why are you here?" He got a muddled reply that was scarcely understandable.

Manfredo repeated. "*Gardish from Gorazan*? Is that what you say? Speak up! Why are you here? You don't wear the legal signs. Are you a pilgrim or a vagrant?" As he listened the blind man tried again.

"I'm called Kardesh from the East, I was born north of Khorasan among the Chipchak nation where my father is son of the Khan. His brother, my uncle, rules now. I'm a pilgrim, but our money ended. Now we beg to stay here." He rattled the coins in his bowl as the footsteps of a man approached and passed.

The priest continued to regard him suspiciously.

"A beggar pretending to be a prince? How do you cross yourself? Where does your patriarch sit?" Manfredo peered at Kardesh closely, straining to understand the reply.

"I'm Christian, my Lord sits in heaven. I came to visit the land of Yesu my Savior. I do penance for my sins, and seek His blessings. I harm no one."

"I'll be the judge of that. How were you baptized? What are your doctrines and customs?" Manfredo was now disturbed enough to call over several keepers of order at the shrine. The different sects had separate places of worship inside the church building. Each provided guards.

"Over here men. This beggar doesn't have our permission to sit at the gate. Bring him into the monsignor's study. We need some answers from him." The men took Kardesh by the hands and lifted him up from his post. The Abyssinian guard picked up the bowl and rattled it. He spoke casually.

"When you come, your money is here in my hand. You will eat tonight. The father wishes to hear more of your story." He chuckled and lowered his voice. "Don't be afraid. He likes to show his authority, but he loses interest quickly. Careful you don't offend him. He's touchy about doctrine and law." Nevertheless, Kardesh was anxious as they led him into the Holy Sepulchre church.

> - - - - - >CHIPCHAK HEARTLAND> - - - - >

"There, it's finished now," the man below said to the man above him. "Give me a hand up, out of this grave." He took the proffered hand to heave up.

"None too soon," his helper said solemnly. "Here they come." He pointed with his chin, past their two grazing horses to a crowd of women coming up the hill from the meadow side. They carried a small, child's casket between them. The sounds of crying filled the air. Two or three men rode behind them. The old priest and his young assistant walked with the group. They circled the open grave and stopped as the two workmen moved back to the outer fringe of mourners.

A tussle arose at the graveside. The mother refused to put the child down. She clung screaming to the coffin, which the women tried to pry out of her arms. The old priest intervened and softly talked to the resisting mother. He placed his hands on her head and started praying. Silence descended like a cloud on all. The man thanked Tanra for the loan of a child to brighten life's short day. He begged that they would arrive some day to see her playing in Yesu's garden. He prayed that they could be together again. The woman sagged in tears, releasing the dear burden. The women began to sing.

Refrain:        All women cry when children die;
                   When heaven calls, we know not why.
                   Then sweet, bright souls all upward fly;
                   Leaving a world to weep and sigh.

1                 They live with pain, all those that stay;
                   Who love with innocents to play.
                   Each mourns the passing every day;
                    With 'might have been,' had they delayed.

Refrain:

2           They wait impatient till we come:
To show us all that they have done.
There they all play in paradise;
Where waters flow and fruit is nice.

Refrain:

3           All women hope to be a bride,
But choice deep touches human pride,
In hearts where spite and envy hide,
And all things good are crucified.

Refrain:

4           Wary, we tread the path o life,
For trouble looms with grief and strife.
Dark shaddows fall on all the days
We should have spent in prayer and praise.

Refrain:

Strangely, the cries quieted and sobs echoed in the new silence. Pats of comfort replaced the tearing of hair and clothes. Pairs and trios of women linked, supporting each other during the quiet words of committal pronounced by the priest who finished with the phrase:

"Rest and play, my child, in Yesu's garden. Store up the joys and discoveries you find there. We will join you some day to hear and share their pleasures with you. Peace to all, in the name of Our Good, Great God, who is Father, Son and Holy Spirit, amen."

### > - - - - - >IN SETCHKIN'S YURT> - - - - - >

"How was it today?" Twozan asked solicitously of Setchkin as he entered the yurt at evening. She sat with her helper near the fire. Weariness showed and she stared into the fire where the food was set. "I was at both funerals. Someone from every yurt was there." She sighed deeply. "At the first burial in the morning there was beautiful music. It was so sad. Such a beautiful child and so young and innocent, dying to save the Khan's wife and baby. She went into labor afterwards. If it is a girl they will name her for the dead child to remember the price of a life. An innocent died to reveal evil-intended poison and save two lives. The priest said it was like Yesu's death for us. A God dwelt, perfect man dies revealing the corruption and guilt of outward religion and government

152

justice. So God's approval is shown by life renewed or resurrected. We too may enjoy God's redemption and eternal life."

"A good sermon and full attendance, but what about the second funeral?" Twozan asked softly.

"There was a handful of relatives and old friends. A married daughter alone, an old friend, myself and a few I didn't know. The relatives demanded and got a heavenly procession from the shaman. The Khan was merciful. Because she told everything, he let her take her own life. She confessed to the priest and died. He touched our hearts with her words of repentance."

ALL WOMEN CRY

All wo - men cry when child - ren die.

When hea - ven calls, we know not why.

Then, sweet, bright souls all up - ward fly,

leav - ing a world to weep and sigh.

Verse They live in pain, all those that stay;

who love with in - no - cents to play.

Each mourns the pass - ing eve - ry day

with 'might have been,' had they de - layed.

"It was a case of weakness, not resisting powerful men's threats and enticements." Twozan commented.

"I loved her in a careless way and she spared my child when ordered to kill him. I have mixed feelings about it all. I'm glad she killed Karga. I could never stand that man. I hear the shaman buried him alone. *Babam*, daddy, is in hiding."

"That makes it easier for both of us," Twozan said. "The women are ready to fold away our yurts and start. But what of those still to come?"

"Let's eat and I'll tell you about our plans to leave" she invited.

## > - - - - - >DERK BEY ON THE VOLGA> - - - - - >

"I wonder why the Wolf likes to use this primitive means to send his messages. He must like riddles." Derk bey commented to the master of the house. A message bundle came to Derk's caravansari during the rain and storm of the night.

"How did it get in the room past two locked doors?" the inn keeper marvelled. "There are no distinctive marks outside. He didn't come on a horse and no footprints. He's a shaman! One who leads the heavenly procession!"

"He's a Muslim, but a match for any shaman. The importance, however, lies in the message, not in the manner of delivery." He opened the small bundle. There lay the fur of a wolf, an old wintered bulrush head a few acorn pods with a small bronze coin. A strand of white silk thread held the rushes and fur together. The cloth bundle was made of plain white wool.

Derk bey drew a sharp breath and smiled. "The Wolf will be by a lake in an oak forest to receive me. He includes the price of one night's stay at most inns and the white silk of a scarf that tradition demands for a host or guest to exchange."

"The wool is from sheep country north of us," the inn keeper mused. "There are a few scattered oak groves there, but not many lakes. It is sheep steppe country: grass too short for horse or cattle."

The invitation is clear. There will be a lake in an oak grove and some kind of shelter or inn. It's a summons I have to meet. My future hangs on my meeting this challenge."

154

"*Soos*, hush now, don't cry." Yasmin whispered. "I'll take good care of you and the baby on the trip. The base has some lovely guest rooms for women. You'll be with Sesli and me. I'm sure you'll come to no harm."

"But my husband, Sanjak, was close by. It's been so long! Now, not someday, I need him now!"

"We've only had just over a half day of travel. Perhaps he'll come tomorrow and return with us. He can have an army career, like my Harun."

"I think his heart is set on return to his homeland."

"You're wrong, who could consider living outside Islam? It would be unthinkable. Everything would be utterly alien and ugly." She turned her back to sleep. Outside could be heard the pacing and call of sentries around the camp and on the horse line.

"Come little sweetheart, don't make a sound," whispered Nooryouz, some hours later. "We'll go to *baba* now." Suiting action to words she crept out of the tent with her bag and blankets and picked her way past a sleeping guard, back to the road they had traveled. She had lived as a shepherdess for months in her escape from Uigur lands. She preferred to walk and so she did for the rest of the night. With the coming of light she found a grove of trees and brush near a water course, made a bed, fed the baby and slept. She did not hear a squad of horsemen ride by on the road.

TANRA'S HEAVENLY PROCESSION

155

# PEOPLE, PLOTS & PLACES IN CHAPTER 13

Baja: exhausts herself seeking a dear friend.
Gabi: Keeps order when his help plays on the job.
Kardesh: gets what no one wants for being himself.
Kynan: gets his assumed name back and his job.
Leyla: finds herself playing another, different, role.
Manfredo: hates heretics with contrary doctrines.
Melek: wants money for information, but shares it.
Nooryouz: escapes one pursurer and hides from another.
Sanjak: finds the army squad seeking his wife.
Sevman: sings at the market and defends his friend.
 Yeet: gets what they need for their Jerusalem stay.


GLOSSARY:
*abbi*: big sister; the oldest is expected to control the young.
*aly'cum salaam*: the response of one greeted in Arabic.
*baba*: father; daddy; papa.
*sadicot*: a portion of one's earnings that given to charity.
*salaam aly'cum*: peace to you, an Arabic greeting.
*ta mom*: okay; I agree; It's alright.

MARKET MUSIC

In the market, Sevman sat with a tambourine in hand he beat the drum face with his fingers. He waved his arms with exaggerated flourishes, crooning his music and looking appealingly at every passer-by. He sang the verse then grabbed up his shepherd's pipe to play through to the next interlude.

1            "Thank you Lord for safe arrival
             For you see our faith is real.
            You've provided all we needed,
            Shown Your faithful love each meal.

Chorus:

            Lord, we thank You for the journey,
            Safely passed with stress and strain.
            So, we pray You, Lord, to bring us,
            Happily to our homes again.

2            Thank You for the dangers passed now,
            They reflect your constant care.
            Food and friendship, daily portioned,
            They all prove that You were there.

Chorus:

**3**      Lord, we come to You in trouble,
For we seek You in our cares.
But when life is fat and easy,
We pretend that You're not there.

Chorus:

PILGRIMS' THANKS

Thank you, Lord, for safe ar - ri - val,

for You see our faith is real.

You've pro - vid - ed all we need - ed,

Shown your faith - ful love each meal.

Chorus

Lord, we thank You for the jour - ney,

Safe - ly past with stress and strain.

So, we pray You, Lord, to bring us,

hap - p'ly to our homes a - gain.

The shoppers passed on their errands or business, but one or another would pause, listen to a verse, smile and move on. A few had a coin to leave. As the sun rose to zenith, Sevman threw his instruments into a bag which he draped over his shoulders and mounted a small cart with wheels that held him a hand-span above the stone path. With two wooden batons held in each hand he propelled himself toward the church several streets away. At the gate he paused to seek his friend, but could not discover him. He gestured toward a passing student of the Ethiopian Seminary. The boy stopped, smiling.

"Melek, Where's my big friend who begs here at the gate? Is he ill?" The boy grinned with delight, held out his hand coaxing and pleaded. "I tell only for a copper coin. You never find him by yourself. I know. You have market money. Now share!"

"Candy make you sick with beggar's money." Sevman grumbled, frowning fiercely. "Tell me and next time I'll bring you some fruit." But Melek shook his head, wiggled his fingers enticingly. He laid his finger across his lips.

"Take it, greedy gut. Now, tell me everything."

Melek moved close to Sevman and spoke in a confidential way. "New priest from Rome take him for question. My uncle, he guard. He take him to Monsignor. Better wait."

The boy ran off to the market and came back with a bunch of grapes. He came over and amiably shared the fruit. "Not wait long. Monsignor always need afternoon nap, before mass and bless pilgrims. More people come now."

Sevman ate sparingly of the offering. The boy scrutinized him. "You come from far Khorasan; not Orthodox Christian, not Muslim or Jew. What are you?"

Sevman shrugged then demanded: "Why was he taken? What did he do, Melek?" The inquisitive boy was a gold mine of information.

"He not wear badge of Christian like men must here. He dress like pilgrim, but he beg like a poor man. Priest is new, curious. he not like differences: no yellow badge and old clothes. No-eyes-to-see'um man too different, he not coward...." At that moment shouting arose. The side door of the church was opened violently. A shriek cut through the stifling heat of mid-day. Inside the door a man was being beaten. He was thrown out bodily. Kardesh hit the dirt.

The priest rushed out. "Dammed heretic! Beast of a Nestorian! How dare you spoil our holy church with your filth! Child of the devil! Get out of here! Never come again or we'll peel your back with whips. If only we were in our country. We have courts to condemn the likes of you. Our bishop wouldn't leave you whole one minute." The priest spit on Kardesh. Then He started kicking at him.

Sevman pushed his cart forward and rolled his wooden cart wheel over the priest's foot, placing himself between them. He reached out with the wooden paddle and hit the priest behind the knee causing him to fall. The noise increased as the priest called the church guards. Melek's uncle and others came running to separate the contenders.

Melek pushed the cart toward the gate, but Sevman pulled at Kardesh to bring him too. Guards pushed the priest back into the open church door.

The uncle came over to help Kardesh stand. He spoke quickly, avoiding a look at the bruised face. Kardesh staggered to his feet. "You must leave before city watch arrives. They like to make a fuss when there are problems in the church quarter and they can fine us. Come this way."

The uncle carried the cart and put Sevman on his back while Melek guided Kardesh. They were taken through the Abyssinian school to a small ally behind the church. There Kardesh gingerly took his little friend on his back and carried the cart in his left hand.

They staggered back to the rock shelter. There they found Yeet cooking lentil soup and joyfully celebrating abundant bread. His first words were loud and jubilant.
"I have a job four days a week. Uncle Gabi will teach me to bake bread. Praises be! We'll never be hungry again!"

> - - - - - >JERUSALEM SHELTER> - - - - - >
"Saida reports life as normal at the Church of the Holy Sepulchre. Father Manfredo has been very nice to her and the number of pilgrims is increasing." Kardesh said.

"The priest insults us on the street. He knows we help each other and Melek said he is asking about our shelter. All this week he has been walking the streets and giving candies to the children who report on us." Sevman stated angrily as they sat round the fire eating.

Kardesh sighed and made the sign of the cross, right to left Orthodox fashion. "Christ have mercy on us sinners."

Sevman grumped on. "He knows we visit St. Helen's church in the valley and has told the priests there."

"We can go to Bethlehem for the Easter season and return after the first week of April," Kardesh suggested. "We should think about leaving. Your pilgrimage is over," Sevman stated. "We can go north through Nazareth to finish visiting all the holy sites and return home."

Yeet was suddenly indignant. He motioned with head and hands. His face was red and his voice loud and shrill. "I can't go. This is the bakery's busy time. Special breads for the season are expected. It's the time when a lot of money is made. I've promised to help. That's what he's training me for. I have a natural talent for it. Uncle Gabi and Rafi both say so." Yeet turned away and pouted.

Kardesh nodded understandingly, while Sevman frowned and complained. "You spend more than four days a week there. They pay you to stack fuel and when they are busy with afternoon sales. But you've spent several nights there as well. You might as well get a room there." He turned his back.

"Who is Rafi? We know of Uncle Gabriel who is generous and good but this other one?" Kardesh asked softly.

"He's from Armenia. Like his uncle. He's named for an angel, Raphael. He's an angel who came here from the Caucasus war. He's severe and a bit sad, but funny when he jokes and sings. We get along well."

Kardesh smiled gently. He stroked his bruised face where the skin was starting to heal. He insisted: "It's time you had some things to laugh over. God uses you to feed us and you're our faithful friend. We'll not be jealous of your good fortune or your choice. We'll go to 'The Church of the Nativity' and see if the pilgrims are generous. Then when we

161

return we'll see how to proceed. God will guide us as he has this whole journey. He sees our sins, but forgives in mercy."

Yeet smiled, but Sevman kept his back turned. His voice was gruff and resentful. "I don't know why I'm here anyway. This has nothing to do with the Jesus of glorious light. He shines in heaven as our perfect example. His beastly birth in a stable; death on a Roman cross, are of little value. The flesh is weak and prone to evil. Only by the imitations of the Christ is there victory over the material universe that binds us to earth and death. The ascetic who punishes the body obtains the victory over it and all creation. Mani has taught us this." Sevman at last turned back to the fire looking smugly self-righteous. He poured the remains of his bowl of soup in the fire. Crossing his arms he looked up at the sky.

>- - - - - - -> CAMPING ON THE CHU RIVER > - - - - - >

"Horsemen approaching, Commander," the sentry yelled at the top of his voice and the trumpet of alarm sounded. The sound of aroused troops searching for weapons and dressing came from the tents. It was just after first light and the warning shout was further interrupted by screams of alarm. "The baby is gone. Nooryouz too," came the call from the women's tent. Commander Harun el Ari had slept in his clothes in the next tent and was immediately present to consult his wife. "The bed is cold they are long gone," she stated. He ran to the horse line and then to the road where a troop had arrived.

"We didn't come to fight, but I want my wife and baby, Sanjak announced.

"My wife says they escaped last night while she slept. They went without horses so they're on foot somewhere. I'll help you search."

"I'll need to confirm that if you'll permit two men to survey the camp," Sanjak retorted.

"You must take my word. I can't allow armed men to wander around in camp. Believe me when I say I can understand your anguish. But no commander can permit what you requested." This refusal was followed by silence.

"*Tamom*, okay, let one woman, Baja hanum, come and talk to your wife. Will you allow that?"

162

"Send her in. Then, pull your men back and we can talk. I'll ride out to you when you've done that."

"They want Nooryouz, Commander," explained Baja. "They don't want a fight if they can help it."

"You look tired Baja hanum," Harun said.

"It's times like these when women need the veil," she replied. "We rode all night and I feel like every bone in my body is out of joint." She laughed as she staggered forward.

"You can look where you like and then you should rest," he advised. "Yasmin can let you rest for an hour. We'll have breakfast when your friends have gone,"

"No friends of mine, Commander, I only know Sanjak and him just slightly. My friend is a lady, the little shepherdess, Nooryouz. She must be in the woods about for she couldn't walk far in a few hours. I have to find her. After that, I'd be glad to let you take me back to the base and home."

>- - - - - - - >GECHIT CITY> - - - - - >

Even Baghdad can't surpass this bazaar, dear friend," Magazi remarked as they passed through the corridors lined with shops, viewing the thousands of articles on display. Both men walked as if on a leisurely stroll examining anything that took their interest.

"The ruler is Jewish, but the market holds men of every faith, every kind of merchandise, every nationality and language. It, truly, must be a second Jerusalem."

"Yes, and set in a near desert with a bone chilling winter. Truly, Allah is great and shows compassion, even on those who are ignorant of our great prophet, peace be upon him. But look," Magazi continued, "a Muslim store selling arms from Baghdad and Damascus."

Abdullah picked up a war bow, strung it and tested its tension.

"*Salaam aly'cum*, peace to you," the salesman stated, rightly presuming on his customer's origins.

They confirmed his presumptions in their response, "*Alycum salaam*, and to you peace. Weapons from so far away, to sell in a cold alien land ruled by Jews?" asked Magazi, "Why live here in exile?"

163

"Allah prospers us while we wait for the day of our liberation. We increase in number, our day will come. I see you like our bow and arrows, Notice the construction of the quiver. The bottom is angled to place some arrows higher for easy access in a moment of action. The recurved bow is an excellent weapon, much superior to the tribal hand work. Notice the metal reinforcement of the bone and horn. The distance and penetrating power are enhanced. Here notice the difference in the arrows."

"I'm impressed, this is a formidable weapon. An army with these could conquer the men of Rome and hold the Straits of the Bosphorus," Abdullah responded. "Now, I seek a special liquid, a milk of snake."

"I see that you are a connoisseur of arms," the salesman responded. "Let me sell you something special from the Nile, milked from the friends of Cleopatra, the beautiful."

"How effective! How long does it take?" Magazi inquired breathlessly.

"There are different strengths, some paralyze. Others kill almost instantly. They are guaranteed and tested on animals. The size, weight and age may vary the effects somewhat. It's a restricted item and I'm not allowed to demonstrate it." They all laughed somewhat uneasily.

Abdullah asked pleasantly," I would like a description of your last customer."

"Are you with the police then? I described the tall stranger already and was told to say no more. Is there some other thing else I can help you with?"

"Let's talk about the price of the bows. We shall want several if you can supply them," Magazi stated smoothly.

> - - - - - >WITH THE EAST BULGARS> - - - - - >

"I thought they would kill us when Perilee described the death of Kerim bey. They were furious." Leyla whispered.

"It's because they have no body to bury. They believe souls wander if not buried correctly." Kynan said.

"What can we do about that?" Leyla responded, "You paid others to bury him -- all the guards, too."

"They think the tribe has lost strength through the souls that will wander looking for their place. I will make the

164

shaman an offer now. Don't object." He rose slowly and held his open hands out in appeal to the gathered men. He confessed, "I bear the guilt of allowing our brothers to be buried by aliens without proper ceremonies. I offer to take the name and place of Kerim bey to complete his duties before the tribe and to attract his spirit and those that served him to his own hearth again. So any harm or malevolence will fall on me and spare the tribe."

There was a moment of silence and then a buzz of conversation and the men discussed the offer. Outside the yurt the women too stopped keening and wailing to listen.

The shaman rose to speak. "Kynan is known to us for he came as a boy and has returned as a man. We know he understands our thoughts and troubles on this matter. He offers to take the dangers from our shoulders to bear it alone. Let the council speak its mind on this matter."

"Let me say," Kynan continued, "that the property and herds of my former master will remain in the hands of his descendants forever, However, half of any increase will be my portion for the work done." Heads nodded agreement and understanding. Then a young man stood to speak.

"I was present at the initiation of this man to the young warrior's barracks. He came as a boy from the estate of Kerim bey. He was loud and arrogant, so some decided to humble him and, in a night of feasting and drinking, they did. I was young and timid and didn't join them. But I remember his anguish and anger. I wonder if he still bears hatred in his heart against those, some here present, who abused him." There was a silence, an older man stood.

"Young warriors lack the experience and the wives of older men. At such times folly seems wise. Pride and seniority rule in young hearts and the excesses of drink and food cost dear. Such unfortunate things happen and none will apologize, for each blames another. The question is: does revenge hide in this man's heart?"

"I held anger and hurt at first. I tried to do big things among my people, but failed. Then, as a war prisoner and living in captive humility, I found Yesu's pardon and salvation. I escaped and rescued a princess. I made my way

165

to you through many adventures. Gratitude filled my heart when I met my old master by the Volga River. The Tarter attack killed me as well. I would now live as Kerim of the East Bulgars and fulfill my destiny where life started. My youthful past is over, my hatred is dead and revenge belongs to Tanra alone. He is a God of justice. Everyone   will face our Creator on a day of judgement. Yesu teaches mercy not revenge is a safer way to go." Kynan finished and sat down.

The old man stood again and addressed the council. "I have heard enough and welcome young Kerim of the Bulgars to join our council and assume the burdens of responsibility. Let me caution him, however, that his Nestorian views of salvation not dominate his good sense of Tanra's great compassion for all His creation and not just those of a particular belief. He sat down again, next to the shaman and silence filled the lodge. It was a warning of possible rivalry that the tribe could not ignore.

"One after another members rose to welcome him.

> - - - - - >JERUSALEM BAKERY> - - - - - >
"More flour Rafi. The pans are full and ready for the oven." Uncle Gabi called out and his wife Safir came to help carry the dough to the oven. There they were dumped out of the pans, placed in the oven with wooden paddles. Rafi came in to the main room carrying a cask of flour on his shoulder. He was working in an open vest in spite of the spring chill. He looked like a well powdered snow man.
The dough was mixed far from the ovens so there would be no explosion with the flour powder filling the air.

Yeet pounded the growing wad of dough with his fist, He grunted with the exertion as he pounded and flipped the mass over repeatedly. Rafi laughed as he went past him.

"Hit him again, Yeet. See how good it feels. You beat your enemies and they resist enough to make you feel good as you pound them." He left and Yeet made no answer.

Returning he said," You are quiet and not your usual self this evening. Is something wrong?"

Yeet shrugged.  "My friends at the shelter must go to Bethlehem on pilgrimage. It … it's too lonesome to stay alone there."

166

"Stay here then. Uncle is so impressed with your work that he wants you to work full time, like family. There's a small roof chamber where we store things or you could stay with me in the small room by the ovens."

Yeet looked annoyed and shook his head.

Rafi smiled and said sadly, "You've never forgiven my challenging you the first day. You're still proud and resentful, the son of a Muslim conqueror affronted by a mere Christian *demmi*. I apologize."

"Not true. I need the top room, if I send for my sister. Fatima's older, but not an *abbi*, she never dominates me. We're very close." Yeet put a hand on Rafi's shoulder. "No apology needed between us, we're friends now. Fatma will like you. I might have to forbid you the use of the roof. Turkish men are jealous with their women."

Rafi nodded and smashed his dough flat with a bang. "Turks accept a bride price for their relatives. That might keep our friendship."

It was Yeet's turn to laugh. He wheeled and slapped playfully at Rafi's chest, back and head leaving white streaks where he touched. Rafi, roaring, pushed Yeet's face into the flour. They stared at the white coatings, laughing and pointing at each other. Uncle Gabi heard the commotion and stuck his head in to yell for order.

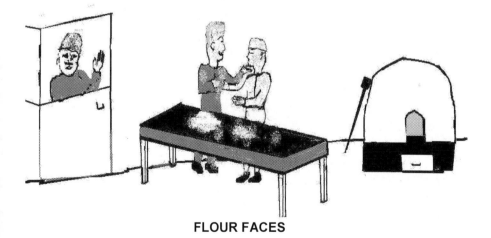

FLOUR FACES

167

## PEOPLE, PLOTS & PLACES IN CHAPTER 14

Abdullah: sells arms and encourages war.
Baja: finds her little friend and makes trouble for all.
Derk: a message causes him to be tied into old problems.
Gerchin: learns much of local politics and then acts.
Harun El Ari: loses a treasure that he hopes to find again.
Isa: a poor village boy practices his Christian faith.
Kadir: knows why the lieutenant will seek Nooryouz.
Kardesh: needs help and finds little in Bethlehem.
Korkmaz: learns and explains what he knows.
Kurnaz: the Vizier gets an offer to use hunting land.
Rafi: enjoys friendly companionship and seeks a bride.
Setchkin: faces a war to find a home.
Sevman: keeps his anger and receives an injury.
Twozan: tells Setchkin the news of their move.
Yeet: finds his job good and old friends frustrating.


GLOSSARY:
*chavush*: sergeant;
*Efendim:* My Lord, term of respect.
*El leri ye*: forward; to the front.
*evit*: yes; affirmative.
*getch mish old son*: may it soon pass; get well soon.
*Haziran*: June.
*Janum*: my soul; beloved; a family term of endearment.
*kai ma kan*: an authority over a district or town in Islam.
*kafir*: infidel heathen; unbeliever.
*Kidron*: a valley running south, east of Jerusalem.
*Nisan*: April.
*Oh kah dar ko lye*: It's so simple: it's so easy.
*Onbasha*: corporal: head of ten men.
*Soos*: shh; hush; quiet.
*zabitler*: the market police; agents of price control.

BUSY BAKERY

"I'll sit beside the gate on the street outside the Nativity Church. It may save us from trouble. Some of the clergy may have heard about us, Sevman. You go to the market but we'll have to eat before we sleep in the juniper grove," Kardesh stated.

"Yeet should be with us. He has found food more important than friends. This uncle and nephew named for angels become more important than blood brothers."

"Yeet always makes more friends on caravan or in strange towns. He has a gift for people, which draws them. We must put aside our desire to keep him ours only."

Sevman insisted, "He should have come. We'll have to spend money for food. The juniper grove may not be safe. His place is with us. You could have left me in the market and he would guide you to the gate. Now I have to bump my cart to the market and back. It's exhausting work." Sevman complained.

Kardesh turned to observe kindly. "If you would eat properly it would be less tiring. You try to gain God's approval by punishing yourself. Yesu died for your sin, accept it. Be glad for every blessing."

"Why shouldn't we be required to do something to show our sorrow over our failures and gain salvation? You came hoping God would heal your eyes if you made pilgrimage. It hasn't helped. There's no miracle for you. In fact, you had the visit of the girl Saida at the shelter. You say she brought food, but she is temptation for you and others. Instead of miracles you are exposed to the greatest temptations that God seekers can know. Lust is the destroyer." Sevman's voice became horse and rough. "We suffer because sex and gluttony rule human lives. Material energy moves to evil. We must cultivate the pure light as Mani showed us. We must become His elect." Sevman rolled off toward the market beyond the square. Kardesh kept himself from angry retorts. He listened to his friend's going and said quietly almost to himself. "*Oh kah dar kolie*, it's so simple, yet so hard for those who would make their own way." Then he turned his thoughts to prayer.

> - - - - - >HARUN'S CAMP > - - - - - >

"*Elleriye*, troop forward," came the call. Yuzbasha Harun ordered his troops forward on the road that led back to the Chu River fort.

Yasmin ran out to see the troop leave. "Where are they going?" she asked young Korkmaz who stood watching with Kadir and Sesli.

"They will follow and take Nooryouz after Sanjak finds her. She's important to the Sultan," he responded.

"But he didn't fight them earlier. Why now?"

"The treasure was lost," Kadir answered. "No need to fight. Once she's found, Sanjak can fight or surrender and come with her, but the yuzbasha intends to take her back as ordered."

> - - - - - >JERUSALEM BAKERY> - - - - - >

"The sun's coming up, Yeet. This is the last batch, so let's get it out so we can get some sleep." Yeet kneaded wordlessly. Rafi stood in his loose shalvar trousers and short open vest. He held the long wooden paddle for removing the loaves from the ovens. Sweat stood on his forehead which he dashed to the ground, wiping his hand on his vest. He threw a glance at Yeet, standing calm and cool.

"How can you work in that full shirt? The cool morning feels so good after facing the hot ovens." He laughed heartily. "Wait until July when the nights are twice as hot as hell. I'd work naked if uncle would let me. He calls it bad advertising for our product." He laughed again.

"I got so cold on the trip across the Iranian plain last winter that I think I'll never thaw out completely."

"Wait until summer little friend. Say, how old are you anyway? You never said, but I'm waiting to see your moustache." He laughed and elbowed Yeet amiably.

"I'm 15 but mother said I'm slow developing, my sister is like that too." Yeet looked embarrassed.

"You mean she looks like a little girl? No breasts yet?" He winked and nudged again. Yeet frowned.

"No, I don't mean that. I mean there are no marriage arrangements because she is choosy and not too eager."

"You know what the parents are expected to do. Uncle is after me all the time." Rafi chuckled. "What does your mother say about that? Do you have an Uncle to insist?"

"Mother is reported dead. We cannot return to our country, so I'm in charge of my elder sister. Mother made me promise to care for her needs even at the cost of life."

Rafi made the traditional consolation statements and Yeet continued explaining. "She said: 'Yeet, brave young man, your life for hers when the need arises. You must put her needs first,'" he said pensively.

"Is she like you Yeet? Friendly, helpful and sincere, are these family traits?" Rafi was serious.

"She is like me in almost every way. I could have her here by the month of *Haziran*, June, if your uncle approved."

"He likes you, Yeet, so I think he would approve of your family. Does she know anything about baking?"

"She knows and would be a better help than I am. She's a sincere Christian and a better person."

"Uncle would pay the bride price and you and your friends would have all your needs met, but you dress and act like a Muslim. The Imam would take her from me, a mere *demmi*. Although you may be an orphan now, by law you belong to Islam. What can we do?"

Yeet remained in thought. "You could say that I lied and carried out a deception: a Christian pretending to be Muslim." He said.

"They would punish you. Then force you to be truly one." Rafi pointed out. "They would say that the pretext shows desire and therefore you are Muslim."

"If they can catch and hold me." Yeet smiled again. "I will wear the yellow patch and temper my actions. I will act the part I have always felt within."

Rafi shook his head and made a face as he looked the boy up and down. "I can't endanger you, my friend. We live in a society of tale-bearers and gossips. They will be quick to pick up any differences and report them. I would have to take Fatima to another city where we were not known."

"Let us trust Yesu for these details."

> - - - - - >SAMARA PALACE> - - - - - >

"I must insist on the use of my new property for your royal hunt, Kurnaz, *efendim*. Your Excellency will find they're all that you can ever need to impress everyone with your wisdom in hosting such a gathering." Thus, Gerchin soothed the Vizier's irritation at losing the property to the new Turk arrival at the palace. He suavely continued, "My guards will do the drive to congregate the animals and your guests will have an unforgettable day and night. My cooks will prepare the banquet with a mix of our and your favorite foods. Allow me the privilege of doing this to show my appreciation of your sponsorship and protection."

"Praise to Allah and thanks to you, Gerchin bey, for  your generous response to my patronage. I have always said that you unlettered men from the wild lands of the north will become great servants of Allah. When all barbarians see how He rewards those who we subjugate to His will, they will be glad. You will find rich rewards in your dutiful obedience to the Sultan. Our Caliph is the shadow of Allah, set to rule the nations of the *kefir*. He will take them from their ignorance to the light of the Koran and Sharia law." Kurnaz was at his eloquent best. Gerchin was not sure how to answer this outburst.  Therefore, he nodded and said, "It will be a good hunt indeed."

> - - - - - >TOOZLU YURT>- - - - - - - - >

"Good news, Setchkin, janum, we have the Khan's permission and supplies. We are ready to move east now. Warriors from the center will

172

accompany us and make sure the colonists are not attacked. They expect resistance from the Kirgiz, but the Tang dynasty in China have abandoned them. They will retreat into the mountains; the Minusinsk Steppes and Angara are ours. Now we will have to contact the Mongols and establish a respect for borders." Twozan explained to Setchkin.

"What about those who are still in the south?" she objected thinking of the desperate families left behind.

"They will come separately and fill the land west of our settlements. We may have to gather hay for them if they delay into summer," he explained.

Let's hope not, that's too much like farming."

"How the mighty are humbled," he laughed. "When it comes to a choice: to live or to die, any effort is good; even being a farmer, unless you love burials!"

She put on an ugly face for him.

> - - - - - >BETHLEHEM> - - - - - >

The dark comes later in spring, but the sleet came with it and the cloak was inadequate to cover Kardesh. The chilling wind blew vigorously. Still Sevman did not come. He had been early all month while they prospered. At last Kardesh stood and taking his staff started across the open area before the church. No pilgrims came to the locked church now. Nothing was to be gained in waiting. He felt his way cautiously, using his stick to test the ground. Pools of cold water greeted his feet. He knew the direction to the market he had traveled with Sevman many times. As he drew near, he heard some light steps running toward him. He halted and found his voice.

"Who's there? What has happened?" He cried, "Is Sevman here somewhere? Why is he late?" The running stopped and a cold hand was laid in his. A child's voice answered him. He recognized the voice: His neighbour Isa.

"I'm supposed to tell you. You must come. He can't guide you, I'll do that. But you must carry him."

"Was he hurt or did he fall sick? The truth now!" He held the little hand firmly, so it could not be withdrawn, but not to cause pain. Isa attempted to withdraw his hand, but the grip tightened. "I'll not let you free until you tell me. But don't cry.

173

I won't hurt you Isa." The child stopped, then spoke quickly, with a trembling voice.

"The men were unloading sacks of salt blocks from the camels. The girth straps slipped on one and the whole load fell over on the singer. His feet, ah, legs are broken again and some blocks hit his head. He's not awake yet."

"Men don't unload at night in the rain."

"The caravan arrived near dark. They unloaded to save the salt. They were standing beside the building where he begs. He was mounting his cart to go to you. I was watching from a doorway. Everyone was sorry." The voice broke in a sob.

"Are we there yet?" Kardesh stooped to touch the head that echoed his feelings. "Come, don't cry. Guide me to him. He straightened up and moved forward. The subdued sobs preceded him. The freezing rain continued to fall. "We're not afraid, God tests us. We must show ourselves brave and faithful. He'll be pleased if we do."

"I'm afraid, not brave. Sevman's in that doorway."

"Pray, Yesu shows mercy when we have no strength left." He felt the doorway's edge of plaster and brick and released the hand that guided. At Sevman's hair line there was a lump that oozed. The body was limp and cold. Kardesh put his ear to the mouth and heard the shuddering breath. He picked up the body and, leaving the little cart, started up. He shouted to the air and street.

"Who will give us shelter? Who will show mercy?" There was the silence of the rain. So he shouted again. "Is there none to show compassion? Men living here who fear Allah and love goodness?" The wind sighed through the rain.

Isa's small cold hand touched, then pulled Kardesh's hand and slowly the blind giant, like Samson, was led away down a street to a small mud brick hovel near the juniper thickets at the edge of Bethlehem. There with Isa's mother, pain was eased; chill banished and hunger satisfied for the moment.

> - - - - - >THE SEARCH> - - - - - >

"Nevrim, Nooryouz, It's Baja hanum," she yelled. "It's safe to come out, darling, Sanjak is here with me. Give us a shout.

174

Everything will be all right.  Don't be afraid. We're here and you'll be safe with us." They rode slowly back the road they had come. Sanjak rode before her seeking a possible spot for hiding. The squad of men rode behind, watching the rear for Harun's troopers.

"We've come too far for a woman to walk from the camp," Sanjak insisted to Baja.

"Nonsense, she's stronger than she looks. Wait! I heard something! *Soos*, be quiet. Is that you darling? It's Baja; I'll help you with the baby if you'll just call. Come dear, talk to me."

There was a breathless pause and then her voice came soft and weak. "Baja, is that you? Am I dreaming?" Sanjak moved silently toward a patch of trees and brush where the voice seemed to come from. "I dreamed Sanjak came."

"*Evit*, yes," he exclaimed, "Here I am, *Janum*."

"Oh Sanjak, I wondered if I'd ever see you again."

"I swear I'll never leave you." Their embrace was fierce and prolonged. Then, the baby cried.

Baja heard the sound of approaching horses and called in alarm from the road. She rode in leading Sanjak's horse and dismounted. "Get on these horses and run away. I'll stay and divert them." They mounted and were off. Their troop followed and all were lost in the brush. The pursuing troop would have continued, but for a piercing scream from a woman with a blanket held around her body where she held a bundle, like a wrapped baby in her arms. Her figure ran staggering toward the wall of brush beyond her. There she was lost from sight, but her screams traced her move away from the road back toward the fort. "I'll follow her," Harun shouted. "Onbasha, get ahead of her; cut her off." They swiftly surrounded the wailing figure. The troop dismounted and approached menacingly around the screeching figure. She stopped.

Baja threw back the blanket and said in a loud voice. "I thought I'd smother in that heavy thing. Well the chase is over I'm ready to go home." a grudging chuckle started around the circle and an angered Harun turned in disgust from the wrinkled but cheerful face.

"Onbasha, go to the fort and ask for a party to ride west to block them and recover her. Chavush, take the squad; follow the escaping band and see if you can catch them. I can conduct the grandmother to camp by myself." The men left laughing.

When Harun and Baja got to the camp, it was empty. Kadir had taken the boy and two women to ride ahead. Harun was left to pack up and bring the gear.

> - - - - - - >UP THE VOLGA RIVER> - - - - - >

"*Do'er*, halt! *Kim gelir*, who comes there?" A challenge rang out from a wooden stockade with upright, sharpened logs that defined its margins.

"Abdullah, the arms dealer honors you with a visit," shouted the well-armed and warmly dressed warrior.

Magazi, riding beside him, was equally set up and held the halter of a well-loaded mule.

"Some of your people are working for the Kazars. I have some things that are so excellent that it will put the Kazars to work for you someday." There was only a pause before the door unbarred and swung open.

> - - - - - >JERUSALEM> - - - - - >

"Courage little brother we are in Kudus, the Holy city. The next climb will put us in sight of David's Tomb and our cave above Silwan pool." A groan was Sevman's only answer. Kardesh moved heavily up to the top of the ridge that looked down on *Kidron* and the walled city. The week of rains had passed and the sun shown weakly during the long walk from Bethlehem. Jerusalem shone washed and bright on the horizon; safely tucked within its walls. A scattering of houses and fields littered the south side of the hill of Zion. Deep gashes marked the winter rivulets and washes. Green grass spread up and down the hills from the welcome rains. Spring filled the air with softness and the bleating of sheep was its music. The sound of the dove was heard in the land.

"We have used most of the day, I must return to my home before dark. Send me away." The little guide, Isa, requested, freeing his hand from Kardesh. He drew back a step.

176

"Come stay the night in our shelter, Isa. It's close now. I know this place. We have food and bedding for rest. You can meet Yeet our little friend from our country."

"Mother will fret and scold if I'm late. The road is not safe at night. I would go now. Please, send me away."

"How can I repay your help? What would you wish from us? Come to the shelter and choose something."

"Mother was afraid of you when you first slept in the Juniper grove. You had a knife with a green handle and you made your beds of branches and cut a room in the trees. When she saw you were good and no harm came to us, she let me buy your bread; run errands for tips." He paused, embarrassed, "She envied your knife. She said: 'How wonderful to have a good sharp knife like that.' Would you give your knife?" Isa looked down at their dirty, bare feet, waiting for a no.

"The handle is jade, an eastern jewel, the metal is Turk bog-iron and it was bought in Perikanda. Samarkand some call it. The knife was given to me by Sevman in Kokand. It is dear to me."

The boy nodded and turned away.

"Wait, you saved our lives. Here, take the knife, give it and the kiss of peace to your mother." Kardesh held the sheathed knife, handle outward, to Isa. "It is little for so much help."

With a look of wonder the child gingerly took and examined the knife. He laughed in delight and tucked its scabbard into his waist band. Then, he turned and ran toward Bethlehem village.

> - - - - - >CAPITAL QUESTIONS > - - - - - >

The *zabitler*, market police, tried vainly to keep the market commodity prices level and fair, but scarcity must raise the price to consumers. The palace and high officials were the normal, big buyers and consumers. A *Nisan*, April wedding announced by a merchant prince for his daughter and, for the same day, a vizier-sponsored hunt sent prices boiling over the set limits.

Excitement grew, as the details became known by the population. Who would go to Samara to hunt? Who would attend the Baghdad wedding? This became a worrisome question for those wishing to advance their position and enjoy the accompanying treats and memorable excitement offered. Everyone took the consequences of refusal very seriously. To reject an invitation was an act so detrimental to one's future that all shuddered at the agonizing necessity of choosing. Debate raged within families, for this question was a survival matter. Ambition, occupation, status influenced each family's arguments. Religion, language, race and rank play an important role in every society. Only a few found an easy choice. Long lasting disagreements, fights, splits, resentments, rejections and partings came as the result of these debates. As one loudmouth clown shouted in the market place, "You say the prices will be back to normal and everything the same after these things are over and done with. Nothing will ever be the same again. It's the end of the world!"

> - - - - - >JERUSALEM BAKERY> - - - - - >

"I'm glad your friends have returned, but I'm sorry one is hurt. I think you people say *'getch mish old soon,'* 'get well soon.'" Rafi looked at him quizzically, truly Yeet seemed more upset than he had ever seen him. He sighed," If you wish I'll get our community's doctor to visit him." Yeet nodded quietly, still moulding the dough into loaves.

"They only returned at sunset and I had to come here, but I've never seen Sevman so desolate. It's like the first time at the hospital... living in despair. He would hardly talk." Yeet shook his head sadly.

Rafi nodded. "I'll go with you in the morning, after work. The doctor's old housekeeper comes for bread from the first batch and we'll send notice with her." They worked silently.

"Does your sister Fatima love people as much as you?" Rafi smiled down at Yeet.

Yeet smiled. "Would you expect and believe less?"   Rafi roared with laughter and nudging Yeet shouted.

"No, you rogue, what sister doesn't outdo the brothers? Uncle is ready to sign the marriage agreement, sight unseen. That means you stand really high in his eyes."

178

"I've sent a letter, as I told you. The caravan should be arriving in Samara. She will leave with Bowzhun's Family blessings and be here for *Haziran*. Then we will have the tea ceremony and you will be able to talk to her. Gaining her consent will confirm and seal the agreement."

"Will she approve, Yeet? Will she accept me?"

Yeet smiled at his friend's nervousness. He gazed at the ceiling. "We're alike, and rarely hold different opinions about people. I know she'll love you, when she gets here."

"You'll stay with us Yeet? Your friends can come too. Uncle has rooms enough. We'll be a family."

"I can't speak for my friends, but where my sister lives, I'll be present to support her and you. As God will permit me, I'll stay with you." Rafi nodded and took the paddle to remove the loaves from the oven and the pleasing smell of bread filled the building.

> - - - - - >JERUSALEM CAVE> - - - - - >

"He's still burning up with fever and is off his head part of the time." Kardesh's detailed report to Yeet was harshly punctuated with his coughs. Yeet looked from Sevman on the bed to an equally sick Kardesh sitting beside the bed.

"You need to sleep now. I'll prepare a meal for you. I'll wake you up when it's ready."

Kardesh shook his head. "No, I slept some a while ago. I ate a bit, but he should wake for food. He didn't eat yesterday except for a few spoonfuls of soup." He stopped with a burst of coughing.

"I think you have fever, too." Yeet put his hand to Kardesh's forehead. Kardesh dodged and turned his back.

"Be a brave fool, you stupid oaf, God give you what you deserve." Yeet broke into tears. Angry and frustrated he rushed out of the shelter.

The coughing stopped. Kardesh slumped over in a stupor beside the delirious Sevman. Quiet fell on the cave inhabitants. The fire smoked unattended. A light drizzle filled the air with chill.

> - - - - - >NEAR THE VOLGA RIVER> - - - - - >

"This has got to be the place," Derk bey murmured as he stopped to admire the discovery. "There's a small hut, better than most and the lake. A tiny birch woods completes the picture, a direct contrast to the bald prairie surrounding it."

Increasingly Derk had started speaking in whispers to himself. He noticed it first on his angry trip in the Kara Kum Desert with the caravan, and then on his desperate return to the Amu River Valley. The lack of accommodation from government personnel increased his concern for his position and future. He needed a success to restore confidence in him, something strong. The Gray Wolf knew of his deductions concerning its head and feared a prompt disclosure and removal from power.

"There's no sign of humans present now, no horse, dog or herd. It has been left so for my accommodation." He rode a circuit of the grounds, woods and hut before coming closer and dismounting to investigate the woods and finally the hut where he found a table set for two and provisions ready to be used. There had been only one set of tracks outside, coming and leaving, so he relaxed.

"He'll come in the evening, so I'll warm the food. Will he come to kill or to deal? Perhaps the Gazelle expected the same things. What can I do about it? I have no other hope or course of action. Perhaps the host wishes to become the head wolf himself, but how could he manage it?" He lit the lamps. He sat debating within himself as the evening approached.

Derk slept sitting up and woke to find a rope tightening around his middle confining his arms to his sides.
"Don't struggle," came the warning. "I promise I won't hurt you. I simply want to talk to you. You're a fast draw with the knife and precaution is necessary," Seerlee bey warned. "We need to talk about the *Bowzkurt's* head. You and I know who he is. So, we are under a sentence of death." Seerlee sat near an oil lamp which he lit. With his hand, he carefully made the shadow of a wolf's head on the wall.

"Success has made him careless," Derk responded slowly. "Now he must seek what he has lost."

180

"A vain hope once the secret is breached. The Gazelle knew and reported to the Kazar Khan."

"So you paid her with death for the breach."

"There were other reasons for her death."

"Things from your past, Simon? Before you came to live with my family and become a Muslim?"

"Of course, we were as brothers with a generous father. I taught you to throw a knife, remember?"

"I remember his anger when you refused the army and became a spy for the Gray Wolf," Derk insisted.

"Avoiding boredom is not dishonor, I make more money and I have constant excitement," Seerlee laughed.

"We serve the Caliphs of Islam, no other task equals it. There alone is our father's honor satisfied."

"You came then to erase the supposed dishonor?"

"I am bound in the chair. I have failed the last three tasks I've been given." Derk proclaimed sadly. "Should you kill me only my family will mourn."

"While, if I die the family will rejoice since honor is restored. Is this your meaning?" Seerlee snapped angrily.

"No, the loss of a brother leaves no room for joy."

"The Head ordered me to kill you, but I'm going back to Baghdad to collect a head for a trophy. Perhaps then the family will find honor restored by the straying one."

"Not if you leave me here tied up."

"You'll be out before I'm out of sight. I know you. Get out on your own, but don't interfere with my plans or you could be hurt." He moved to the door.

"Do you realize there may be murderers on your trail? The Wolf is known for eliminating witnesses." Derk insisted. "Dead, you'll help no one!"

"Dead or alive, I'll see the job finished." After these words, Seerlee left Derk alone to work on his bonds.

# PEOPLE, PLOTS & PLACES IN CHAPTER 15

Abdullah: falls in events that cost him everything.
Attila: was always too fond of showing off his money.
Baja: loves good food and the occasions to enjoy it.
Derk: finishes his task and tries a contact for the Sultan.
Kaplan: the tiger sees an enemy and recognizes a friend.
Kardesh: suffers loss of friends, health and home.
Magazi: arranges for his final trip back to Gechet.
Saida: An Abyssinian girl helps needy pilgrims.
Sanjak: tries to persuade Erly and runs for home.
Setchkin: has a surprise for her husband.
Sevman: involves his friends in new problems.
Tanra : Turkish word for God.
Twozan: finds acceptance with neighbors at a future cost.
Yeet: finds no joy in saving his friends' health.


GLOSSARY:
*Allah shue koor*: Praise to Allah; Thank God.
*felucca*: a sailing vessel common in the Mediterranean.
*ger: yurt*; Mongol dwelling tent.
*Tanra'ya sue koor*: thanks to God; praise Tanra
*tebrik ede'reem*: my congratulations.

ENEMY SHIPS

"I don't like carrying this money around. Shouldn't we hide it with the other?" Magazi asked nervously.

"We have found a gold mine selling weapons to the Tartar outposts. We carried samples of our weapons; why not samples of their earnest money?" Abdullah replied happily. "The talk of attacks by the Russ and forest tribes makes them free with their gold." He patted Magazi's money-belt.

"Ships on the river!" The call came from the fort's corner tower. Trumpets blared and gongs sounded.

"Quick, let's get up the mosque tower. The imam will be there watching," Magazi urged, running toward the brick mosque.

"No, the wall is better for defence. This way! Allah, Allah, look at the fleet. There must be twenty ships."

The flotilla sped in on the current and spread along the quay before the main entrance of the wooden fortress. The snarling animal heads of the boats were facing the village. Then, from the bow of each boat, a small ballista flung a missile: a two foot-long six inch diameter log. Each was hollowed to hold a handful of burning coals. They streaked across the sky to land with a resounding thud against wooden walls or thatched roofs. Again the weapons threw their deadly cargo and small boats pushed off the far side of the ships to carry warriors to the shore.

"Down, be quick!" Abdullah pushed Magazi and jumped to the foot of the inner wall to escape the coal-filled rain from the sky. "Now, run back to the mosque. The brick won't burn."

The arcing curtain of fire was now continuous above the advancing warriors. They were shouting their war cries and carrying battering rams. Each ram was carried by ten men with their shields slung protectively over their backs. Ladder men ran beside them. The rams attacked burning gates while the ladder men looked for areas without flames. When the gates burst open the fire from the ships stopped.

From the mosque tower a flight of arrows cut down the men rushing through the gate. Other gates were opened and the village guards slaughtered. The mosque was the last citadel to fall in the burning Tartar fort.

> - - - - - >ATILLA'S DILEMMA > - - - - - >

Atilla sat contemplating his life's journey. In China, he had felt a mix of racial superiority to the local heathen, Kafir, as he esteemed them. Yet their ingenious adaptations to need and environment surprised him. The food was delicious and the crafted goods were attractive. He made his fortune shipping goods. In spite of the immunity of Muslims from the expulsion orders, he had determined to leave the senseless violence and political disruptions of the restored Tang dynasty and return home.

The journey with diverse refugees had further brought him to question his own culture and beliefs. After a period of uncertainty, he found again his religious sense of rightness.

He enjoyed his association and banter with the Christians present in his travels, but was secure in his traditional beliefs.

Now in Mecca he was again in a quandary. The feeling of unity and rightness was edifying. Yet on the personal level the actions of men who served those who made the haj was mercenary and sometimes rude. He had paid for a glass of water for a poor man suffering thirst. The vendor verbally

184

assaulted him for his good deed. "The Imams are supposed to prohibit those who lack money enough. Now you encourage them by your proud intervention. May Allah rid this world of all such fools."

Atilla concluded sadly that perhaps sin was more general than supposed. He found encouragement, but no perfection in Mecca. He debated his desire to see Egypt, whose marvels did not historically include Islam. Perhaps he should travel to needy lands beyond the seas. He knew what his Christian friends would say. Was his call not noble? To be a hoja would bring honor at home, but rather than return he would take the harder road. He would go to a foreign land, take a wife and bring the kafir to surrender to Allah. His resolution brought renewed confidence.

### > - - - - - >A HIDING PLACE> - - - - - >

The tiger paced his beat, seven paces from one wall to the other. The hut had become his cage and his anger filled the room. His political dreams had collapsed with the confession of the old nurse and the death of the crow. Desires for revenge had replaced his careful planning. The sounds of new arrivals meeting his body guards brought fresh hope to the caged animal. Kaplan paused and opened the door to the small meadow enclosed in thick woods. A Tartar squad was dismounting to unload a small barrel from a pack horse. It was placed at his feet and the messenger's voice brought greetings.

"Here is the head you have requested of my master the Khan of Kazan. It is brought at great price for we came up the Kama River to evade the angry Bulgar patrols. This man, Kerim, was dear to them."

"No less precious to me. I have the price here, but I would see the head of the one who killed my son, Kynan, first. I must be sure," the giant man insisted.

"There could be no mistake," the messenger insisted. "He rode the black and the lady at his side the Fergana mare. I led the raid. Our riverside spy heard the page's announcement: 'Make way, Kerim *efende* of the East Bulgars arrives.'"

"I can't wait to see the wretched fool who killed my treasure and stole the girl." He loosed the top and pulled the cord that fished out the vinegar preserved head of Kerim. He dropped it on a cloth and gasped.

185

"But this is a man near my age. He's no passionate lover. He's the man who was to prepare my son for service in the court of the Bulgar Khan. His daughter was only four years younger than my boy."

"He is Kerim of the Bulgars and rode the horse of your description. Only two girls and one youth escaped our attack. The reward is ours."

"The mistake is yours and I'll not pay blunderers. You have killed an honourable friend and ally."

"I didn't run these risks to return empty handed."

In an instant knives were drawn, but the Tartar was quicker and had plunged his weapon deep into the big man's belly. Twisting the knife he shouted to his squad. "Attack! Teach these fools that no one can mock Tartars. We are the rulers of the steppes and rivers. No one trifles with us. Kill them all! Burn the camp!"

> - - - - - >JERUSALEM CAVE> - - - - - >

"Sevman, you hear me? Yes, I feel you nod your head. You must try to listen. We pray you'll get better," Kardesh 'insisted.

"I have failed the light. Will God give me another chance?" Sevman's voice was low. His eyes were fixed above.

"Yesu forgives our failures, His death sealed our pardon. With his stripes we are healed. You must believe and obtain his cleansing."

Sevman lifted his head upward. "No, my sin and failure is too great. I remain bound to this fallen world. The Demurge holds my spirit. I must pay with my next opportunities, bound to my karma."

"Yesu knows our slavery to this world. He frees us for the present and the future. Tell Him of your love for God and rightness. He understands and forgives, you'll feel it. Tell Him about your fears and failures now. He'll receive you as you are." Kardesh continued between coughs.

"I wanted good, but evil is disguised and pervasive. God help me. I go without rightness. I take Him all my faults."

"You will learn of Him to bear your cross. He'll carry your faults away. You can be glad. Sleep now to sorrow; awake after to salvation, confidence and health."

Sevman nodded, but fought to keep awake. He whispered. "My faith is small, my pride too great. I seek humility, but I find a cunning mime within; pretending one thing while being another. Christ have mercy on me..." His voice faded to silence and he stared out into the darkness.

> - - - - - >CHIPCHAK WAR CAMP>- - - - - - - >

"*Barish, esenlick olson*, peace, be tranquil, we wish you blessings and prosperity," boomed the voice of the tall, impressive chief who spoke from his small sturdy pony. Dismounting, a company of Mongol chiefs repeated the greetings expected as they approached, bowing slightly before the assembled Chipchak leaders at the *ordu*-eve.

"Be always welcome in Yesu's name, oh People of the Gobi and the Baikal steppes." returned Twozan.

"We bear gifts and beg permission to approach," spoke the chief. Each man unpacked from his horse a bolt of white silk which they placed at the feet of the Chipchak leader. They resumed their places.

Twozan, with a motion, called forth boys to carry the gifts to the women who were assembled behind them. There was an outcry of delight as the women examined the offered goods.

"We have seen with approval your expulsion of the Kirgiz by your effective army. We are disappointed by the lack of a summons to aid you in their dispersion. It would have pleased us to help," stated the chief.

"It was but a small affair not worthy of your great attention," replied Twozan. "The Lion Horse people had a small quarrel which they settled easily. The pressure of your trribes with the attack of our was enough."

MONGOL GREETINGS

"We have heard and seen the quality of your tall, chestnut coloured animals," the chief retorted. "We would like to acquire some of these splendid beasts." The Mongol assembly nodded agreement.

"Unfortunately the stock is small, special and always reserved for our tribe only," Twozan explained.

"Yet, it is said that in ancient times the emperors of China received the breed," he retorted, insisting.

"It is true that Kaya the great, traded with the Kin dynasty and the practice continued for a short time. But the Gobi Desert requires a special, tough, resilient horse which you now ride." Twozan countered.

"Horses we will share with you as the need arises." the spokesman asserted. "Perhaps you will come to the same conclusion about your chestnut coloured horses with time."

"Tanra alone knows the future," Twozan quoted. "He is Creator and brings blessings to such as seek Him. In Yesu we have redemption from our sin and ignorance, bought at a price of sacrifice and pain."

The Mongol chief studied the ground. Twozan continued, "But come, food awaits your arrival."

"Yes, I smell its cooking and see your women in attendance on it. Are you as selfish with your maiden's marriages as you are with your horses?"

> - - - - - - ->AT THE BURNT CITY >- - - - - - - >

"Strip them before you carry them out to the raft," ordered Wolfstrand the warrior to his Kazar slave, a youth of uncertain age. "No use sending goods down to the Tartars." He paused to study the still form of Abdullah. Cut off his thing and stuff it in his mouth. That will make them take notice, by Thor," he swore with a coarse laugh.

"He fought well and held you back. Why dishonour the brave?" The boy asked as he continued stripping him of armour and weapons.

"As you like, weak fool of a Christian. Will your God give you credit for squeamishness?" Wolfstrand sneered as he walked away. "I go to enjoy some of the women we captured. You finish here." He swaggered away while his servant worked on.

"Why take him to a raft?" asked Magazi who sat leaning against the mosque wall, his shoulder cut open from an axe blow.

"What?" The boy jumped with fright. He had taken the man as dead. Now, he looked him over. Seeing no danger he answered, "The Tartar raft will be sent down river to frighten the Kazars and Jews. All the dead and dying will carry the raven's feast down to their cities. It lets them know we're coming. Next year King Olaf will have twenty more ships," he stated, leaving Abdullah's corpse and drawing near Magazi to study him.

"I will give you a reward if you put me on the raft with him." He tossed out a small purse of coins from his money belt. He closed his eyes in weakness.

"I would have had it anyway, when I stripped you," the boy protested, gathering the purse. "They'll torture you to death as a prisoner."

"Promise by your God to put me on the raft as if dead, beside him. I'll give you a place where ten coins are hidden." They both paused to consider.

"I'll have to take your armour and outer clothes... But I'll do it and leave you your knife," he agreed.

"At the inn of the Black Bilah under the linden tree where a stone rests, with a snake carved on it, you'll find it. Dig under it and be blessed in your life."

> - - - - - >JERUSALEM CAVE> - - - - - >

"The priests won't bury him. All know he was a heretic and Manichee. No cemetery will receive his body; not Orthodox nor those of Rome nor Muslims will give him ground. We must go out to the desert." Saida spoke between tears.

"He is a light burden, I'm use to it." Kardesh said between coughing spells. His face was flushed and feverish.

"No, I'll have the wood cart for the day. It's all arranged." Yeet was solemn and calm but his eyes stared out of dark circles. He suppressed a shudder and continued. "I took him from the hospital in a cart. I'll see him out now."

Saida sighed and added. "My brother knows of a small cave very near. He found it when he was herding goats; He blocked it so it's still unused and unknown to others. No one will find him there."

"The neighbours have brought food for the friends who come to the wake. After, we'll go there, secretly."

> - - - - - >ARMY VILLAGE>- - - - - - - >

"Home at last," exclaimed Baja. "It feels like I've been gone for years. Come in Yasmin, don't be shy. This is the best kitchen in the world. You'll all be hungry. Just sit a while and I'll have everything ready. Come help, Sesli, you need nutrition to plan a wedding. They are life changing moments. They need attention. You go get wood for the fire, Harun bey; Kadir, and you help, Korkmaz. You men have only to follow orders. We women take care of all the details in things as important as this. Too bad you can't stay longer Yasmin. I've lived and I'll die in this house."

> - - - - - >RED SEA SHORE> - - - - - >

"I take this boat to go to the south lands to spread the rule of Allah and his messenger; peace be upon him." Atilla proclaimed in grandiose tones to the ship's crew. "My sword is dedicated to this purpose. Surrender to Allah or die. I will proclaim it to the idol worshiping heathen. All Islam will see and be glad."

The crewmen smiled and nodded in happy agreement. The captain commented, "We find your example and keen words encouraging, for in the east and south are many enemies of Islam. Pig eating, ignorant savages who need to be redeemed by the warriors of Allah. War in the Sudan is fierce and unrelenting." The crew continued to listen as the two men: the man who commanded the boat and the man who paid for its journey, matched words.

**ATILLA'S SWIM**

190

"Truly you are an unusual man," began the captain. "For we take many pilgrims to Mecca on the Haj, but we see few return with such money as you possess. For one man to hire a boat is a sign, of great wealth." The crew all agreed.

"Allah *sue koor*; Allah be praised, He is truly great. The unbelievers will tremble as he beats them to submission and surrender; they will believe. Allah knew I would need a good *fellucca* and I found you at the fishing village where the authorities said pilgrim bearing boats would not come. I was rightly guided."

"Naturally, we came from the pearling waters where we hunted... for pearls, of course. But you came up for your swim in the Red Sea, remember?" the Captain urged.

"Yes, I have bathed in the Yellow River, in the Amu River, the Euphrates River, the Jordan River, the White and Dead Seas, now I add a sea of red color to my exploits," bragged Attila as he doffed his robe to splash off the side of the ship. "It's warm," he said as he pushed farther off.

"Enjoy it," the captain shouted. "Up sail," he added to the crew. "Did you drag the meat after you dumped all the garbage?" he asked the cook.

"Yes, three fins were following us" he answered. "Allah ordains it," the Captain repeated piously, as shouts for help came behind the departing ship.

> - - - - - >LAKE BAIKAL> - - - - - >

"It seems to have gone well this week," Setchkin reported to Twozan. "What do you think?"

"With a lot of extra guard duty, vigilance and food, I'll be glad to see the last of them for a while. But they'll be back."

"Will they leave us in peace?" she inquired anxiously.

"They are accustomed to raiding China for any need. They'll have that tendency with anyone. However, our other victories: our horses and our women impress them. They may decide to leave us alone or incorporate us into their system of alliances and groupings."

"They kept referring to us as the chestnut horse tribe; does their language have a word for lions?"

"Yes, but you can eat chestnuts, not lions. They want to feel safe and superior to us. Feel we are human enough to win points in our relations.

They want our horses and women, but fear us too." He paused and then continued carefully. "We have to learn their language and customs, our lives merge with theirs. We will get little support from the homeland now that the army has returned to the capital."

"I can't imagine living in a *ger* instead of a yurt. It sounds like the growl of an angry dog, ger-r-r-r!"

"Get used to it. They will eventually get what they want from us. We must not become expendable."

"I hoped I'd have our child in safety," she said.

"We're having a baby?" he asked, startled.

"It started when we got home and were safe at last. Now I'll worry." She sounded petulant and annoyed.

"We're as safe as we would be in Kaplan's corral. Your father makes all the homeland tenuous for us."

"If what the midwife say's is true, it'll be a girl. It's different from the first time. Doesn't bother me as much."

"She'll grow up with her brother riding the country, loving Yesu, speaking both languages naturally and be the center of blessings to all of us," he said aloud. Silently he wondered whom that baby girl would have to marry twenty years down life's road.

> - - - - - >CHU RIVER CAMP>- - - - - - - >

Sanjak urged Erly to accompany him north; to move the last refugees. But Erly adamantly refused.

"We are hunting during the spring migration, the Chu River is flowing again and the birds are stopping over. We'll get ahead in meat and strength to travel. We had a hard winter here. With the supplies from the fort we'll make it across the dry country before the hot weather arrives."

"Remember the Abbasids are not our friends now. I rescued Nooryouz and the Uigur troop will be around searching for her. We haven't any good defence."

"I agree, so take her and go. I'll lose more by rushing. You can take off now and get ready for us at the home end of things. You go; we'll stay a month more." Erly ordered.

The positions were definite and opposite so Sanjak prepared to travel with a small group of followers. They intended to run far and fast.

> - - - - - >VOLGA RIVER> - - - - - >

"How long have you searched for them?" inquired the Tartar boat-man as they touched on the upper, windward side of the raft of stinking flesh. Birds, like a black cloud of smoke followed the progress of the raft.

"For a month, before I got news of them in Kazan," Derk reported. He examined the two cadavers on the raft's edge. "Why are they less picked over than the others?" His voice was muffled by the cloth worn over his face.

"The little one has protected them. He died later, see, he has a knife. There's a slash on his wrist."

"He became too weak to protect himself." Derk observed. "Let's go, I'll finish my report and try to make contact with the conquerors. We'll let this raft go on down river and unnerve the Kazars."

"I'll go with you. I had relatives in Kazan. Perhaps I can ransom them," his Tartar companion said.

"Wear your best. We'll go representing the Sultan. Remember the enemy of my enemy is my friend," Derk quoted. Both nodded wisely, it was a political idea widely quoted. They forgot the tribal saying that 'wolves love only their own pack, and not even that at the kill.'

RAVENS' FEAST

## PEOPLE, PLOTS & PLACES IN CHAPTER 16

Ali bey: seeks information by beating children.
Ana: comes to Jerusalem by caravan from Mt. Hermon.
Derk: seeks to convince Kazar's enemies to be his allies.
Gerchin: plans his way to the top of all his dreams.
Jon: finds good customers and earns a wife.
Kardesh: makes friends and is useful on a mountain.
Kaya: finds safety on the Chu River by farming.
Kerim: discovers new realities about family marriage.
Kurnaz: leads the charge to slaughter the innocents.
Leyla: enjoys her position as matron and mother.
Maril: finds in marriage all she sought in life.
Melek: is excited by the arrival of Rafi's bride.
Nooryouz: is grateful to be safe in her new home.
Onat: defends his army base and family to the last.
Rafi: Gets a letter that sets the marriage date.
Saida: is interested in marriages and Rafi's new bride.
Sanjak: leads the retreat toward the homeland.
Seerlee: seeks desperately to save the Gray Wolf's head.
Yeet: ends his life in an orchard near Mount Hermon.
Yusuf: gets the opportunity to speak about his faith.

## GLOSSARY
*delikanla*: youth; teenager; literally: crazy blood.
*dough roo*: true; correct.
*evet*: yes; certainly.
*jizya*: a Muslim tax on Christians.
*ordugar*: headquarters; army post.
*peckee-yee*: very well; excellent.
*Sari Su*: a wadi; yellow water; seasonally dry course.
*vatan benim*: my homeland; my country.
*yayla*: an alpine meadow; high mountain grassland.

DRAGON SHIP

Saida brought the letter to Rafi with the borrowed cart. Yeet wrote that Kardesh remained very ill. He said they had started back to their own country. He affirmed that Fatima, now called Ana, would come in a month: *Haziran*, June. She would arrive and stay at the nunnery on Ascension Hill, above the Garden of Gethsemane, until the wedding. He thanked the community for their affection and help. He promised never to forget them and the church that guarded the head of John the Baptist in its sacred walls.

> - - - - - >ESCAPING NORTH> - - - - - >

"Let's keep on the march," Sanjak ordered, "Our pursuers may be close on our trail." They were riding north away from the River Chu and toward Lake Balkash. A substantial group of young men and women were accompanying them. Tired of a winter of deprivation and boredom they were eager to go on to the tribal homeland.

"Look back, there's a troop of Abbasids at the Chu camp, shouldn't we run?" an outrider called.

"That would draw them immediately to pursuit. We will continue at the same pace. We go to Lake Balkash to hunt waterfowl. Let the women be veiled to conform to their expectations. Hide Nooryuz and the baby among them. Bring out your nets and birding arrows. We may have to pass their muster and approval to proceed.

"We are out of the Abbasids' borders. I'll not submit to their inspections," a young hot-head shouted.

195

"If you will ride with me, you will obey, *delikanla*. Sanjak responded sternly. "We go as one or not at all. We can't afford to have two heads."

> - - - - - >LAST PILGRIMAGE> - - - - - >

Leaving Nazareth Yeet and Kardesh journeyed across the lake side to the highlands of Gilead. The heat of spring was tempered near the heights of Mount Hermon and the hills about were filled with caves. How bright the snows of Hermon appeared! They were now in retreat from the increasing heat of the sun. In the distance a small village appeared enclosed by fruit trees of great size. The plants were pears, plums and, in sheltered spots, peaches and almonds. All were nourished by the unfailing melt of the snowy heights. "You must change into your new clothes, Yeet," Kardesh ordered with a smile. "The water will be cold, but the sun is warm and you have privacy here. I'll rest in the orchard. Then, we'll go on to the Christian village."

A MAIDEN'S BATH

196

"I guess it's time to make the change but I'm afraid. I've been a boy too long," Yeet complained. "How long have you known I'm a girl?"

Kardesh laughed and said. "You were too fond of gossip with Leyla. You wouldn't tease her by calling her Leylek, the stork. You were careful to obey Tayze when she came down hard. You pitied Sevman too much, in his many injuries and despairs. You chose knives rather than muscles for defense. You always went alone to answer calls of nature. Tayze worried about you in a way different from the boys. Women knew and some boys suspected something different about you."

"You make me feel like a failure," Yeet confessed. I thought I was fooling everyone."

"You did fool a world of people who knew you only slightly. Only those you lived with suspected anything. Most of us were sympathetic. We know the hard lot of girls in Muslim society. But there's no way out for most of them."

"Oh, Kardesh I do hope I'm doing the right thing. I love Rafi, but I'm afraid to continue in Jerusalem."

"Don't stay in Kudus, go north, it's too hot there any way. Find mountain country where you can be free."

"Rafi says that there are mountains northwest of Antep that are only lightly controlled by the Sultan, There we might find a place to bake bread."

"Tanra must be your guide. Now, go bathe and change. I'll rest here," Kardesh ordered.

> - - - - - >ERLY'S CAMP> - - - - - >

"We've come for Sanjak and his wife," shouted the Abbasid sergeant to Erly bey at the *ordugar*.

"They've gone on down the Chu to the central camp, I assume. That's where Kaya bey has planted his farming colony. I haven't time to take care of everyone's problems. We have to procure food for our departure," Erly grumbled grimly. "Go see."

"There's a party riding north." reported the sergeant Major suspiciously. "Where do they go?"

"To the lake for birds, check them out if you like, but you'll miss Sanjak if he uses the Sari Su Wadi to run."

"Damn you and all tribesmen," shouted the frustrated sergeant, but he led his men west down the Chu toward the other encampments. The Sari Su was the logical road north.

> - - - - - >VOLGA SEARCH> - - - - - >

"We are near the place of last sightings, *Efendim*." The Tartar boat master Instructed. He signaled the team of mules pulling the tow-lines. These pulled the beautifully crafted boat north, against the river's current. The vessel contained a squad of liveried guards and rowers. The team master watched and pulled the boat against the bank to stop.

The team stood waiting for instructions, when from the north a huge Viking ship hove into view and swiftly descended with the current and wind to intercept the smaller ship. Soon the fanged dragon head of the ship rested beside the boat flying the black Abbasid colors.

Derk, wearing the red turban and military dress called for a truce. Avaricious faces looked down on the smaller craft with contempt and rudely joked in their strange language. Derk made a gesture of peace; a salaam of greeting.

The face of a Kazar child of perhaps ten or twelve years appeared at the Viking ship's rail. He sat and required them to surrender. Then, after that, inquired as to their business.

OFFERS CUT OFF

198

"We are an embassy of the Sultan of Islam, the shadow of Allah, resident in great Baghdad. We come to offer an alliance of aid against a common enemy; the cursed Kazars and Jews of Getchet. With our aid you'll beat them."

Laughter followed the child's translation. The captain replied with amusement, "When we harpoon a whale or a walrus we know the creature is ours with a little more work. In its weakened state, sharks often attack it. They intend to steal what we know will be ours. They are rivals not allies. So you and your Sultan are competition, not trusted friends. Aysengar, or Yuhudigar, whatever you call the second Jerusalem, will be ours. We have no need to share their goods. If your great Baghdad is on a river, we will descend on it some day. Then, our ships will convince him that we need no help."

"Surely, so far from your base you will need aid and supplies. We have teachings and science that Allah has given us that will profit you," Derk insisted.

"Surrender now and you will live. We will let you work with the slaves on the farms and provide labor for our advance. Otherwise, you will be sent down the river to feed ravens." The Captain spoke his threat through his childish interpreter.

There was a brief pause before Derk tried another offer. However, the whir of a throwing axe cut short any further talk between the two parties.

> - - - - - >ARMY BASE> - - - - - >

I thought you should know immediately sir," reported the orderly, holding the prayer rug in hand.

"*Dough roo*, quite right," returned the general staring at the blood stained rug. "You've tried to remove the change in color? Could we dye it?"

"Everything sir, nothing covers or removes it. Every month it has spread and today it covers the rug."

"Well done, Corporal, You will burn-up the rug tomorrow without fail," Binbasha Onat ordered.

"But Sir, you love this rug as your life." The orderly protested vigorously.

"Therefore, I shall not need it in the future. Truly it reflects my life, but I'll not need it now."

"As you say, *efendem*. I'll do so tomorrow."

As he left Onat's mother entered. "What was that all about? Why would you burn a prayer rug?"

"It is the hand work of a Christian lady I was ordered to kill in Kokand. It was the most difficult act I ever did. She was blind, but knew my voice from a previous encounter when I told her of her husband's death. She knew why I was ordered to do it and she prayed while I approached her. She begged Allah's forgiveness for my ignorance. It angered me at that moment. But I have had to live with it since then."

"Why haven't you told me this before son? You remember my mother? Your grandmother was a Christian. Many of our tribe were. She would recommend repentance and prayer. God forgives much when asked through Yesu's suffering and victory." She reached out to comfort him.

"My pride won't let me beg, Mother. Prayer won't change Allah's will. Our Allah is not weak and made pliable by sobs and tears. He always gives what is best, not what is wanted by people."

"Love is moved by tears, son. If Allah loves his creation, He must be pliable and willing to listen. Besides do you find all happenings to be the best? Is there no room for human rebellion and indifference to be a cause of much of those happenings which are not for our best? Not everything that happens can be Allah's will. Think and pray while there is time." His head rested on her shoulder.

"There is no time now, Mother. The lady has appeared to me in a dream. She is as she was at the loom before her death; face transfigured and sadly announces my death. She forgives me and says her daughter is happy and safe far away. Now the blood stain fills the prayer rug. I have no recourse. I must die and you return to Kokand to the old family house." They were both crying now.

"I will pray for you son. There is mercy with Tanra."

> - - - - - >MOUNT HERMON VILLAGE> - - - - - >

"We seek a place to stay for the summer," Kardesh said to the village headman. "We are Christians and my sister

200

here will be married in another month," he indicted the lovely, veiled girl who guided him. "Her name is Ana and she is betrothed to a Christian baker in Jerusalem. She will go to that city after a while here."

"We welcome you to our village. We have a widow whose house is large, but her child is ill. She may not want a guest who cannot care for himself," the headman replied.

"I have some experience in healing; could we visit the lady?" Kardesh inquired.

"The child has been ill all winter," the headman stated, "and she is dependant on a brother to farm."

"Let me sit here before the house and pray before we call," Kardesh requested. They sat as he had asked while he prayed and rested. Then, the door opened.

"You see mother, there are visitors here. I knew there would be when God woke me and I was well." A small, frail child stood looking out at the group waiting before the house.

"Come in and welcome," the boy shouted, as the astonished mother looked on. Kardesh stood feeling for Ana's guiding hand.

The headman stood astonished and spoke quickly, "There are other families who will want a visit. I will contact them now," as he rushed away to spread the news and visit other sick families.

> - - - - - >EAST BULGAR YURT> - - - - - >

"I've got the herds and workers numbered and in place," Kerim stated. "The man was less prosperous than when I worked here, for there has been several areas neglected and overgrazed. We need to cull the herds, reduce their numbers for better results. As overseer I will correct these things."

"The extra meat will go to celebrate our Perilee's wedding," Leyla mused. "The preparations are coming along. Orhan's family has agreed and I'm telling her what to expect."

"You mean you're telling her about what we've done all winter?" Kerim was indignant.

201

"Girls shouldn't be ignorant of these things. I'm older and have the duty of instructing the young."

"You're seventeen, two years older. Your limited experience is less than a year," he exploded.

"Tayze told me about a woman's function and needs. I pass everything I've confirmed, on to Perilee. Women have to stick together against men's bullying control," Leyla insisted.

"Men protect the wife and home, many of us die doing just that," Kerim protested.

"*Evet*, yes, and we love you for it. But women don't make wars. Men do! Women must make their babies safe. It's not easy to have babies. I'm going to find out how difficult in the next eight months."

"We're having a baby?" he asked excitedly.

"I'm having it; we started it. Your part's over. That's why I've continued to sleep with Perilee."

"Do you mean you won't sleep with me now?"

"I had to be sure first. Now we can sleep and play, but I can't let you in where the baby is. Tayze said that it might hurt the little one. We'll have other ways to play and show love." Her gaze was tender.

"Just until the baby's born. Right?" he pleaded.

"Tayze says conception is rare until after the baby is weaned, but it isn't safe to indulge much."

"You mean two years old? That long?" he gasped.

"Sex is for reproduction. Babies take time. You talk a lot about the Creator, Tanra, and His love for people. Your Savior Yesu was a celibate, remember? I've heard that some of His priests are too. You'll be able to learn from them. When the baby is crawling we can start a bit at first. It's something to look forward to, don't you think?"

> - - - - - >MT. HERMON VILLAGE> - - - - - >

"Here, this is the cave where our hermit lived." The child indicated the place to Kardesh and Ana. They followed their new friend, the little boy who had been sick until they arrived to visit his home. Now healed, he was busy showing them the places of importance near his village.

"It faces the sun and is bright, but not hot." Ana noted, "The west wind cools it."

"He loved to look at the lake and valleys of Israel," the child stated with a smile. I climbed here every day and he would tell stories about Isa and quote Scripture. He prayed for our village and we miss him so, since he died. He sat on this large stone before the cave and taught us many things about God."

"It sounds like pleasant work," Kardesh said. "Would you come visit me if I stayed here?"

"Every day," the child responded.

"Does someone own the cave?" Ana asked cautiously?

The boy shrugged, "Nobody complained."

"Ana, can we bring our goods and live here? It will save his mother time and us money." Kardesh eagerly asked.

Ana's response was thoughtful. "She needs the money, so we will ask her to send a meal each day. I can leave enough of the bride price for that."

"Yes, and I can deliver it to him," the boy agreed.

> - - - - - >GERCHIN'S SAMARA ESTATE > - - - - - >

"The breakfast is ready and the beaters are in place, Gerchin *efendem*. First light is almost on us. If you are to get some of the animals that are night hunters you must start before they return to their lairs. The early hunters are about to emerge hungering," Gerchin bey's helper stated.

A CUNNING PLAN

203

"Start the drive. We can't wait for the late guests. They will miss the early excitement. A just penalty for sloth and lack of preparation," Gerchin laughed, with a good natured sneer. "Signal the men at the yayla on top to start the drive down the mountain now."

"*Peckee-yee, Efendem* I'll light the signal fire." He made a nod and arm motion to a waiting slave.

"Send Kurnaz *efende* to me when he arrives. We must drink together and be friends up to the end."

"The ground is prepared just at the stream bank as you ordered, *Efendem*. It is impossible to detect. Sand and small border plants covering wet clay, a slick place with loosened earth several fingers deep just above the pool.

"It should do the job. Have several bowmen ready, just in case. Accidents are a perennial part of hunts. I want the excitement to build by drinks and spilled blood until the incident occurs at the climax of the hunt." Gerchin smiled in self satisfaction. "Will we bag a wolf or just a fox?

The tribesman looked in admiration at his Khan. "I'm sure the Sultan will find a worthy successor."

"The accounts gathered by the unfortunate Sorba bey, or his accomplices were left at my door. These have assured me of an opportunity to denounce and replace a venial vizier and perhaps even a gray wolf."

> - - - - - >MT. HERMON VILLAGE> - - - - - >

"This is Ana, my dear sister," Kardesh indicated to the Caravan Master. "She leaves the family to form her own. She's a great traveler and will cause you no trouble at all," he assured the man.

"I guarantee a safe and prompt delivery to the nunnery," promised the Damascus based caravan director. He always went out of the direct route to visit the village of orchards at the foot of Mount Hermon. "I could take you as well and even return you here again if the need arises," the man said.

"We lack funds and God's approval for such a trip." Kardesh explained. "They have a journey to make elsewhere before they settle down to family life."

"I'll be back through here in a month with news," promised the caravan leader.

> - - - - - - >HIGH IN TANRA DAH> - - - - - >

Mangore's troops met a harried messenger from the old Tang fort on the Illi River. The summons was urgent. Kirgiz tribesmen had appeared in force and surrounded the fort. Meanwhile, numberless Kirgiz families passed south into the high ranges of the Tanra Dah Mountains, called by the Chinese the Tien Shan, Heavenly Mountains. Yearly rain brought the high *yayla*, alpine meadows, into a green carpet of food for grazers. They provided a living for those willing to endure the long cold season and the storms that raged on its slopes at all seasons. The loss of Tang Chinese support and tribal pressure from neighbors sent the Kirgiz south into the highlands used by local grazers in the summer and avoided in winter. Desperation drove the Kirgiz into this high, fridged, sparsely occupied land while the Uigurs fought Tibetans in the south of the Tarim lowlands, where irrigation produced the crops.

"We will break through to reinforce the fort until help can arrive," Mangore insisted to his sergeant. "Manly will send help; we can be sure of that."

In Aksu, below the mountains, Manly was defending the irrigated lowlands from Kirgiz incursions. There would be no help to spare for the north.

> - - - - - - >ABBASID ARMY POST> - - - - - >

"Binbasham, we're under attack. The north post has sent an alarm. The East post doesn't respond. We are under attack from two directions." The alarms sounded as the adjutant ran to General Onat's house. Onat *Efende* was up and dressed, while the adjutant explained. The sound of metal, sword on shield, echoed from the perimeters of the base. The sounds of swift horses came from the streets. The village was over-run and the houses smoked with the fire of torch and arrows. Villagers and army stumbled about in the faint light of dawn. People were retreating westward on the road to the Syr River where most of the base troops had gone to quell the rioting and restore peace. Onat *Efende* formed a rear guard to protect those panicked families and troops that were rushing away from the Kirgiz shock troops. There had been only two points of resistance in their invasion and occupation of the highlands. The Illi River fort and the Sultan's base near the pass. The burned Uigur village below the pass offered no resistance whatever.

Onat Pasha got an arrow below his armour in the abdomen, so his personal guard made a stand in the ruins outside the village where Kirgiz horsemen overtook them. His mother wrapped him with the prayer rug the sergeant had rescued and brought with them. They prayed as the attack ceased and warriors sacked the village and base. The dying commander would not repossess the base. There was nothing left to go back to there.

> - - - - - >MOUNTAINS NEAR KOKAND> - - - - - >

"Sir, these are only Kirgiz refugees, no men, just women and children. I'm sure that means the stories about Kirgiz troops is false. These say they're survivors of a war near Lake Baykal. Their men are dead and they hide here, below the high mountains." The police sergeant reported to Ali bey, the commissioner in charge of the police squad. "Fergana army troops report fighting in the villages in the Tanra Dah Mountains above Kokand."

KIRGIZ RESISTANCE

"Yes, Sergeant, but our own refugees in Kokand city report that men burned their homes and ran them out of the village of Usk. The men may be off fighting elsewhere. Bring me one of the boys to question. There, that one will do."

They caught a boy and hauled him before Ali bey. He slapped the child's face, then shook him violently. He shouted: "You'll tell me the truth now, boy, or you won't walk for a week. Understand? Now, where are the men who came with you?" He held the collar of the struggling boy.

The crowd of protesting watchers opened their bundles to reveal quivers of arrows and bows. The women and children took, armed the bows and shot at the police.

The captive boy drew Ali bey's knife from its scabbard and used it on him. Ali bey dropped him and fell with an arrow in his chest. "Kirgiz widows and orphans are as able as warriors," someone among the refugees shouted boldly.

> - - - - - >IN THE CHIPCHAK CAMP> - - - - - >
"This is our new home then?" inquired Nooryouz in the guest yurt of the Khan Erden.

"*Vatan benim*, my homeland," Sanjak agreed. "It is a land of endless green meadows and silver birch trees."

"It certainly is big and, well, it's so huge it scares me. I feel safe only in the wife's yurt. She is so kind. I know nothing can hurt me there."

"Khan Erden wants us to stay here. He values my experiences with the Tang, Uigurs and Abbasids. He will send Erly east with the last of the refugees."

"Tanra's country for us," she sighed, "Yesu brought us through to find it and be safe."

"Yes, as He does with all who believe and obey."

"Oh Sanjak, I learned a song the women were singing. Do you want to hear it?"

"Of course, if it's one I know, I'll join you."

> Praise to Yesu, glory Yesu.
> Yesu, the Creator's son
> Come with courage, come with purpose.
> Come to save us all.
> Kind, He healed the weak and ill.

207

Praise to Yesu, glory Yesu.
Yesu, the Creator's gift,
Come with blessing, come with treasure,
Come to share His love.
 Kind, He took our sin and loss.

PRAISE TO YESU

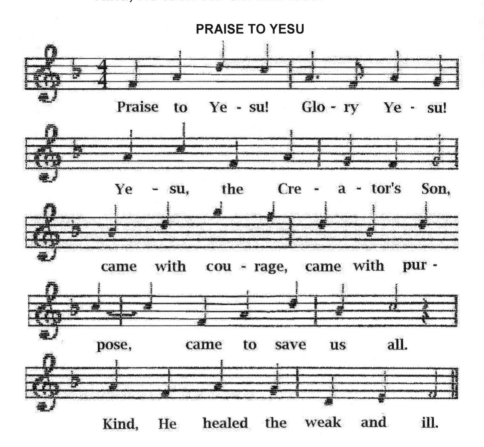

Praise to Ye - su! Glo - ry Ye - su!

Ye - su, the Cre - a - tor's Son,

came with cou - rage, came with pur -

pose, came to save us all.

Kind, He healed the weak and ill.

> - - - - - >MARIL'S WEDDING> - - - - - >

In Baghdad the guests were all invited to the bridal breakfast for there were two: one for the bride entertaining ladies and one by the groom with the men, some of whom had started the celebration the night before and aimed to continue all day. The public deposited their gifts, a reflection of their wealth and standing in the community; only to receive gifts and favours worthy of the host, as they joined in the celebration. The Cathedral was filled beyond capacity and the most notable preachers and authorities, civil and religious were there. Great care had to be taken with protocol for the highly placed are sensitive to their status and recognition.

At the celebration, after the Christian ceremony was over, they sat down to the wedding dinner. Jon was able to relate some of their experiences on the return from China. Maril told of their escapes as shepherds crossing borders to come home.

Presents were opened with fanfare and displayed with recognition and hugs for the givers. After a long, exhausting day of display, and over-indulgence, the public tended to drink itself to sleep. The happy couple was allowed to retire and rest, but were expected to display a stained proof of virginity the following day.

Several times persons who had not been invited or registered as guests, or who had entered without proper recognition, were expelled from the estate grounds.

Yusuf bey used the banquet to expound on the blessings accompanying the invitation of God to the marriage feast of the Lamb. There, Isa would receive his believers.

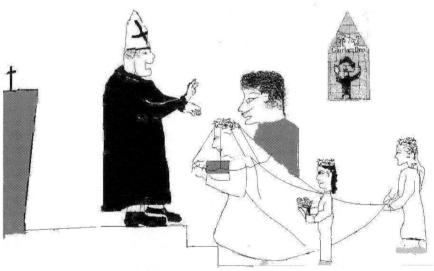

MARIL'S MARRIAGE

They would be God's chosen ones to enjoy fellowship with each other and the man who was God's chosen instrument to bring salvation to the world of fallen sinners. God would rejoice with the redeemed ones forever.

The audience listened, some with enthusiasm and others with doubt or indifference. Such ideas seemed far from the day to day world of work, worry, pleasure and gain.

That day a large ominous column of smoke marked the location of Samara to the northwest. It became an omen.

The wedding was considered a gala affair and talked about for years, but pride digs its own pitfalls. It marked a time of great changes as the Sultan increased the Christian tax or *jizya* that Muslims traditionally receive from that older community of people.

> - - - - - >SAMARA HUNT> - - - - - >

The drivers and tribesmen guards came roaring down the mountain driving all before them. Any panicked creature that doubled back was killed by the alert tribesmen. The smell of blood carried those remaining, down the hill toward the u-shaped valley. Below, at each end of the valley, groups of princes and aids awaited, with the Sultan, the arrival of the promised slaughter. The upper end of the valley, where the Vizier and assistant were located, faced a small stream below the mountain. It rested under a small, waist-high bank descending to a meadow. There the abundance of animals would pose an easy target for arrow, spear, sword or even knife. The breakfast and drinks had loosened every tongue and the thrill of sound and smell of blood permeated every head. As the animals arrived the eager shooting and slashing started. The line of shooters wavered as some tried to get in a shot and others pushed to stay ahead of them. Each arrow was marked to claim the prey for the owner.

From behind a cry arose. A lathered horse and rider tried to gain the front row where Kurnaz shot. "Make way, an urgent message for the Vizier," voices cried in the midst of the noise. The beaters were descending the slopes and the animals were all concentrated, so the front row drew swords and rode forward – a wave of armed men and horses rushed into the mass of panicked creatures. They pushed forward, jumping down the bank of the creek. The impatient riders hit the wet clay and slipping, went down, along with the worn rider behind the Vizier. The messenger's lathered horse fell on top of the growing pile, while the rider, Seerlee bey, died with an unmarked arrow in his back. Later, it was reported that the messenger was a reputed agent of home security.

The mob was too excited by the hunt, so the dead and wounded were left until the slaughter ended.

Servants and slaves prepared the roasted feast near the hunting lodge. Some of the brush, grown from winter rains, caught fire on the dry, south side of the mountain. The flames devoured the sides of the mountain to the *yayla,* alpine meadows above. A cloud of black smoke arose. The column of smoke could be seen from Baghdad.

The Sultan and guests enjoyed the feast. The tragedy did not penetrate dazed heads until the next day. Assessments could be made only after cobwebs and hangovers of the Vizier's celebration had passed.

THE HUNT'S END

In the wild, the death of a wolf pack leader is immediately replaced by the next ranking male, or is fought out by rivals. Among larger herd animals the same need is felt. However, domestication occurs when wild beasts live in continuous contact with humans. Even physical changes occur. The wolves' tails curl up, ears flop down, they learn to bark and work for the human master. There are no records of wolves living naturally with people; only dogs live with humans.

Wolves live on in reduced numbers in scattered places around the world. Although protected and studied, their importance is insignificant. Domesticated dogs are their significant replacement. This most important animal is bred in countless forms and uses, all related to human existence.

Wolves live on in reputation and legend among us; strong, resilient, persistant, silently seeking out their prey. However, we fear them no longer. Their day is over forever.

The death of the vizier was remedied quickly, by a Sultan occupied by pleasure. Gerchin was careful to make himself visible, affable and available to his master. He also hired the Vizier's assistant as his own.

The loss of a head was but slightly felt by the Grey Wolf Secret Society. The place and reason for the loss, as well as his identity was still unknown. After a brief pause, orders were forthcoming again though there were some noticeable differences in style and methods employed by the head.

The excitement caused by the Syr Valley turmoil and the Kirgiz invasion caused distraction enough to take peoples' attention. The Ibn el Ari clan found joy in the birth of an heir through Yasmin, wife of the younger son, Harun, now safely settled in Merv.

The smuggling of valuable Chinese and Uigur goods was promptly revived by younger gangs in competition with the needy Kirgiz. Life soon settled down in Dar Al Islam and new events continued to hold peoples' momentary attention.

> - - - - - > JERUSALEM BAKERY> - - - - - >

Melek was brimming with excitement when he saw Rafi at the bakery. "Saida has seen Ana at the nunnery on the mountain near the Ascension Place. She's got nice things.

212

She has brought some from the Far East. Saida has seen them all. Ana is lively and full of fun; Saida laughed lots. Ana wants the announcements and preparations to start for the wedding."

"Great!" Rafi responded excitedly, "What does she look like?" He paused, "I mean: she saw her?"

"She is Saida's size and build, but she wore her veil. She said she promised Yeet to wear it until after the wedding."

Then, seeing Rafi's disappointment, he added: "She said she was saving the best for last; no one would see her before you do. But she told Saida about the cities: Kokand, Khiva, Baghdad and Samara. She's traveled all around and met so many people. She lived with the Bozhun household. They are really rich, but she is like a poor relative, she said. It's funny, said Saida, but listening to Ana is almost like listening to Yeet's voice."

EVEN WOLVES CHANGE

213